FLIGHT TO THE REICH

Submarine WWII Series
Book Three

Charles Whiting
writing as
Leo Kessler

SAPERE
BOOKS

FLIGHT TO THE REICH

Published by Sapere Books.

24 Trafalgar Road, Ilkley, LS29 8HH

saperebooks.com

ISBN: 978-0-85495-141-3

BOOK ONE: ESCAPE FROM VARNA

CHAPTER 1

At dawn the fog came drifting in from the Russian coast.

At first it was nothing more than a few stray grey wisps, hardly noticeable. At a steady ten knots, the lean steel shape of the U-70, looking every inch the predatory killer she was, ploughed through the limp sea, the bridge party seemingly unaware of the growing mist. Gently, softly, the wisps curled themselves around the submarine, slowly thickening and thickening, chilling the deck look-outs, clad in their thin summer uniforms, leaving the conning tower dripping with cold condensation, as the coast began to disappear from sight.

On the bridge, as it grew steadily colder, with the moisture dripping down their hard intent faces, the officers' original high spirits vanished. They leaned forward peering into the grey murk, sunk suddenly into a brooding chilled lethargy. The prey they had been stalking for over a week ever since they had sailed from Varna on the Black Sea coast had eluded them yet again. This sudden fog had put paid to everything!

Soon the U-70's tour of operations against the Red Fleet in this supposedly warm inland sea would be over and the crew would be shipped right across Europe by train and thrown into that infinitely more cruel Battle of the Atlantic, in which, in this year of 1943, they stood little chance of surviving more than a couple of weeks. For even the 'old hares', the few surviving aces among them, could no longer out-trick the massed Anglo-American attackers, with their mini-carriers, airborne radar, and all the rest of their damned sophisticated anti-U-boat devices.

'Sink the *Stalin*, Lords,' *Kapitänleutnant* Harsch, their skipper, had bellowed at them just before they had sailed from Varna. 'Put the pride of the Ivan's Black Sea Fleet to the

bottom of the ocean and you'll be living like the King in France for the rest of this year, at least. There'll be no North Atlantic for us, take my word for it!'

But where was the damned *Stalin*? asked *Leutnant zur See* Christian Jungblut, the U-70's second-in-command, as he stood next to the skipper on the dripping bridge, eyes narrowed to slits. His harshly handsome face was set and taut as he tried to penetrate the grey curtain of the sea mist. Personally he wasn't scared of going back to the bitter battle of the North Atlantic. He had run the gauntlet of the Anglo-American navies out there four times already and survived. He'd cope all right.

It was the crew he worried about. They were all greenbeaks, still wet behind the spoons, save for a handful of veteran, hard-bitten petty officers like Chief Petty Officer Frenssen. How would these callow teenagers, for that was what they were for the most part, fare against the ruthless English, who had been fighting the U-boats since 1939? Not very well, he imagined. He looked down at the youthful, unlined faces of the look-outs on the wet, slick deck below and frowned. They needed time and training — lots of it — before they could hope to face up to the merciless, cruel skippers of the English Royal Navy. The Tommies would eat them up before breakfast and spit out the pips with that damned awful tea that they slurped all the time, when they weren't drinking pink gin...

The U-70 was now crawling across the still, leaden surface of the Black Sea at a snail's pace. The fog thickened even more. Now Harsch called out a double watch. Look-outs were posted everywhere on the deck, ears straining for the slightest sound, as they drifted through the dripping grey murk, searching for that damned elusive *Stalin*. Down below in the fetid, green-glowing interior of the sub, which stank of diesel oil and stale human sweat, the specialists crouched over their instruments, eyes peering at the dials, headphones clasped tightly to their ears, faces glazed with sweat, as they tried to pick up the soft throb of a ship's screws. The air was charged with tense, nervous, electric expectancy. *Where was the damned* Stalin?

Watching the skipper, Jungblut told himself that the older man burnt with impatience. He had never seen a man in whom the raging fire below the surface was so obvious. He was desperate for glory. Even now he fingered his throat, with surprisingly delicate hands for such a big man, as if he wanted to feel the comforting hardness of the Knight's Cross of the Iron Cross hanging there. His neck was bare of that decoration, which adorned Christian's own throat.

Harsch, in spite of being an 'old hare' who had first served in the U-Boat Arm back in 1918 as a teenage cadet, had had an unlucky war. Time after time he had run out on patrol, full of high hopes of some great prize, only to return miserably with some low tonnage merchantman or Tommy fishing boat to his credit. Once, back in 1941, when the Tommies had still held Crete, he had spotted one of their troop trains chugging along the coastal railway and in his despair at the lack of prizes had actually fired a torpedo at it and blasted the locomotive to smithereens! Thereafter they had joked in the officers' messes whenever he had made an appearance, 'Look who's there, comrades! Why, it's *the Locomotive Killer*!'

Christian Jungblut forgot the skipper and concentrated on the task at hand, as the U-70 ploughed forward. There was no sound now save for the muted, monotonous throb-throb of the surface diesels and the steady tense pacing of the look-outs as they strained to see through the gloom. Once 'Smutty', the cook, poked his head up from below and cried happily, 'Cap'n, coffee with a nice dash o' firewater in it, *sir*!' But Harsch had ignored his offer of the hot drink, laced with schnaps. He did not seem even to hear and the greasy-looking cook, with his over-long matted hair, had disappeared below once more, muttering to himself. Twice the look-outs yelled out excitedly, that there was something to port and then to starboard. But both times the sightings were false and the skipper turned on them, his green eyes blazing with fury, the obscenities tripping from his tongue in a merciless stream.

By four that June afternoon, with the fog as thick as any Hamburg waterfront pea-souper, Christian Jungblut had about given up the *Stalin* for the day. He knew the Ivans. Their radio and radar systems were exceedingly primitive. They made most of their contacts visually. As soon as they couldn't see, most skippers of the Red Fleet headed back to the nearest port for safety. In all probability the pride of the Red Fleet, the *Stalin*, was already on its way back to Sevastopol. Thus it was just as he was about to suggest to the skipper that the U-70 should dive beneath the Black Sea so that the men could eat and rest, that from below came the urgent cry, '*Achtung, Brücke*! We're getting some noise, sir!'

Savagely Harsch snatched at the speaking tube. 'Captain here,' he barked harshly. 'Sure it's not a shoal of fish?' Even as he spoke, Christian could see by the look of almost desperate longing on his hard face that he was hoping against hope the operator was right and he was wrong.

'No, sir,' the excited young voice came floating up. 'Definitely not fish. I'm getting her loud and clear. Sound of ship's screws. *Big screws*!'

Harsch swung round on Christian, eyes gleaming excitedly. 'Did you hear that, Number One? It could be her — the *Stalin*!'

'But, sir,' Christian began to protest, 'surely the *Stalin* has now returned to —'

'*Object, port bow, sir!*'

Christian and Harsch flashed a look to the deck. It was the Moses, the youngest member of the crew, a seventeen-year-old volunteer from the naval arm of the Hitler Youth. The handsome blond youth was almost jumping with joy as he stuck out his arm to indicate something he had seen through the rolling fogbanks.

Both Christian and the skipper flung up their binoculars as one, as Moses, remembering what little training he had received back at Mürwik, yelled in the approved official manner, 'Object — *green-one-zero*!'

Behind them, towering above the two officers with his massive bulk, Chief Petty Officer Frenssen breathed in disbelief. '*Great crap on the Christmas Tree* — it's her! It's the frigging pride of the Popovs. *IT'S THE* STALIN!'

It was, too. There was no mistaking that tremendous shape, clearly outlined in a break in the fog. As if framed like a picture, there she sailed at a mere five knots; the SMS *Stalin*, all thirty-five thousand tons of her, her two forward turrets housing the largest guns of any ship of the line in the whole world, six huge 120mm cannon, that one single rakish funnel behind the bridge clearly distinguishing her from the rest of the Black Sea fleet. And the great battleship was completely unescorted! There was not one single destroyer in sight!

For one long moment they gazed in stupefied awe, like open-mouthed yokels, then she was gone, swallowed up almost instantly by the rolling banks of grey fog.

Slowly, very slowly, *Kapitänleutnant* Harsch turned to Christian, face set in a look of disbelief. 'Was it —? Did I really see the *Stalin*?' he stuttered and gasped.

On another occasion, Christian might well have laughed at the look on the skipper's face, but he remembered the first time he had glimpsed a great warship they would soon destroy and how he had felt then as a callow youth. So instead of laughing, he said quite seriously, 'Yes, sir, you did. There —'

'There was no mistaking it — the silhouette!' Harsch cut in excitedly. 'It was *her!*'

Green eyes blazing, he spun round, and cried, 'Well done, Moses! There'll be an extra tot of firewater for you tonight!' He looked at the flushed pleased youngster in a way that Christian found momentarily distasteful. He knew not why. Then the look was forgotten as the skipper started to reel off his orders. *The chase was on!*

Harsch peered through the bright circle of calibrated glass at the Soviet battleship. There seemed no end to her. Here and there he could make out chinks of yellow light where her blackout was imperfect, or where someone perhaps moved a blackout curtain on the upper deck. Even at periscope depth he could hear the steady throb-throb of her mighty screws as she headed back for the safety of the great harbour of Sevastopol.

Momentarily he raised his head from the periscope and ordered the engineer to raise the speed immediately. Christian, standing next to the skipper, felt the increasing turbulence as the U-70 moved into the *Stalin's* wake and he guessed Harsch intended to trail the *Stalin* until he got within firing range. With a bit of luck, the Soviet asdic operators might confuse the sound of their own tremendous engines with those of the U-

70. He smiled in admiration. In spite of his bad luck, *Kapitänleutnant* Harsch was a real old hare; he knew all the tricks.

CPO Frenssen, however, seemed unimpressed. He tugged at his red bulbous nose, the product of many years of cheap beer and even cheaper schnaps, and growled *sotto voce*, 'The Popovs can't be that frigging dumb, *Leutnant*. Even their operators must know the difference between a thirty-five thousand ton displacement battle wagon and a piss-pansy short-assed sub!'

Christian flashed him a momentary smile. 'Aren't you just the right little bundle of joy, *Obermaat?*' he whispered, as the skipper bent over the periscope again, battered white cap back to front. 'Smile — and give your frigging face a treat.'

Frenssen muttered something and relapsed into silence, while Christian tensed, waiting for the skipper's orders, as they grew ever closer to the mighty rump of the great Soviet battleship.

He didn't have long to wait. Without taking his gaze off the *Stalin*, the skipper snapped, 'I'm going to attack from the port beam, Jungblut. If we can manage it, I want to get a fan of four kippers the whole length of her. I don't want to leave her floating so they can come out from Sevastopol with the tugs and tow her into harbour. I want the bitch to go down — straight to the bottom right off!'

Christian nodded his agreement, but said nothing. He knew it would be to no avail anyway. The skipper was too excited now to listen to another opinion.

As the U-70 started to swing out to leave the wake of the *Stalin*, Harsch sang out his orders, voice barely under control, 'Tubes one to four ready for firing!'

'Tubes one to four ready for firing, *sir!*' the torpedo mate replied dutifully from the end of the tightly packed sub.

'Target Red 90,' Harsch barked. 'Speed fifteen knots. Range … twelve hundred metres!'

Christian whistled softly to himself as the gunnery mate repeated the instructions. The skipper was going in damned close. If anything went wrong at that close range… He dared not take that particularly unpleasant thought to its logical end. The Black Sea was not his idea of a last resting place.

Christian looked around him in the tight confines of the operations section. The men's faces were glazed with sweat and they kept licking their dry lips. Here and there men swallowed repeatedly, or rubbed their hands over their unshaven young faces, unaware that they were making the movement. The tension in the air was electric. It was now kill or be killed — and even the rawest greenhorn among them knew it. *Kill or be killed!*

'Skipper to torpedo mate,' Harsch rasped, the knuckles of his big red hands holding the grips of the periscope were white with nervous tension, 'stand by to fire!'

'Standing by, sir!' the mate yelled back.

Christian licked his lips. This was it.

Suddenly *Kapitänleutnant* Harsch did something completely out of character, or at least, at the time, Christian Jungblut thought it out of character. He turned abruptly and looked at the handsome, sweat-glazed face of young Moses and said, 'Here, Moses, come up to the 'scope.'

'*Me*, sir?' the youngest member of the crew said in surprise, while the others stared at him and then at the skipper in complete bewilderment. An invitation of this kind now, just before they were to attack, was unprecedented.

Frenssen frowned and Christian stared at the skipper, realizing for the first time just how decadent that long upper lip of his was.

'Yes,' Harsch said easily, as Moses stumbled forward. 'You were first to spot the *Stalin*, my dear boy. You deserve the honour of taking a *last* look at her before we send her to the bottom of the Black Sea.' As the Moses bent hesitantly to look through the tube, the skipper put one hand familiarly on his skinny young shoulders. Frenssen's frown deepened.

And then *Kapitänleutnant* Harsch was his usual business-like self once more. He shoved the Moses to one side, bent to peer through the periscope and yelled, 'Fire when ready, *Obermaat!*'

'*On ... on ... on!*' the excited gunnery mate yelled, indicating that the torpedo settings were correct.

Christian clenched his fists, hot sweat trickling down the small of his back and wetting his already clammy shirt.

'*FIRE!*' Harsch cried.

There was a soft hiss. Compressed air escaped from the tubes. In an instant it was followed by a wild flurry of bubbles, racing towards the surface. Christian tensed. Four times the boat trembled and lurched as the one and a half ton torpedoes shot into the water and streaked lethally towards their target.

Harsch, glued to the periscope, began to count off the seconds as the torpedoes raced through the water. '*One, two, three, four —*'

Suddenly, startlingly, there was a tremendous bang. Even the water and distance could not mute that horrific explosion. Christian reeled back and just in time caught a stanchion to prevent himself falling as the U-70 dropped a good three metres under the impact. At the tube, Harsch screamed wildly, beside himself with completely unrestrained excitement, '*We've done it! We've done it, Jungs! This time I've cured my throatache for good!*'

Christian's heart leapt. He knew what the skipper meant even before Harsch invited him to peer through the periscope. He'd 'cured his throatache' because the Führer would award him the Knight's Cross for this one. *He had hit the* Stalin!

With trembling fingers he pushed his cap back to front and bent to peer through the periscope, automatically turning up the intensifier to get the best possible image. He gasped. The *Stalin* had obviously been holed just below the waterline and she was sinking fast. Quite clearly he could see the panic-stricken efforts of the crew to lower the lifeboats, to toss Caley floats into the sea, which bubbled and raged at the points where the *Stalin* had been holed, and to jump in after them ... mouth gaping he watched in awe as the great battleship started to yaw dramatically to one side, her radio masts dipping into the water with a sudden angry crackling of violent red and blue sparks.

A rating, perhaps a look-out, panicked like the rest, launched himself into a spectacular dive from one of the topmasts. He misjudged the list and failed to make the water, his target, and slammed to the heaving deck in a mess of broken bones and gore. An instant later the *Stalin* listed even more, with a great metallic rending of tearing plates and frantic hiss of steam escaping from the ruptured boilers.

Christian groaned. In spite of his feeling of triumph at this tremendous 'kill', he was suddenly overcome with the daemonic madness of this cruel war at sea where great ships and all aboard them were sent to the bottom in such a relentless, heartless manner.

Harsch had no such scruples, it appeared. 'Take her up, Number One,' he bellowed above the excited cries and yells of the crew, who now knew there would be no Battle of the Atlantic for them this summer. 'The Big Lion' would ensure they stayed in the Black Sea. Once back in port, there'd be whores and booze, as much as they could fuck and drink —

and then some! Even that hoary old hare Frenssen was carried away by the mounting excitement. As the U-70 started to rise, he pulled out his precious flatman and took a sly slug at the fiery Bulgarian plum brandy, saying, as if to himself, 'It's gonna be roses, roses all the frigging way from now on!' But for once Chief Petty Officer Frenssen — 'Frau Frenssen's handsome son,' as he often called himself with his usual lack of modesty — was going to be proved wrong.

'Stop both!' Harsch cried, as the U-70 broke the surface and Christian raced up the dripping metal ladder to fling open the hatch of the conning tower. 'Deck party prepare to rescue survivors.' Harsch saw the looks on the faces of his crew and chuckled. 'Not for humanitarian purposes, Jungs,' he explained. 'For me the only good Popov is a dead 'un. No, all I want are a few survivors to prove to the big shots back in Varna that we have actually sunk the *Stalin*. Now move it! *Dalli, dalli … los, los!*'

On the bridge, Christian watched the dying Soviet battleship sink. The air was full of the cloying stench of escaping diesel and he felt like being sick, his ears filled with the fearful cries of the Russian sailors trapped on the stern, which now towered high in the sky. But his eyes were not on them, as the *Stalin* prepared to take her final plunge beneath the boiling, white waves. They were fixed on the lone figure standing rigidly to attention among the shambles of the tilting bridge. It had to be the *Stalin's* captain, Christian told himself, a brave man who had already decided his own fate. He would go down with his stricken ship. Suddenly Christian's heart went out to the unknown Russian and he felt the comradeship of the sea which transcended all national boundaries and the vagaries of armed conflict.

Harsch, however, had no time for such sentiments. 'Move it, Number One!' he cried triumphantly, feasting his gaze on the sinking ship. 'Let's get that dinghy over the side. We want to collar at least three of 'em. Make one of them an officer if you can. Intelligence likes to deal with Russian officers best.'

'Yes, sir,' Christian answered, tearing his gaze from the lone captain, and clattering down to the deck below where the sailors of the deck party were feverishly attempting to loosen the shackles holding the dinghy in place. Frenssen urged them on. 'Come on, you bunch o' piss-pansies! Move them cream-puff asses of yourn! The skipper needs a nice Russian sailor —'

'Knock it off, Frenssen!' Christian cut in sharply, his mind still full of that doomed Soviet captain. 'Let's get a couple of the poor bastards aboard and be done with it.'

Frenssen looked at him queerly, but said nothing. Instead, as soon as the last hinge was loosened, he heaved his huge bulk against the big rubber dinghy, the muscles rippling brutally through the thin material of his shirt and threatening to burst free of the fabric, and heaved it overboard with a splash.

Five minutes later, as they were hauling the first of the spluttering, oil-soaked survivors aboard, ignoring the cries of the others all around them, there was one final great metallic rending, followed by an unearthly, banshee-like wailing as a tremendous jet of steam shot straight into the sky.

Christian took his eyes off the pathetic, panic-stricken survivors and caught a final glimpse of the *Stalin* sliding beneath the greedy sea, that lone Soviet captain still standing upright on his shattered bridge to the very end. Sadly he raised his hand to his battered cap in salute. 'Poor shits,' he whispered.

'We're all poor shits, sir,' Frenssen echoed, 'all of us…'

Five minutes later the *Sturmoviks* came hurtling out of the sky, great metal hawks of death.

CHAPTER 2

'*ALARM! A-L-A-R-M!*' Christian yelled urgently as the klaxon shrieked, and Frenssen flung himself behind the twin machine-guns mounted on the bridge.

'The buggers have spotted us!' Frenssen yelled and thrust the twin guns round with a nudge of his powerful shoulders. 'They're coming in!'

'Stand by for air attack!' Christian cried, as man after man tumbled by him to slide down the iron ladder and land in an awkward bundle at the bottom. But there were still a good half dozen of them left on the deck, together with their prisoner. Before he could get them below, Christian knew the *Sturmoviks* would be onto them. They would have to stay on the surface and fight it out.

But Harsch thought differently. He had sunk the pride of the Red Fleet. Now all he wanted to do was to escape and report his great success to the authorities back in Varna. 'Come on down, Number One!' he cried from below, his broad face urgent, perhaps even a little frightened. 'We've got to crash dive. *Come down!*'

'But I've still got men up here!' Christian shrieked above the ever-louder roar of the diving planes. 'I can't —'

'Abandon them!' Harsch yelled, cutting him short brutally. 'We have to sacrifice the few to save the many — and the boat!'

Christian gasped with shock. For a moment he stared down at Harsch speechless. In the U-boat Arm, you never abandoned a comrade, whatever the reason. It was the unwritten law of the service. 'But you can't — can't mean that, sir,' he stuttered, finding his voice at last. Behind him Frenssen cursed mightily and then pressed the trigger. The twin machine-guns opened up with an ear-splitting roar. '*You can't*!'

'*Leutnant* Jungblut, I am giving you a direct order to come down here at once. Do you hear me?'

Christian's face hardened, his lips curling in contempt. 'I think even you would hardly dare to flood the boat with your Number One still on deck — *sir*,' he said icily and then forgetting Harsch, he turned and stared up at the sky, as the first of the *Sturmoviks* came falling out of the leaden sky.

'Lead him in, you big rogue!' he yelled above the tremendous racket, as Frenssen peppered the sky to the dive-bomber's front with a lethal hail of tracers, the twin barrels of his guns steaming furiously. Then suddenly he saw the *Sturmovik* attack was a feint. Half a kilometre to their right, coming in low over the sea, almost skimming the waves, there was another plane! Hastily he flung up his binoculars. The plane itself was almost obscured by the tossing waves but there was no mistaking the twin torpedoes beneath its ugly grey belly.

'Torpedo bomber!' he shrieked crazily above the terrible racket as the first *Sturmovik* levelled out and a myriad small bombs started to tumble out of its bomb bays. The U-boat rocked alarmingly as huge fountains of boiling angry white water shot up into the air on both sides of it. With a shrill scream of fear, one of the ratings went over the side. 'Torpedo bomber at three o'clock, Frenssen. For chrissake, Frenssen' — he shook the giant angrily — '*at* three o'clock, damn you, man! *THREE O'CLOCK*!'

The *Obermaat* swung the twin machine-guns round. The torpedo bomber was barely a quarter of a kilometre away. It was now or never. At this range, the pilot couldn't miss the U-70. Frenssen *had* to knock it out of the sky — or else...

Frenssen knew it, too. He squinted through the ring sight for a second and then pressed the trigger. A solid wall of flying white steel leapt up to block the torpedo plane's progress. Slugs stitched the sky in a deadly Morse. Suddenly the torpedo plane staggered.

'You've hit it!' Christian screamed wildly. 'You've hit it, Frenssen!'

'Stick *this* up yer filthy Russian arse as well!' Frenssen yelled and fired off another tremendous burst.

Crazily pieces of gleaming metal flew from the torpedo plane's fuselage. Almost instantly a thin white stream of escaping glycol started to pour from its port engine. Christian flung up his binoculars once more. Behind the gleaming spider web of cracked cockpit perspex, a dark shape slumped over the shattered controls. It was the pilot, dead or unconscious.

The starboard engine stopped. With a tremendous smack, the torpedo plane hit the sea. For a moment it was obscured by a huge spout of wild, white, furious water, then came a great white, incandescent, blinding flash.

Christian involuntarily closed his eyes for an instant and Frenssen ceased firing. When he opened them again, the plane had vanished completely, save for one lone wing slopping back and forth on the grey-green swell.

'Well done, Frenssen!' Christian cried exuberantly. 'You old rogue, you've gone and —'

The rest of his words were drowned by a tremendous explosion, followed an instant later by a blast of hot acrid air. Christian yelled in alarm as it propelled him against the side of the conning tower. Dimly he heard screams and cries for help and then the other *Sturmovik*, which had sneaked up on the U-70 while they had been occupied by the torpedo-plane, was hurrying high into the sky, with Frenssen firing a fruitless angry burst behind it.

Groggily, Christian raised himself and shook his head. His vision slowly came back into focus, but already his ears were telling him that something serious had happened. The U-70 had slowed down considerably and there were muffled cries and yells coming from within. The U-70 had been hit.

What had been the dinghy party lay sprawled out on the deck near a gaping ragged hole in the hull, bodies ripped and torn by the *Sturmovik's* bomb, a mess of dripping gore. He swallowed hard, sickened by the sight. Not one of the dead was older than eighteen. In the U-70's moment of triumph they had paid the price of victory.

He tried to assess the hull damage as the U-70 started to yaw alarmingly and thick black oily smoke began to pour from her diesels. Obviously the U-70's steering had been hit.

Next moment *Kapitänleutnant* Harsch's angry shout from below confirmed it. 'That damned bomb has bent the damned rods,' he yelled. '*Verdammte Schei*☐*e*! Now the gold watch has really fallen into the damned piss-pot!'

Christian stared down at Harsch's brick-red angry face and called, 'Anyone hurt, sir? We've got six fatalities up here.'

'Don't talk to me of casualties, Number One,' Harsch waved his hand, as if brushing away some importuning insect. 'We have serious problems with the steering and as soon as that damn Russian fly-boy reports he's hit us, they'll be after us with a vengeance. Planes, surface craft, the works!'

Christian flashed a look at the sky. The fog had vanished and it would be another two hours at least before darkness came. They would simply have to sweat it out. 'I suggest we reinforce the deck, sir,' he said.

'Impossible!' Harsch barked. 'Totally impossible! We'd be a sitting duck on the surface.'

'I appreciate that, sir,' Christian said patiently. 'But can we risk diving with the steering gear out of order? It's a chance *I* wouldn't take.' He looked directly at Harsch's angry eyes.

'*YOU are* not obliged to take the decisions, Number One,' Harsch began to blurt out, then he caught himself and said, 'I suppose you're right, Number One. We might go under and never get up again. All right, this is what we'll do. I'll let you have every possible free man on the deck. Arm the lot of them and man the 88mm cannon. With a bit of luck we might make it to Varna before they attack. If we don't, we'll fight them on the surface.' He bit his bottom lip. 'I'll dive only as the very last resort. *Klar?*'

'*Klar,*' Christian snapped back hurriedly. Harsch bellowed out his orders and there was the clatter of heavy sea-boots as the men selected for the deck started to seize their weapons.

Frenssen wiped the sweat off his forehead and said, 'If the Russians come back, sir, we're right up to our hooters in shit!'

Silently Christian nodded, and then he steeled himself to clear away the gory mess on the foredeck before the rest saw them. It wasn't going to be pleasant at all.

Survival was now the only thought of the tense and silent deck crew as they listened to the muted sound of hammering from below as the engineer's crew tried desperately to straighten the buckled driving rods of the steerage. Sliding through the water at a mere five knots an hour, smoke belching from the diesel exhausts, the crippled U-70 was manned by fearful, apprehensive men, who knew they were sitting ducks. Their triumph in sinking the *Stalin* was forgotten. Even the normally loud and boisterous Frenssen was silent and thoughtful as he stood next to Christian on the wet buckled deck, still stained with the blood of the dead men Christian had gently eased overboard, and who were now bobbing in the U-70's wake like ghastly swimmers.

Time and time again Christian raised his binoculars and searched the darkening horizon for some sight of land, but the coast around Varna remained obstinately out of sight. There was nothing but the rolling grey-green seascape, bare of anything. 'If only the damned fog would come back!' Christian cursed more than once, clenching his fists in impotent rage. 'If only!' But the mist refused to do so and visibility, in spite of the approach of evening, was still a good couple of kilometres.

Thus they sailed on, every man wrapped up in a moody cocoon of unhappy thoughts, the look-outs turning their heads from side to side slowly, like wooden puppets worked by a tired puppet-master, to search the horizon for the first sign of an approaching enemy.

An hour passed. Christian estimated that they couldn't be more than ten kilometres from Varna now. They ought to see the first dark smudge of the coast at any moment. Then they could break radio silence and appeal to the harbour authorities for assistance. There was half a flotilla of E-boats based there. They could afford the protection the crippled submarine needed. But it would be fatal to give away their position too soon. The Russians' radio systems might be primitive, but at this moment, he guessed, the whole radio listening network of the Russian Black Sea Fleet would be on the alert trying to pick up any signal the U-70 might transmit. After all, the Russians knew she had been hit and might well be in need of assistance.

'By the Great Whore of Buxtehude, where the dogs piss through their eyeballs!' Frenssen cursed thickly, 'what I wouldn't give for a half litre of good Hamburg suds, a real old sergeant-major of a head…' His words trailed away to nothing as he saw that Christian wasn't listening. Instead he was staring intently at the horizon to the west, eyes narrowed to slits. Suddenly he whipped up his glasses and focused them hurriedly.

'It's them — *the bastards*! They've rumbled us!'

'Russians?'

By way of answer, Christian sprang to the voice tube and yelled urgently. 'Skipper — Jungblut here. Two enemy motor torpedo boats approaching fast. Two enemy MTBs to port, sir!'

Harsch didn't hesitate. 'I'll break radio silence and contact Varna. Sparks, raise the port. You, Number One, try to hold them off the best you can.' He shrugged slightly. 'If the worst comes to the worst, we'll risk a dive.'

'Yes, sir,' Christian answered smartly and leaving the captain to signal Varna, he ran to the side of the conning tower. 'Gunnery Mate, prepare to engage the enemy!' he yelled, as the noise of the racing engines grew ever closer.

'Ay ay, sir,' the *Maat* replied dutifully, as his gun crew sprang to their positions, the number one already swinging

the long 88mm cannon round to face the approaching enemy. Next to Christian, Frenssen did the same with the twin machine-guns. 'Come on, you bastards,' he muttered to himself, as he squinted down the ring sight, 'come on to Daddy!'

Christian allowed himself a momentary grin and then he flung up his binoculars and focused them on the two enemy craft.

They were going flat out. A white bone of water in their teeth, they were skimming across the surface of the sea at a good forty knots an hour, tiny black figures running back and forth across the steeply tilted decks, obviously preparing their craft for action. He frowned. He didn't recognize the type; they were new to him. But in addition to what looked like twin 20mm cannon, it looked to him as if the enemy MTBs were armed with torpedoes. If his guess was correct, they'd come in at top speed, break to port or starboard at the very last moment, and launch their deadly tin fish at the sub. He'd have to do some devilish quick thinking to outguess those damned torpedoes. He licked suddenly parched lips. He hoped to God that the U-70 would respond smartly enough.

Down below on the deck, the gunnery mate bellowed 'Fire!' and the 88mm opened up with a resounding crash. With a sound like ripping canvas, the great shell howled across the water to meet the enemy. It fell in a great burst of whirling white water some hundred metres to the front of the MTBs, obscuring them from view for a few moment. But then they were there again, hurtling forward. Christian bit his bottom lip. The Russians had scented blood. They were not going to be put off so easily. God, he only hoped the skipper had now raised Varna and aircraft were on their way.

Suddenly he spotted the dreaded tell-tale flurry of bubbles exploding on the surface in a trail headed directly towards the U-70. He flung himself to the voice tube. '*Hard to starboard!*' he yelled frantically. 'Great God in Heaven — *hard to starboard! There's a torpedo heading straight for us!*'

Next to him, Frenssen fired off a long burst as the leading MTB broke to the right, exposing the whole length of her superstructure. Wood chips and bits of mast flew everywhere. A Soviet gunner perched in a kind of cage slumped forward over his machine-gun, a dozen bright red buttonholes suddenly stitched across his chest. He yelled in triumph as dark black clouds of smoke started to issue from the MTB's engine room, and the boat's speed began to decrease.

But Christian had no time for Frenssen's victory. He gripped the side of the conning tower with white-knuckled hands as the deadly fish flashed closer and closer, with the U-70 turning dreadfully slowly to get out of its path. 'Damn you, come on!' he whispered to himself, eyes bulging from his head like those of a madman, willing the submarine to move more quickly. '*Come on, you bitch!*' Beads of sweat broke out on his forehead and he tensed his muscles for the impact of one and a half tons of high explosive.

With maddening slowness the U-boat continued turning. Only an effort of sheer naked willpower stopped Christian from screaming out loud. And then the crisis was over. By what seemed to be less than a metre, the torpedo flashed by the hull of the U-70 and continued out to sea. Christian let out a sigh of relief, his legs soft rubber beneath him, all energy drained from his body. But he knew there was no time to relax. Already the second MTB was coming in for the attack, swinging round in a great wide arc, her white wild wake flashing high in the air as she tried to attack from the port side, making the whole length of the crippled U-boat her target.

At once the gunners took up the new challenge, the 88mm thundering away as the sweating crew loaded and re-loaded, the deck at their feet littered with steaming yellow shell cases. Frenssen, too, was firing all out, deliberately aiming at the racing craft's tiny bridge, hoping that a lucky burst might put the captain or his equipment out of action. But it wasn't to be. The second skipper had learned from the misfortune of his comrade, whose craft was limping away from the action at a miserably slow speed, trailing smoke behind it. As he prepared for the attack run, he threw his craft wildly from side to side, as though it was a speedboat and not a 100 ton MTB. At any other time his virtuoso performance would have been a joy to watch. But not now. The 88's shells were landing impotently to the side and rear of the wildly bucking, zigzagging craft. This time, Christian told himself, they hadn't got a damned chance in hell.

But he was wrong. Down below *Kapitänleutnant* Harsch worked feverishly to bring the U-boat round to face the oncoming enemy bow-first, thus presenting the smallest possible target. At the same time he readied four more torpedoes, the torpedo men working all out to reload the tubes, each one of them well aware they were fighting for their very lives.

Harsch shouted up urgently to Christian. 'Give me a bearing on the bastard — *quick*. Number One!'

Christian realized what Harsch was attempting to do. Hastily he shouted out the bearing. Harsch did not hesitate. As the torpedo mate poised over his now ready torpedoes, he called out the setting and then, 'Fire one, two, three — four!'

Christian felt the boat tremble abruptly. He flashed a glance over the side. The water bubbled furiously and there was that familiar swift ripple as the first torpedo shot from the tube and raced just below the surface towards the attacker. Christian swallowed hard. Could the skipper pull it off?

Then it happened. A great hollow boom. A sharp rending sound. A ball of angry red flame. Suddenly the MTB's stern rose straight up into the air. Christian could see her twin screws quite clearly, spinning purposelessly, cutting empty space. The stern slammed down once more and the craft broke in half. At once her bows disappeared under the water, leaving the stern to settle more slowly, thick black smoke mushrooming towards the evening sky.

Christian somehow found his voice and croaked, 'Save your ammunition! Cease firing… cease fire!'

On the deck, the loader allowed the shell cradled in his brawny arms to fall, while Frenssen slumped back gratefully against the bulkhead and wiped the sweat from his brick-red face. '*Grosse Kacke am Christbaum*,' he cursed thickly. 'Somebody up there' — he pointed a forefinger like a hairy sausage at the sky — 'must like us. I thought we was gonna have a nip tucked into our arses this time.' He sighed again.

Christian forced a grin. 'You weren't the only one, *Obermaat*,' he agreed wearily, as the first of the bodies and debris from the sinking Russian MTB started to drift by them in horrific profusion. 'You certainly weren't. *Phew!*' Then Christian stiffened as Harsch came clattering up the ladder, his face radiating self-satisfied happiness. 'Well, Number One, what do you say to that?' he asked, looking at what was left of the MTB, ignoring the shattered Russian corpses bobbing up and down in the waves. 'First the *Stalin*, then two, well, one motor torpedo boat, plus a plane. Not bad going at all for our first battle patrol in the Black Sea, eh?' He beamed at Christian.

'Yes, sir,' Christian agreed readily. 'Very good indeed. I don't doubt that you will be soon receiving *greetings* from the Führer himself.' He emphasized the word 'greetings', for those greetings were always accompanied by the telegram announcing the award of the Knight's Cross.

Harsch's beam increased. 'Very good of you to say so, Number One. I'll see what I can do for you.' Behind their backs, Frenssen muttered something about having a whole chest full of 'tin'; he'd rather have a full flatman and a packet of 'lung torpedoes' any day.

Harsch did not seem to hear. Instead he said, his smile vanishing, 'Funny thing, though, Number One.'

'What is, sir?'

'We tried to raise Varna, as you know, but we couldn't get anywhere. All the operator got was a lot of mumbo-jumbo in what he took to be Russian.'

'*Russian?*'

'Yes. Don't know what to make of it, Number One. He had the correct wave-length, net, the lot. Yet all he got was Russian. Strange, what?'

Silently Christian nodded his agreement and stared at the faint smudge on the darkening horizon that was Varna. What looked like smoke seemed to be rising above the port. He shook his head and told himself he must be imagining it…

CHAPTER 3

Now they were sailing by the dunes that had once been Varna's pre-war pleasure beaches. They rose in humps of deeper darkness, clearly outlined by the lurid red flames that rose into the sky above the port, dotted here and there with abandoned vehicles half-sunk in the sand and twisted into fantastic shapes by shell fire or bombs.

Slowly the U-70 edged its way forward, no one speaking, save for the captain when he gave his orders; and even his voice was subdued and awed, his triumph vanished now at this strange spectacle. They nosed their way around a burning freighter, its deck littered with wreckage and dead seamen. The ruined face of one looked as if someone had thrown a handful of strawberry jam at it. The Moses gasped and turned away quickly trying not to vomit.

To their right, they could see the local sugar refinery burning fiercely and unattended, as the whole mole seemed to be. It was as if they were sailing into a ghost town. Christian frowned and looked at Harsch as they neared to the main landing mole. 'What do you make of it, sir?'

Harsch shook his head. Somewhere to the rear of Varna there was a tremendous explosion that rippled the water at their keel and sent yet another huge cloud of smoke mushrooming upwards. 'God knows, Number One. The only thing I can think of is that' — he hesitated a moment, as if he feared to express the thought aloud — 'the Russians have broken through.'

'But, sir,' Christian protested, 'they were well over a hundred kilometres away when we sailed out on patrol.'

Harsch shrugged. 'Perhaps it was one of those damned long-range Cossack groups of theirs. A sort of spoiling raid. But I'm sure our men have the situation well in hand. The Russians are no match for our brave stubble-hoppers, what?'

'Of course, sir,' Christian agreed without conviction. From what he had seen so far of Varna, this did not look like some 'spoiling raid'. It had all the marks of a full-scale offensive. 'But don't you think we ought to make a few contingency plans, sir? Ensure that we are fuelled up immediately, take on extra rations —'

'Don't panic, Number One,' Harsch interrupted. 'The *Wehrmacht* will sort it all out. It will all look quite different by the light of day tomorrow morning, take my word for it. As soon as we tie up, I shall report to the Port Commandant. He'll put me in the picture, then we'll see. After all,' he added proudly, puffing out his chest, 'it isn't every day that the U-boat Arm sinks the flagship of the Red Fleet. I'm sure our people back in Berlin will want to know about that immediately. Now then, Number One, will you take charge? I think I'll go down and change.' He looked down at his shabby leather overalls, which were well-encrusted with sea salt as all their uniforms were. 'These rear echelon wallahs are sticklers on niceties of dress. And we mustn't offend those swine, must we?' And with that, obviously feeling highly pleased with himself, he nodded to Christian and clattered down the ladder into the hold.

Frenssen waited until he was out of earshot before saying, 'Don't like it, sir, don't like it one bit. Wooden eye — be careful, that'd be my motto if I was in charge here.' He closed one eye and touched his big nose significantly.

Christian didn't comment, but he knew what Frenssen meant. Something very strange was going on at Varna and he didn't like it one bit. He felt himself surrounded by a deadly, evil atmosphere. He shivered suddenly and when Frenssen looked at him, his face hollowed out to a dark-red death's head by the flames, he said apologetically, 'A louse must have run over my liver, Frenssen.'

Frenssen nodded dourly, 'Know what you mean, sir.' They both fell silent as their nostrils were assailed by a horrible stench of blood and mutilation. Not a breath of air was blowing to dissipate the appalling odour. Even the teenage deck crew stopped their excited chatter at being back in port again, and stared numbly into the red gloom, puffing silently at their cigarettes.

Kapitänleutnant Harsch, when he reappeared on the bridge, spruce, washed and changed into his number one white summer uniform, complete with dirk, was full of himself. 'Well, Number One, how do I look?' he demanded. 'Smart enough to meet that fat Port Commandant, with his War Service Cross Third Class,' he chuckled, 'earned presumably from bedding all those ugly grey auxiliaries, what?'

'Yes, sir. Very smart,' Christian agreed hastily, though Harsch's appearance was furthest from his mind at this particular moment. 'Very impressive.'

'*Gut*,' Harsch snapped, tilting his cap to a suitably rakish angle. 'I'm taking the Moses with him by the way — just in case.' He indicated the pale-faced young rating who now popped his head into the tower, a machine-pistol hanging from his shoulder.

Frenssen flashed Christian a look, but he ignored it. Instead he asked, 'Your orders, sir?'

'Just sit tight, Number One. *Ruhig Blut,* that's the order of the day. But if you so wish, you can refuel over there,' he indicated the fuelling jetty. 'Otherwise sit tight and let's see what the Port Commandant has to say. Come on, Moses.'

Christian bent over the edge of the conning tower and yelled. 'All right, you men, get the skipper's dinghy over the side!' Then he snapped to attention, as the captain began to scuttle down the ladder. Clearly, he could not get ashore soon enough to report his tremendous victory. Behind him, the Moses trotted dutifully, his youthful face a mixture of pride that he had been selected by the skipper — and apprehension.

Two minutes later they had disappeared into the red gloom, the Moses rowing mightily, while Christian stared moodily at the burning horizon, wondering just what exactly was going on in Varna…

'Don't look so worried, Moses,' *Kapitänleutnant* Harsch said encouragingly, as they clambered up the dripping ladder to the debris-littered jetty. 'It's all something local, my boy, believe you me.'

'Yes, sir,' the Moses said, gripping his Schmeisser more tightly and staring to left and right, half-expecting hordes of Russians to spring out of the glowing darkness.

Harsch laid his hand on the boy's skinny shoulder and pressed it, perhaps a little too hard. 'Now you just stick close to me and I'll see you're all right.'

'Thank you, sir,' the Moses answered and then barely concealed his gasp of relief as the skipper took his big paw away. He had never been treated so familiarly by an officer and it was a strange feeling.

Together they started to move forward, aware now of a muted rumble in the distance, broken occasionally by sharper cracks that were followed by spurts of cherry-red flame. Obviously there was still life in Varna, Harsch told himself. But it was conspicuously absent from the docks, normally swarming with human beings day and night. Where in three devils' name had everybody gone? He frowned and then thought of the *Stalin*. The lurking sense of apprehension and danger vanished. God be praised, he told himself, they would never call *him* the 'Locomotive Killer' again.

Five minutes later they saw the first sign that there was still life at Varna docks. From the second-storey window of the large building to their immediate right, bright white light was streaming, totally disregarding the blackout regulations. Moses licked his dry lips and clutched his machine-pistol more tightly in hands that were already damp with sweat. 'Somebody's in for a rocket, sir, if the police catch him. Just look at that light. You can see it kilometres away!'

'I know, Moses. All the same, let's go and have a look-see. At least, somebody must be alive up there. Can you hear the noise? Sounds like some machine or other working. Didn't know those rear echelon stallions worked at night. Come on.'

Together they crunched over broken glass, kicking aside what appeared to be bundles of files, which were everywhere, their nostrils assailed now by the smell of burning paper, and started to mount the stairs.

They didn't get far. Moses gasped suddenly and flung his hand to his mouth again, as if he might vomit. 'Sir,' he said thickly, face suddenly white with shock, as he stumbled to a stop on the stairs.

'What is —' Harsch stopped short and gasped, 'Oh, my dear God — what a mess!'

Through the open door of the office to the right, he could see them; the dead grey mouse, lying sprawled on the paper-littered desk, legs spread wide, her grey issue knickers crumpled about her ankles, dark red blood already congealing at her shattered temples. At the next desk, on which rested two empty bottles of cognac, slumped a dead officer, service pistol still clutched in his lifeless fingers.

Harsch knew instinctively what had happened. They had got drunk and rutted like animals, then he had shot her first before turning the pistol on himself. But why?

He caught the Moses gazing at the dead woman and snapped hastily, 'Come on, Moses. There's enough piggery here as it is. *Los!*'

'Yes, sir,' the Moses answered obediently, tearing his gaze away. 'But what's — what's going on, sir?'

'I don't know,' Harsch snapped. 'But I'm soon damn well going to find out. Let's see what that chap with the machine has got to say. Move it!'

The Moses 'moved it'.

They turned a bend in the stairs and saw what seemed to be the only person alive at Varna docks. He was a tall, harassed staff officer, who was feeding papers into a shredder with a hand that trembled visibly, while drinking from an open bottle with the other. Next to him, sprawled in an armchair, was a fat captain-quartermaster, whose face — what was left of it — was vaguely familiar to Harsch. He too had committed suicide. Perhaps he had been too drunk to chance putting his pistol to his temple. Instead, he had played it safe and put the muzzle inside his mouth. He had blown the back of his head off. The welter of gore was still dripping slowly down the wall behind him. Harsch stepped forward. Behind him the Moses retched miserably and began to vomit.

'*Herr Kapitänleutnant*' Harsch began.

The staff officer at the shredder jumped visibly. The bottle fell from his fingers with the shock and shattered on the floor. There was sudden stink of cheap cognac. 'Oh, my God,' he gasped, lean face drained of all colour. 'I thought it was them.

Oh, my God!' He wiped the sweat off his brow and for one horrified moment, Harsch thought he'd break down and cry.

'*Herr Kapitänleutnant*' he said firmly. 'My name is Harsch, skipper of the U-70. We have just run in — after sinking the *Stalin*!'

The other officer did not seem to understand. His lips were moving, though he was making no intelligible sound, and a nerve was ticking and twitching at the side of his mouth, obviously out of control. The man was at the end of his tether. It was no use telling him about the *Stalin*. 'Now pull yourself together, man!' Harsch barked, wondering whether he should strike the other officer across the face to bring him back to his senses. 'What in three devils' name is going on here in Varna.'

The other man licked cracked lips and said hoarsely. 'Sorry. I forgot myself for a moment. The panic, the mass suicides.' He waved his hand at the room a little helplessly, as if it should be explanation enough. 'Forgive me.'

'But why the panic … the suicides?' Harsch persisted, aware now that the sound of gunfire was growing closer. He thought too he could hear the rumble of tanks. 'And why are you shredding official documents?'

'Haven't you heard, *Herr Kapitänleutnant*?'

'Heard what?'

'The Russians are rolling up the whole Black Sea coast. We're surrounded here in Varna. There's no way out. Those who don't want to fall into the hands of those swine have taken the officer's way out.' He indicated the dead captain-quartermaster.

'But you're sailors. There's the sea,' Harsch objected. 'That's a way of escape isn't it?'

Surprisingly the other man began to laugh, but it was a strange kind of laughter, verging on the hysterical, one that could easily end in tears.

'Pull yourself together!' Harsch bellowed and slapped the other officer hard across the face. 'Damn you, man, get a grip of yourself. And you too, Moses. Stop that vomiting. At once, do you hear?' Harsch was beginning to feel the first cold finger of fear trace its way down the small of his back. He shivered. God, he didn't want to be trapped here now at the very moment of his tremendous victory.

The other man stared at him, eyes filled with tears, his pale face clearly revealing the livid marks of Harsch's fingers. 'Sorry,' he said slowly, voice shaky. 'I don't know what got into me. I must pull myself together. I've got my job to carry out, you know.' He indicated the shredder. 'Mustn't let this top secret stuff fall into their hands. Must get it finished before they come.' Still talking, he picked up another bunch of papers marked in bright red '*Geheime Reichssache*' and started to feed them into the clacking machine.

'But you haven't answered my question, *Herr Kapitänleutnant*,' Harsch snapped. 'Why haven't you attempted to escape by sea?'

The other man didn't take his gaze off the machine. 'Simple. Some of them did. The E-boat half-flotilla for example. They made a dash for the Bosporus. Once they were through it and into the Sea of Marmara, they reasoned, they wouldn't have any trouble with the Turks. Although they're officially neutral, the Turks hate the Russians passionately.'

He shrugged. 'They never got that far. The Russians were waiting for them at the entrance to the Bosporus. They were slaughtered to a man.'

Harsch gazed at him aghast. 'Do you mean,' he stuttered, 'that the whole ... of the Black Sea is sealed off? *Is that what you mean?*'

'Yes. Since Wednesday the Black Sea has been a Russian lake.' He went on shredding.

As the rumble of the guns grew ever closer and Christian recognized the characteristic howl of the Russian multiple mortars, the ones the stubble-hoppers called the 'Stalin Organs,' he knew they were in serious trouble in Varna. Refuelling was well under way, with the men bustling back and forth, loading fresh rations. But there was still that damned great hole in the deck. If they had to make a run for it, their crippled steering gear would be trouble enough, but if the U-70 attempted to dive with that hole... Damn the skipper, with his head full of honours and decorations. Someone had to face up to the realities of the situation. He'd order the immediate patching of the hole.

Obermaat Frenssen, for his part, had more personal problems on his mind just then as Christian started to give orders for the patching to the engineering officer. As he stood on the jetty, listening to the rumble of the guns, supervising the young ratings carrying out the re-fuelling, he told himself, 'Otto, old horse, if we're gonna have to make a run for it, there are two things you need before they lock you back in that tin box for another couple of weeks.' He grinned at the thought and then snarled at a rating, who seemed to be carrying out his duties too slowly. 'Hey you, slime-shitter! Move your hind-flippers a bit faster — or you'll feel the tip o' my dice-beaker up turd-dispenser, right sharpish. *Move!*'

The rating fled, leaving Frenssen to continue his ruminating. 'Yer, there aren't many pleasures allowed to your ordinary humble sailor-boy in this world. But he should be entitled to his share o' guzzle and women before he turns up his toes for Folk, Fatherland and Führer.' He rubbed his unshaven jaw with a hand like a small steam shovel at the thought. 'Guzzle and women,' that was the order of the day.

He looked at the men busy with the fuel pipelines and then at the other ratings busy on the U-boat's deck. There was no one on the bridge save look-out. The number one had disappeared below. Nobody would miss him for a few minutes. God, he had so much ink in his fountain-pen, he didn't know whom to write to first! It wouldn't take him long to grab a little arse. A quick knee-trembler against the wall over there and a nice slug o' the local firewater and he'd be a happy man for the next couple of weeks or so. The prospect of a woman and a drink became ever more attractive. He tugged at his black pants, as if the front had suddenly become too tight for him, and rose to his feet. One last look at the U-70 and he was gone, moving with surprising quietness for such a big man. Moments later he had vanished into the glowing shadows. *Obermaat* Otto Frenssen was on the hunt for 'guzzle and women'.

But the big petty officer was not fated to enjoy those simple basic pleasures. Hardly had he moved off into the shadows when he became aware there was something wrong, seriously so. It was the smell which alerted him, the unmistakable bitter odour of black tobacco he had come to associate solely with them. *Makhorka*, they called it in their language. He stopped and crouched next to a pile of packing cases, the hunt for 'guzzle and women' totally forgotten. Out there, somewhere in the glowing darkness, *they* were present — the Russians!

As he crouched, he patted his pockets. *Nothing!*. He didn't even have the jackknife he occasionally used on his corns. He was completely unarmed. He cursed softly and wished he had remembered to bring with him his 'Hamburg Equalizer' — his brass knuckles; they would have been the ideal weapon for what he knew was to come. 'As usual,' he moaned to himself, 'blinded by lust!' He shook his head at his own foolishness and waited.

There was a soft sound of horse's hooves, as if they were muffled by rags, and suddenly, startlingly, outlined a stark black by the red glow, he saw him. There was no mistaking that rakishly tilted fur hat and the gleam of the drawn sabre. 'A frigging Cossack,' he cursed. 'That's all I needed — a Cossack armed with a sodding penknife!'

The Cossack poised, half-raised in his saddle, turning his head slowly from side to side, listening. Frenssen tensed. He knew the Cossacks were half-savages, and like most savages they had phenomenal powers of hearing and smell. 'In half a mo, his hooter'll get a frigging fix on me,' Frenssen told himself grimly, feeling his heart begin to pound with growing excitement, 'and then the piss will really be in the flower pot!' He clenched his fists and prepared to act, as the Cossack rose a little higher in his stirrups, resting his drawn sabre over his right shoulder as he did so.

It was now or never, Frenssen told himself. As yet the Cossack suspected nothing. He drew a deep breath. His massive chest swelled. The muscles of his arms felt like hard rocks. He was as ready as he ever would be. It was time to tackle the Russian piss-pants!

'*Crap!*' he yelled at the top of his voice, as he launched himself. 'And a thousand arses bent and took the strain! *For in them days the word of the King was law!*'

The Cossack's horse whinnied with fright and reared up on its hind legs, its forelegs pawing the air, just as Frenssen had predicted it would at the sudden noise. '*Boshe moi!*' the Cossack cursed and pulled furiously at the bit. It dug cruelly into the animal's mouth and made it flail the air even more with its forelegs. Then the rider saw Frenssen. His sabre sliced the air violently.

'Hey, you up there, watch that frigging penknife!' Frenssen yelled angrily. 'You nearly sawed off one of my frigging flippers!' In that same instant he reached up and grabbed the Cossack. Caught completely by surprise, the Russian slithered from his saddle, and tumbled together with Frenssen to the ground. The thoroughly unnerved horse didn't wait for a second invitation to escape. It bolted, leaving its master to his fate.

The sabre clattered to the concrete. The Cossack, a head smaller than Frenssen, but slim and wiry, brought up his knee. It just missed Frenssen's groin and caught him a painful blow on the hip. 'Shite-hawk,' Frenssen cursed, 'try to ruin a man's sex life!' he grabbed for the Cossack's throat, seized by a frenzy of mad, blinding rage.

The Cossack dodged. He thrust forward the two fingers of his right hand, inserted them into Frenssen's nostrils and tugged hard. Frenssen's head nearly fell off with the excruciating pain. He yelped with the agony of it, hot blood flooding his mouth.

Instinctively he brought up a hand and chopped at the Cossack's exposed Adam's apple. The Cossack gurgled something. The terrible grip vanished abruptly. Snorting blood, Frenssen drew back a fist and with all his huge strength launched a massive punch at the Cossack's face. The latter screamed shrilly as his nose burst, splattering blood everywhere, through which his teeth gleamed like polished ivory. His head flopped to one side and he was gone, either dead or unconscious. But Frenssen had no time to check. Already he could hear the muted sound of further horses.

He wiped the blood from his right fist on the Cossack's black coat and crouched, grasping the sabre, eyes searching the gloom for the others, nerves racing. He had to get through the bastards, he told himself urgently. He had to warn the others. The Cossacks would slaughter those piss-pansies of young ratings re-fuelling the U-70 before they knew what had hit them. He wondered what old 'Locomotive Killer' Harsch would say if his precious boat was captured — *by horsemen*!

Suddenly all thoughts of Harsch vanished from his big cropped head. To his immediate front there were two more fur-hatted riders, carbines slung over their backs, sabres in their right hands as they urged their horses forward through the mess of packing cases. He pressed himself back into the shadow cast by the wall, hardly daring to breathe. If they spotted him ... Frenssen decided he would not think that particularly unpleasant thought to its logical and frightening conclusion.

The Cossacks trotted closer. He could hear the soft jingle of their harnesses and muted clatter of equipment. He tensed, the palm of his hand gripping the sabre wet with sudden sweat. A nerve started to tick urgently at the side of his face. Christ, he prayed, don't let the Russian crap-arses see me!

Now they were only metres away. His body froze as the horse of the leading rider threw up its head and shuddered in the deep throaty way horses have when they are nervous. Frenssen stopped breathing. *The shitty old nag knew he was there, lurking in the shadows!*

Its rider muttered something and jerked at the bit. The horse's head shot up and it snorted painfully. It was so close Frenssen could feel the hot air on his stony face. Would they spot him at the very last moment? He prepared to fight for his life.

Then they were past, clattering off into the red gloom, leaving him leaning limply on the wall, his body lathered in sweat, gulping for air. He had done it again, he had got away with it. 'Holy strawsack,' he swore fervently to himself, 'somebody up there must frigging well love you, Otto!'

Then he was running all out back to the U-70, as if the Devil himself were after him.

CHAPTER 4

'Fill the shitting hole with mattresses, Engineer!' Christian cried desperately. 'Plug it with anything. *Los!*' He swung round on a panting exhausted Frenssen, his face glazed with sweat. 'You, you big ox, man the twin machine-guns. Come on... Christ in Heaven, *where's the fucking skipper?*'

The re-fuelling party abandoned the hoses, which snaked into the water, disgorging diesel in huge, bubbling gulps and belches; and the deck crew doubled forward to man the 88mm cannon, swinging its long barrel round to face the land — and the Russians.

Hurriedly, as the lurid flames over a dying Varna grew higher and higher and the caulking party below pressed and tugged and squeezed mattresses into the gaping hole in the deck, Christian yelled into the voice tube, 'Engine room, start both. For chrissake, start both!' He cupped his hands to shout above the noise of shelling and cheering that came from the port, and cried. '*Leinen los!* Cast off those lines, you deckies. Come on, *Leinen los!*'

As the U-70's diesels whined and groaned, thick black smoke pouring out of the exhausts, the deckhands frantically undid the hawsers that attached the boat to the mole. Even the dullest among them could tell from the racket coming from Varna that the Russians were not far away now; and all of them knew what their fate would be if the Russians captured them. Like the SS, paras, and members of any police formation, they would be slaughtered out of hand. The Russians didn't take submariners prisoner!

Christian smashed his clenched fist down on the conning tower with frustration. First off, the damned skipper, with his shitting dreams of glory, was missing. Now the damned engines were refusing to start and already he could hear the clip-clop of horses' hooves approaching. Those would be the Cossacks Frenssen had mentioned. 'Get ready to fire, you big ox,' he commanded. 'I don't want any of those buggers getting within range of the boat.'

'Don't worry, sir,' Frenssen replied loyally, squinting down the ring sight in anticipation. 'But I don't know what good this farting little popgun is going to be against *that*.'

'Against what?' Christian snapped in irritation.

'Tanks, sir. Can't you hear the friggers. Them is Russian tanks out there.'

Christian groaned. 'Shit on shingle, not that as well!'

Frenssen nodded grimly as he cocked the twin machine guns. Christian left him to it. He squatted over the entrance to the boat and yelled, 'Come on, Engineer, get those shitting engines working. They'll be on us at any minute, damn you!'

The harassed engineer officer, his face sweaty and oily, dark circles of worry under his eyes, snorted. 'Have & *frigging* heart, Number One. What do you want me to do — stick a *frigging* broom up my arse and sweep the place out as well? I'm trying to fix *the frigging* hole and get the frigging buggers started at the same time. I can't do *frigging* everything, you know.'

In spite of his fears and the tension, Christian grinned. He said. 'All right, Engineer, do your *frigging* best — *please!*'

Now it was the engineer's turn to grin. He tugged a piece of cotton waste from his back pocket, wiped his face with it and cried, 'Don't worry, Number One. I'll get the friggers started for you —'

'*Leutnant* Jungblut!' Frenssen's urgent yell broke into the conversation, 'It's the skipper … with the Moses!'

Christian turned and peered over the side. *Kapitänleutnant* Harsch had thrown all dignity to the wind. He was running all out for the U-70, followed by an obviously terrified Moses. Behind them came the clatter of racing horses' hooves. The Cossacks had spotted them! 'Give them covering fire, Frenssen!' Christian cried in alarm, as the first of the riders came careering round the corner, waving their sabres excitedly above their fur-capped heads and yelling '*Urrah!Urrah!*' in the frightening manner of attacking Russian troops.

Frenssen didn't need a second invitation. He pressed the trigger. At a rate of a thousand slugs a minute, white tracer hissed towards the Cossacks. They didn't stand a chance. Horses and riders crashed to the ground in a confused, bloody mess, with the mounts whinnying piteously.

Another wild group came charging round the corner. Some were shot down immediately. Others sprang boldly over their dead and dying comrades and disappeared into the packing cases. Almost instantly they flung themselves from their mounts and opened fire. At the gun, the first rating flung up his hands wildly, as if appealing to heaven itself at the injustice of what had just been done to him, and then fell over the side.

Christian groaned. The situation was getting completely out of hand. And the rattle of tank tracks was louder. When would the engineer get those damned engines started?

Gasping frantically for breath, Harsch stumbled up into the conning tower, slugs pattering off its metal skin like heavy tropical rain on a tin roof. 'They're everywhere … everywhere!' he gasped, as a white-faced frightened Moses pushed by him to drop to the bottom of the conning tower in a panting heap. 'Varna's virtually taken … as is the rest of the coast… We've got to get away, Number One … while there's time… The Russians are sealing off the exit to the Black Sea!'

Christian bit his bottom lip with worry. Below the engineer tried desperately to start the engines, which obstinately refused to do so. 'You mean we've got to be off, get through the Bosporus — with the boat the way she is, sir?'

Holding his hand to his heart, chest heaving madly, Harsch nodded numbly.

'Christ on a crutch, sir, that's really a tall ord —'

'*A tank, sir!*' Frenssen's urgent shout broke in abruptly.

Christian flung a look at the jetty. In a shower of angry blue sparks, as its tracks dug into the concrete, a T-34 slewed round the corner, its machine-gun already spitting fire.

Another one appeared behind it. 'Oh, my God!' he gasped. Down on the deck the gunnery petty officer bellowed, '*Feuer!*'

The 88mm cannon erupted. Blue flame shot from its muzzle. *Crump!* The shell exploded against the T-34's turret. The Soviet tank rocked wildly, crashing back on its rear bogies. Someone cheered. But when the smoke cleared the T-34 was still moving, a great gleaming silver scar on its turret where the shell had struck it.

'HE is no good!' Harsch roared above the racket. 'And who heard of a U-boat carrying armour piercing ammo!'

Christian groaned as the gunners fired again and once more struck the leading tank harmlessly, the shell bouncing off its thick metal hide like a glowing ping-pong ball.

Frenssen pressed his trigger, deliberately aiming at the driver's slit in the T-34, but he was equally unsuccessful. The T-34 came on, the long overhanging 75mm cannon swinging round on the submarine. In a minute they would open fire, Christian told himself miserably, and that would be that. At that range they couldn't miss.

From below there was suddenly a throaty cough, followed by a high-pitched, teeth-grating whine. Christian's heart skipped a beat. He looked at the skipper. Harsch stood, fists clenched and white-knuckled, face drawn, as if physically willing the U-70's engines to start up.

On the quay the leading T-34 skidded to a stop. Christian knew what that meant. The Soviet tanks were old-fashioned. They did not possess a gyro-stabilizer and had to stop when they wanted to fire. The enemy gunner was about to fire at them.

Below the banshee-like howling continued, rising and rising. Again thick black smoke jetted from the exhausts. The whole boat shuddered and trembled under the strain. The plates creaked and protested. Still the dire keening continued. 'Come on, come on,' Christian cursed through gritted teeth, sweat pouring down his face. 'Come on, you bitch, *start*!'

The gun of the T-34 on the quayside ceased turning. The Soviet gunner had them exactly in the centre of his sights. Christian could imagine him, closing one eye, holding his breath, his hand stealing out to fire the great overhanging cannon. He tensed.

A sudden flat crack. A belch of angry red flame. The thirty ton tank reeled back. A howl. A tremendous screech. '*DUCK*!' Harsch shrieked hysterically. Something smacked the conning tower a tremendous blow. Christian grabbed frantically for support as the whole boat heeled and trembled. He saw to his horror that the whole inner left side of the conning tower was glowing a livid purple and was actually beginning to melt. Already great molten steel tears were starting to drip and trickle down the side. He swallowed hard, his nostrils assailed by the stink of melting steel, his body lathered in a sweat of absolute terror. The Russians had used an armour-piercing shell. If it managed to penetrate the conning tower, it would whiz round and round, tearing everything in its path to ribbons. They would all be ripped to pieces. For what seemed an eternity he watched the dull glow run the length of the conning tower, as if the shell had life and intelligence of its own and was desperately trying to get in and carry out its gory, lethal work of destruction. Then suddenly the glow vanished and he heard the abrupt hiss of water and steam as the shell fell harmlessly over the side.

In that very same instant, the engines of the U-70 burst into a full, throaty, pulsating life. Harsch reacted immediately. '*Both into reverse!*' he screamed into the voice tube. 'Clear the deck crew —'

Across the way, the T-34 fired again. A shell slammed into the U-boat's side. She reeled and heeled, as if struck by a giant fist. A burst of machine-gun fire from the tank's turret scythed down the deck crew running for the conning tower. The gunnery petty officer flung up his hands dramatically and pitched over the side into the dirty, oily water of the harbour. Frenssen fired one last angry burst at the first tank, the tracer bouncing off its thick hide in a glowing white rain; then he too was sliding down the ladder into the interior of the U-boat, just as the second T-34 skidded to a halt and began firing. 'What are you going to do, skipper?' Christian cried above the din.

Harsch cupped his hands to his mouth. 'There's nothing for it, Number One! We've got to take her down to periscope depth, as soon as the water's deep enough. Up here they've got us with our nuts in the wringer. In a minute one of those blasted Russian tanks is going to strike lucky —' Another shell smacked into the U-70's side and they both clutched frantically for support. 'Now come on, let's hoof it, Number One!'

'Flood!' Harsch commanded, as Christian flung his whole weight behind the wheel that sealed the hatch to the conning tower. It snapped closed metallically.

'Flood!' the engineer yelled back. One by one he counted off the tanks as they filled with the harbour water... It became much quieter inside the boat now as they switched from the diesels to the electric motor. Abruptly red glowing lights broke the yellow gloom the length of the boat and the various operators tensed over their instruments.

The bow of the U-70 tilted. The whole boat shivered and trembled. The ratings swallowed and tried to avoid looking at each other. They knew they were between the Devil and the deep blue sea. If they stayed on the surface, the Russians would get them. If they dived too deeply, it was anybody's guess how long their steering would hold out. It might take them to the bottom for good. Then there was that hastily repaired hole in the deck. If that gave way under the pressure of the sea water, they'd flood and sink without a chance in hell of ever surfacing again.

'Twenty-five degree load,' Christian sang out with more confidence than he felt. His legs seemed to be made of soft rubber. He would dearly have loved to sit down, but he knew he couldn't. The youngsters were nervous and tense enough, he had to set an example.

'Periscope depth,' he called out a moment later. Small sharp explosions began to peck and nip at the submarine's steel casing. Obviously the Russians up above on the quayside were tossing grenades at the clearly visible boat. They could do little damage — perhaps buckle or spring a plate here and there — but if one of the Russians got lucky and hit the poorly patched hole on the upper deck, then that would be that. They wouldn't make it.

'Periscope up!' Harsch commanded. Swiftly he turned his cap back to front as the gleaming steel tube hissed upwards. He grasped the twin handles and peered into the optic. All about the operators, their faces hollowed out to grim skulls in the red light, waited for him to speak. Christian told himself the skipper was faced with one hell of a task. He was going to have to steer his half-crippled boat through the mass of sunken shipping in the channel which led out of Varna, with the Russians already alerting their patrol craft and air force that the U-70 was trying to escape just below the surface.

In an atmosphere of fearful apprehension, the boat limped forward into the channel, the noise of the grenades dying away now as they drew away from the Russians. No one dared speak. Even Frenssen, no respecter of persons at virtually any time, kept his big mouth shut. For whatever he felt about the skipper, he knew too that his, and all their fates now depended exclusively on Harsch's skill and nerves. He was their only link with the outside world. He alone could make the decisions.

Softly, carefully, Harsch called out his orders and each time Christian said a silent prayer that the U-70's damaged steering gear would respond in time. Obstacle by obstacle the submarine crept out to sea, manoeuvring with painful, creaking slowness. Once there was a dreadful, heart stopping, rending sound that seemed to go on for ever as the U-70 scraped the length of some obstruction or other. Frenssen cursed softly and abruptly the back of Harsch's cropped head was wet and gleaming with sweat. The tension was almost unbearable.

'Increase both — ten,' Harsch ordered, some fifteen minutes after they had entered the channel. 'Easy does it!'

The engineer repeated the order and the Moses couldn't contain himself any longer. 'We're through!' he cried out aloud. 'We're through!'

'Be quiet back there!' Harsch snapped severely, not taking his gaze off the periscope for a moment. 'We're not through yet — by a long chalk. But we've got to make speed before the Russian planes jump us. Hold her steady now.'

The Moses hung his head, as if ashamed and his face flushed crimson with embarrassment. Frenssen frowned and looked curiously at the handsome young boy.

The U-70 plodded on, but the strain on her structure at being underwater again was beginning to tell. Even before the engineer approached him, Christian could dimly hear the trickle of water and the first splashes as it started to run across the deck. 'I don't want to tell the skipper just yet, Jungblut,' the other officer whispered in Christian's ear so that the crew wouldn't hear, 'but that damned plug where the shell came through is beginning to leak and I don't know how long the other damn hole will remain sealed. There's a hell of a great gash there, you know.'

Christian nodded and gestured to Frenssen. Swiftly he told the latter what the engineer had said and then commanded, 'All right, you great ox, don't just stand there like a wet fart waiting to hit the side of the thunderbox! Get a couple of your cronies — old hares — and see what you can do. But for God's sake don't alarm the green beaks. They're jittery enough as it is.'

Frenssen forced a grin. 'Don't you worry, sir. Frau Frenssen's handsome son'll soon sort it out.'

Christian grinned too and made an obscene gesture.

The chief petty officer shook his head. 'Afraid I can't do it, sir. Already got a double-decker bus up there.'

'Be off with you!' Christian said and then forgot Frenssen as he concentrated on the skipper, who was still glued to the periscope as if he had been fused to the metal, his voice reduced to a harsh croak as he issued his orders The strain of command was all too obvious. Suddenly Christian felt for him. He didn't particularly like Harsch. He was one of the old school of skippers — *der letzte Dreck*, the scum of the earth, as they called themselves with bitter pride — who had been trained on the three-master sailing ships of the Kaiser's Navy. 'Hell ships', they called them, where they had lived off food no self-respecting pig would have touched and where they never averaged more than a couple of hours sleep a day. Through the Revolution they had been spat and jeered at by their own ratings, their medals and badges of rank torn off their tunics by the howling mob of mutinous sailors.

Thereafter had come the long years in the civilian 'wilderness' when the new Republic had been forbidden to possess U-boats. What had Harsch done in that bitter time when six million Germans had been employed? Sold brushes from door to door and toothbrushes on street comers from his 'belly shop', as the tray of wares suspended from the neck by a strap was called. Even when he had been recalled to the *Kriegsmarine* and given his own boat after those long years of waiting, he had been unsuccessful. He had seen Prien, Kretschmar, and the like become celebrated aces, known throughout the Reich, heaped with honours, famous U-boat skippers, who had sunk great ships and thousands upon thousands of tons of enemy shipping. No wonder Harsch was a bitter, lonely man, who remained remote and had little real contact with his much younger officers and men. Now the fates of all his crew were in his hands — a crew who had not understood his private fears and worries and who had been contemptuous of this 'Locomotive Killer' with his overweening pride and greed for glory.

The sudden rush of water around his ankles made him forget Harsch for a moment. He knew instinctively what had happened. Frenssen and his old hares had failed to stop the leak. The water was rushing in unhampered. It wouldn't be long before it flooded the batteries of the electric motors and then there would be all hell to pay. Something had to be done — and done quickly.

Harsch realized it too. 'Number One,' he snapped harshly.

'There's nothing for it. We've got to surface and take our chance.'

'I agree, sir,' Christian said without hesitation.

Hastily Harsch spun the periscope three hundred and sixty degrees. Christian waited tensely. Someone up front started a deep, tight, hacking cough, as if the first of the gas was already beginning to leak from the batteries under the influence of the water rushing in.

Harsch clapped the handles of the periscope together with an air of finality. 'All right, take her up,' he commanded. '*Surface!*'

Compressed air streamed into the buoyancy tanks. Water rushed out with an obscene gurgling sound. There was the familiar noise of a submarine breaking surface, rocking as if punch-drunk from all the punishment she had suffered in the last forty-eight hours. The hatch opened with a metallic click and suddenly fresh air streamed in and fought the gas and the stench of oil, human fear, and stale sweat. Hurriedly Harsch pelted up the ladder into the conning tower, followed by Christian, both of them sucking in the blessed air greedily. For a moment or two the officers simply stood there under the velvety, star-studded night sky, listening, ears strained for the first sound of danger. But there was none. Although they could still see the red glare on the horizon which was a dying Varna, they seemed to have outdistanced their pursuers. For the moment at least, they appeared to be safe.

Harsch leaned towards the voice tube. 'All right, Engineer, ventilate the boat and start the pumps working. Start up both!'

'Start up both, it is, sir!' the engineer replied. The diesels started to pound, accompanied by the steady throbbing of the pumps fighting the water threatening to swamp the U-70. To Christian's way of thinking, they could be heard all the way to Moscow. He looked at Harsch, his face set and determined in the silver light of the stars.

Finally Harsch spoke. 'As you must realize Number One, we haven't many options left. The U-70 is in pretty bad shape. I'm scared to take her down again and we'd be a sitting duck if we continued on the surface, especially as it gets light. We've had all the luck we can possibly expect as it is.'

Christian nodded his agreement. 'So what do we do, sir?' Harsch didn't answer. Instead he cocked his head to one side in the same moment that Christian too heard the faint drone of aircraft. 'Russian,' Harsch said. 'They can only be their aircraft. They're looking for us. So what do we do?' He answered his own question. 'We steer in clear to the Bulgarian coast, hugging the coastline the best we can. It's pretty low in this area, but it should afford us some cover. By dawn I want to have found some little cove or inlet where we can hide during the daylight hours. With a bit of luck, we can do the necessary emergency repairs on the U-70 and then prepare to attempt to enter the Bosporus…' His words trailed away and he looked at Christian almost pleadingly, willing him to say they had a chance.

The younger officer considered a minute, listening to the faint persistent drone. Their chances were slim, he knew that. The Bulgarians had been shaky allies of the Third Reich ever since Hitler had forced them to declare war on their fellow Slavs, the Russians. Now he guessed they'd go over to the

Russians wholesale. The local fisherfolk and villagers, therefore, couldn't be trusted. That was the first thing. Then there was the problem of finding a hiding place on the coast not yet occupied by the victorious Red Army. It would be only a matter of days, perhaps even a mere twenty-four hours, before they captured the whole length of the Black Sea coast right up to the border with Turkey. That was the second thing. Number three, could they with their limited resources manage to knock the battered submarine into reasonable shape once more?

Harsch looked at Christian's face and seemed to read what was going through his mind. Very quietly he said, 'What other alternative do we have, Number One?'

'I agree, sir. If we surrender, they'll shoot us out of hand. If we don't and continue at our present rate, they'll blow us out of the water as soon as it's full light.' He laughed, but there was no warmth in the sound. 'I think, sir, there's nothing for it but — march or croak.'

Harsch's laugh was cold and bitter. '*Jawohl, Jungblut,*' he cried, '*da haben Sie recht... Marschieren oder krepieren!*' So the decision was made. Slowly the drone of the hunter's plane began to fade away in the night sky. They were on their way. *March or croak...*

CHAPTER 5

The glare of the morning sun — a blood-red ball standing on the stark, black peaks of the far mountains — cut their eyes like a sharp knife. Eyes narrowed to slits, they all watched tensely as the battered U-boat started to nose its way slowly, carefully, through the perfect, sun-dappled water of the little cove.

While the deck crew crouched, weapons at the ready, Harsch and Christian on the bridge surveyed the land anxiously through their binoculars. Behind them Frenssen manned the twin machine-guns, ready to spring into action at the first sign of trouble. All was tense expectancy in spite of the calm beauty of the morning, with the birds chirping merrily in the line of stunted firs that lined the little cove. The heady scent of pine resin wafted towards them as they came closer to the haven.

But there seemed nothing to fear. The little cove had an almost peacetime air about it, with its gently sloping, golden-sanded beach unmarred by even a single human footprint. The war might have been a million miles away.

'Well, it *looks* all right, perfectly safe,' Harsch conceded, lowering his glasses. 'What do you think, Number One?'

Christian let his glasses fall to his chest, enjoying the morning warmth after the long night's miserable cold. 'It looks all right to me too, sir,' he agreed. 'You wouldn't think there was a war on to look at that place. Ideal holiday spot. All you want now is a stall selling ice-cold Bavarian beer, and a few buxom blondes running around in skimpy bathing suits.'

Behind them Frenssen grinned hugely and commented, 'Just my collar size, sir!' But Harsch was not impressed. Instead he said a little grumpily, 'All right, Number One. Don't let your imagination run away with you. Concentrate on the job in hand. Let's see if the, er, natives are friendly first before we start romanticizing.' He bent to the voice tube and ordered, 'Dead slow, both ahead, engine room.' The speed of the U-70 decreased even more. Now she advanced into the lovely little cove at a snail's pace.

'We'll anchor below that little cliff,' Harsch continued. 'It'll give us shelter from the sun and we'll cut some of those trees down to camouflage the deck while the men work. Won't do us much good if anyone is looking at us from the sea, but it should cover us from the air.'

'Yes, sir,' Christian said, as the boat started to move into the designated anchorage.

'Priority number one,' Harsch went on, as a couple of the deckies sprang over the side bearing the hawsers on their shoulders and struggled towards the land, up to their necks in water, 'is the repairing and caulking of the holes and the steering system. Every available man is to be put to work on those two vital tasks. Understood?'

'Understood, sir.'

'That should leave a handful of men, who, commanded by *Obermaat* Frenssen here, will dig a defensive perimeter on the top of the cliff, up there among the trees.' He bent to the voice tube and rasped, 'Stop both!'

A moment later the diesels ceased their steady throbbing and the U-70 rattled to a halt. Almost immediately, now that the slight wind had ceased, they felt the impact of the morning heat. Christian felt himself begin to sweat. It was going to be a very hot day.

Harsch didn't seem to notice. 'Frenssen takes charge of the perimeter, Number One,' he continued, 'and you're in charge here.'

'Yes, sir. And you sir?' Christian enquired politely.

'As soon as the perimeter party goes ashore, I follow. I want to have a look-round on the land.' He gave Christian a sudden and surprising smile. Abruptly Christian realized he had never seen the skipper smile before.

'Do you think that's wise, sir? After all, we don't really know—'

'Don't be an old woman!' Harsch cut him off, though he continued to give Christian a toothy smile. 'I shall take precautions. Besides, I'll take one of the ratings with me — to give me a bit of extra muscle.' His smile deepened as if he were pleased with his choice of expression. 'Yes,' he added, almost too casually, 'I'll take the Moses with me. Now then, let's get marching, Number One, what?'

'Yes, sir,' Christian snapped dutifully and then Harsch was gone, leaving Christian with his own thoughts for a moment, before he dismissed them hurriedly to get on with the urgent tasks before them...

The morning passed swiftly. In spite of the heat, the crew, stripped to the waist, worked hard and cheerfully, some of them even singing and whistling as they set about their various jobs. Christian, here, there and everywhere, knew why. It was a reaction against the almost unbearable tensions and dangers of these last terrible days since they had sunk the *Stalin*, Even the old hares of the pre-war *Kriegsmarine* might well have cracked under that kind of strain. More than once they had thought themselves finished, when they had been attacked by the Russian dive-bombers or when those tanks had come rattling down the quayside so alarmingly at Varna. But somehow they had survived. Now, with the resilience of youth, they had thrown off their cares and worries and were enjoying the hard, back-breaking work, set against the background of the idyllic little cove, with its blue, sparkling, crystal-clear water.

At twelve he called a halt. The work was progressing well and he knew the men must have some rest, for now the sun had reached its zenith and the heat was tremendous. Each man received four hard-tack biscuits, a small hard salami, and a canteen of tepid water. But after drinking their water, most of them left the food and, stripping naked, dived into the water. White wet naked bodies flashed and gleamed in the sun.

It was just about then that Christian decided he could leave the boat in command of the engineer officer. He wanted to have a look at Frenssen's perimeter and he was a little worried about Harsch and the Moses. They had still not returned from the skipper's 'look-round', though it was now two hours since they had left, the Moses lugging his machine-pistol as usual. Still, Christian told himself, as he waded ashore, enjoying the coolness of the water, the skipper was an 'old hare'. He could look after himself.

Frenssen's men had dug in at five metre intervals in the shade of the stunted firs, now loud with the monotonous chirping of the cicadas, which never seemed to stop and would have maddened anyone else but the imperturbable Frenssen. The latter now squatted in the shade next to the fresh brown dry earth of his foxhole regaling the young ratings with one of his impossible, immoral stories. 'Believe me, you bunch o' cream puffs,' he was saying lazily, face brick-red with the heat, 'it takes a stiff rod to catch a big fish. Get it?' He guffawed coarsely at his own crude humour. 'And take it from me, *Jungs*, I know whereof I speak.' He tugged at his flies, as if his trousers were too tight for him. 'I remember back in '37 when

I decided to honour the U-boat Arm with my services.' He beamed at the young men. 'That winter the dustbin lids froze over so I thought that if I didn't want to starve, I'd better *volunteer* my services for Folk, Fatherland and Führer. Anyway, as I was saying, I had just got out of recruit training in Mürwik, full o' piss and vinegar. In them days I could get a blue-veiner, a real old diamond cutter, just by *looking* at a woman. Couldn't keep it down. *Jungs*, did I have the hots in them days —'

'*Obermaat* Frenssen,' Christian cut into his reminiscences with feigned boredom as he came sweating up the incline, 'isn't it just too hot for your tales, however sexy? Can't we talk of other things? Like the defensive situation perhaps?' He smiled pleasantly at the big rogue, who he knew was the backbone of the crew, and waved to him to stay where he was squatting on the ground.

Frenssen forgot the days when he could get that celebrated 'blue-veiner, a real old diamond cutter' and was business-like immediately. 'Nothing, sir!' he reported. 'The place seems to be deserted. I did a little bit of look-see myself an hour ago as soon as we got these positions set up. But there's nothing out there.' He indicated his front with a wave of his big paw. 'Not even any tilled land or any sign of human cultivation. Looks as if any natives there might have been around here have got the word that the Russians are on the way and have done a bunk.'

Christian nodded his thanks and, pushing back his battered cap, with its tarnished gold insignia, focused his glasses on the front, sweeping carefully from left to right, searching the horizon. But there was nothing, just as Frenssen said. The terrain was empty, shimmering in little blue tremble waves in the fierce noonday sun. He frowned and dropped the binoculars to his chest. 'And the Old Man and the Moses — any sign of them?' he asked, licking his lips.

Frenssen was hesitant. '*Nix*,' he growled after a while. 'They went off in that direction, and that's the last I've seen of them.' He looked at Christian, suddenly challengingly. 'I hope he ain't gonna get that kid in trouble, sir? You know that Moses is still wet behind the spoons. A real innocent, as bloody green as the growing corn.'

Christian ignored the remark. The whole subject was becoming distasteful, something he didn't feel qualified to deal with. In fact, he didn't want to have to deal with it. Instead he said, 'Better keep a weather eye out for the pair of them, Frenssen. If there is no sign by the time the midday break is over, report to me down on the boat —'

'Sir,' one of the youths squatting in his hole to the right broke in suddenly, 'there's something over there ... at three o'clock. Some dust and, I think ... people!'

Hurriedly Christian flung up his binoculars, while Frenssen snapped off the safety on his machine-pistol and cocked it smartly. In an instant the languid, relaxed mood of the young ratings had vanished. They tensed in their holes, weapons at the ready, all eyes focused on the little cloud of dust slowly moving towards them.

Christian peered through the circles of bright, sparkling, calibrated glass, waiting to make out who was causing the dust. If it were the Russians, then that would be that. They'd have to make a run for it, with or without the skipper. He didn't want to bog the men down in a fire-fight. They possessed only hand-fire weapons. They'd be no match for properly armed Russian infantry. He waited, feeling the sweat trickle unpleasantly down the small of his back.

'Well?' Frenssen hissed.

Christian didn't reply. The glare and the dust the strangers were making made it difficult for him to get a clear view of them. At the back of his head a wild little voice cried out urgently, 'Come on, come on, *who are you?*'

Suddenly he had one of them in the centre of his glasses. Hurriedly he adjusted the binoculars more finely with fingers that trembled. A ragged figure came into view. He flashed a glance at the helmet the man was wearing. It seemed the familiar one. He lowered the glasses to focus on the uniform. Yes … yes… It wasn't the earth-coloured smock of the Red Army. He gulped.

'Sir, for chrissake,' Frenssen demanded in a choked voice, 'the frigging hot piss is trickling down my right leg! Put me out of my frigging misery. *Who are they?*'

'Well, Frenssen, you big rogue, if I'm not mistaken — *they're ours!*' Christian whooped suddenly in joyous relief. 'They look like our own hairy-assed stubble-hoppers!'

'Thank Christ for that!' Frenssen sighed fervently. 'Miracles never cease.'

Ten minutes later the 'stubble-hoppers' began to straggle into the sailors' positions, who stared at them in silent awe, as if they were visitors from another planet. They were old hares all right. Men in their late twenties and early thirties, filthy and obviously lice-ridden, their thin faces hollowed out and worn by the burning sun to nut-brown skulls, their fading *Wehrmacht* uniforms ragged and stained, and surprisingly enough devoid of the combat badges and decorations that usually covered the tunics of such veterans. But their boots were in excellent condition, Christian noted with some wonder. 'God, how they pong!' Frenssen whispered out of the side of his mouth to Christian as they came ever closer, dragging their feet with infinite weariness, 'like the ruddy monkey house at the zoo.'

'Don't worry about the smell,' Christian ordered. 'Send one of your chaps down to the U-70. See what they can rustle up in the way of food and water. The poor chaps look all in —'

'Exactly,' a familiar voice cut in. 'These poor fellows deserve everything we can spare them. They've been on the run from the Russians ever since the Red Army broke through our main line of resistance.' It was the skipper, his uniform thickly powdered in the same white dust that covered those of the others. Behind him was the Moses looking strangely sullen for reasons known only to himself.

Christian stiffened to attention and asked, 'But who are these men, sir?'

Before Harsch could answer, an incisive, unmistakably Prussian voice rasped, 'Lieutenant, we are the last survivors of Battle Group Kirsch. We have been fighting, retreating, and fighting now since the spring, covering one thousand kilometres.'

Startled, Christian swung round to face an immensely tall lieutenant-colonel of infantry, eyes blazing fanatically from an emaciated face, beneath a head wrapped in a dirty, bloodstained bandage. 'Glad — glad to meet you, Colonel —'

The other man grinned at his discomfiture, but there was something cold and disconcerting about that grin, as he sized Christian up. 'Colonel *Kirsch*' he supplied the name and, bowing stiffly at the waist in the old-fashioned manner of the Kaiser's Army, returned the startled lieutenant's salute.

'Jungblut, *Herr Oberst*,' Christian introduced himself hastily, '*Leutnant zur See* Jungblut.'

'*Angenehm*,' the other man said and added, 'We went in two thousand strong and this is what is left of us. A mere fifty-odd.' He held out a thin hand to indicate his men, but there was no compassion in his cold blue eyes, no feeling, just an overweening fanaticism.

'Colonel Kirsch says that the Russians are a good forty kilometres behind him, Number One,' Harsch said cheerfully. 'We'll have the rest of this day and perhaps the most of tomorrow to make the U-70 seaworthy.'

'Yes,' Kirsch agreed. 'I think for the time being the Russians have shot their bolt, the steam has gone out of their attack. Naturally their losses have been tremendous in men and material. They'll need a little time to bring up fresh supplies of both. For a little time we'll have some peace from the red rabble. Now, with your permission, *Herr Kapitänleutnant*' — he made another stiff little bow — 'I should like to rest my men within your perimeter here. God knows they deserve it. These last forty-eight hours have been hell for us.'

'Why of course, *Herr Oberst*...' Harsch began, but already the tall Prussian colonel was beckoning to one of his non-commissioned officers, a huge hulk of a man with a savage, brutalized face, rent on one side by a terrible livid scar from eye to jaw that made his face look as if it had been torn in two. '*Sergeant-major*' he commanded, 'get the men into the shade at once.'

'*Jawohl, Herr Oberst*' the NCO growled in a surly fashion in the unmistakable accents of deepest Bavaria. 'All right, you bunch o' cardboard soldiers, you heard the CO,' he commanded without saluting, 'get into the shade. We don't want yer to burn yer frigging delicate skin, you arse-with-ears.'

Slowly, almost sullenly, the survivors of Battle Group Kirsch stumbled into the trees, hardly deigning to notice the young sailors who gaped at these tough, hard men, with their tattered uniforms and scarred faces. To Christian's way of thinking they looked like those brutalized *Landsknechte*, the seventeenth-century mercenaries who had fought for which-ever side had paid the most during Germany's terrible 'Thirty Years War'.

'I shall personally see to the food and drink,' Harsch said hastily, obviously delighted with the news that the Russian advance had stopped for the time being.

'Get an earful of that, lads,' the big sergeant-major growled with an ugly smile, 'the boys in blue are gonna provide fodder. I hope they don't forget the frigging finger bowls!' The men sniggered and the NCO looked at Harsch with open contempt.

Christian frowned. They were Germans all right, these hard men, and they had obviously been through some shattering experiences in their two years in Russia. Yet he didn't like them for some reason he couldn't quite establish.

Frenssen, however, was quicker off the mark. A little later as the weary infantrymen squatted in the shade, munching the hard-tack and sipping the water Harsch had had brought up for them, he took Christian's arm and led him out of earshot. 'Notice their boots, sir?' he asked softly. 'Look at them dice-beakers that Bavarian barn-shitter, the one with the scar, is wearing?'

Christian nodded. 'You mean they're all in a good state of repair?'

'Yessir. The leather and the hobnails might well have been done yesterday. You can see how new the leather is on Scarface's boots.'

'Yes, I can see that. But what are you getting at, Frenssen?'

Frenssen looked at Colonel Kirsch for a moment. He was talking to Harsch, who was quite animated and cheery for him. Obviously he was relieved that the pressure was off for the time being. For his part, Kirsch's harsh lean face showed nothing. His eyes were quite blank, as if his mind was a million miles away. 'Well, sir,' Frenssen said, 'if those hairy-assed stubble-hoppers have been fighting and retreating for over a thousand kilometres, as their CO said, how come their boots are in such good shape, sir?' He looked pointedly at Christian. 'The way things were at Varna yesterday, I can't exactly see 'em standing around in their foot-rags while somebody repaired their dice-beakers.'

Christian stroked his chin thoughtfully, but said nothing.

'And there's another thing as well, sir,' Frenssen continued. 'Their pong.'

'So what? Stubble-hoppers don't tend to take foam baths when they're in the line, Frenssen. What do you want them to smell of, attar of roses?'

'It's not that, sir, don't get me wrong,' Frenssen said urgently, looking about him to see if anyone might be listening after all. 'It's the smell of tobacco, that black Russian muck that they smoke in bits of rolled newspaper, that *makhorka* of theirn. He lowered his voice significantly. 'Now where in the name of hell would they be getting Russian lung torpedoes, eh, sir? Who's been supplying the buggers with Russian *cigarettes*?'

But to that overwhelming question a puzzled and somewhat uneasy Christian had no answer…

CHAPTER 6

Night fell suddenly, as it always does in that region of the world. One moment all was a beautiful warm, golden glow, with the sun hovering over the silent, perfect sea; the next it had vanished abruptly, casting the sky a deep, starless purple hue. Almost immediately the temperature dropped and with the change there came the usual mist drifting in silently from the sea, muffling all sound, even the hammering from the submarine anchored below.

In their holes the weary young ratings shivered as the cold damp sea mist curled in and out of the trees before settling down upon them like a silent soft grey cat. But the stubble-hoppers, who were still keeping to themselves, did not seem to notice. They either slept, propped up against the trees, boots still on and weapons kept close at hand, or they remained shirtless, in spite of the sudden cold, busily occupied in searching and killing the lice with which the seams of their shirts were infested.

Obermaat Frenssen, for his part, had no time for the cold. His suspicions of the strangers had grown apace since the afternoon conversation with *Leutnant* Jungblut. All afternoon they had kept stubbornly to themselves, refusing to be drawn when the ratings had attempted to question them about their experiences. His own attempt to strike up a conversation with 'Scarface', as he had now named the hulking Bavarian sergeant-major in his own mind, had failed too. Even his offer of a slug from his precious flatman had been turned down in a surly contemptuous manner by the Bavarian. 'Ner,' he had said, pushing out his hand as if physically warding off the sailor, 'yer can stick that Bulgarian muck in yer hat! When I want to gargle my tonsils, sailor, I use good old German schnaps!'

There was something strange too about Scarface's relationship with his CO, that lean autocratic Prussian, *Oberst* Kirsch. Twice, when the latter had passed on some order or other to Scarface, the big NCO had not even bothered to rise, nor had he addressed his CO with his military rank, an unheard-of thing in the Greater German *Wehrmacht*. Everything the colonel had said had been received with a kind of bored contempt by the other man. Indeed their relationship had been that almost of equals, or perhaps better that of an subordinate talking to a superior, with Scarface in the latter role. It was all very puzzling but there was nothing tangible he could pass on to *Leutnant* Jungblut.

Now as his greenbeaks snored and twisted in an attempt to keep warm in their suddenly cold foxholes, Frenssen determined to keep awake and watch the stubble-hoppers, in particular the big Bavarian, propped up against a tree some thirty metres away, puffing moodily and in silence at a little clay pipe and obviously using *makhorka* tobacco. There was no mistaking the pungent odour, even at such a distance.

Time passed leadenly. The fog grew thicker. Now there was no sound save the muted snores of the weary men in the perimeter and the hammering from below. Even the stubble-hoppers had drifted off into sleep now. But not Scarface. Carefully Frenssen had edged in closer, using the cover of the fog, and now he could still see the dull red glow of his pipe. He was awake and smoking, while Colonel Kirsch snored in a delicate refined sort of way some five metres away.

Instinctively Frenssen knew why Scarface was remaining awake. He was up to something. But he wanted the rest of them asleep before he did anything. Frenssen cursed to himself. He should have disobeyed *Leutnant* Jungblut's order not to post sentries. With the Russians kilometres away, the lieutenant had said it was not necessary; let the weary greenbeaks sleep. Now unless he kept his eyes on him all the time, Scarface could sneak off into the fog at any time without being challenged by an alert sentry.

Frenssen found himself grimly trying to fight off sleep. His eyes felt as if they were filled with grit and his eyelids seemed to weigh a ton. Over and over again he blinked wildly and forced them open with an effort of sheer naked willpower, but his head dropped to his chest and he began to snore immediately. Still Scarface puffed at his pipe, as if he would smoke all night. Frenssen drifted in and out of sleep, fantasizing in his exhausted state. More than once he imagined he could hear the muffled clip-clop of hooves far off. There were the calls, too, like the distant hooting of owls, which jerked him from his sleep, but when he looked around, cocking his head to one side to catch even the faintest of sounds, all was silent. Nothing but the hammering from below and the snoring of the men...

It was dawn when he awoke. The sun was already up, perched on the rim of the mountains, the great dark shadows racing across the plain below as it grew ever lighter, vanishing like silent black hawks. He rubbed his eyes, wondering where the devil he was. Then he remembered his self-imposed task. He sprang to his feet and stared at the tree where Scarface had sat. *Scarface was gone!*

Kapitänleutnant Harsch and *Leutnant* Jungblut were already on the bridge when he reached the U-70, panting for breath. They were watching the new shift frolicking about in the water, laughing and jumping up and down, splashing each other like a lot of frigging schoolkids on their first outing to the sea,

Frenssen couldn't help thinking. He noticed, even in his excitement and worry, that the Moses was keeping to himself, quietly soaping himself away from the others, his naked body turned, presumably so that no one should see his privates. Frenssen dismissed the slim handsome boy with the white unblemished skin from his thoughts and wondered how he was going to tell the lieutenant about his night-long vigil and the seeming disappearance of Scarface. After all, he might well just have wandered off to have a private crap. Even people like Scarface might be fussy about taking a crap in the presence of the others. He had met a few sensitive souls like that in his time.

'*Herr Kapitänleutnant*,' Frenssen spoke, flinging the two officers a tremendous salute, 'permission to speak, *sir*!'

Both officers swung round, Harsch taking his eyes off the Moses' naked form reluctantly and frowning when he saw who it was. 'What are you doing down here, *Obermaat*?' he asked severely. 'Come on.'

'You are supposed to be in charge of the perimeter, Frenssen.' Christian added his complaint to the skipper's. 'Remember?'

'Yes, sir, I know, sir,' Frenssen answered hastily, still standing rigidly to attention. 'But, you see, sir, something has come up, like.'

'Nothing that authorizes you to abandon your post without specific order to do so,' Harsch barked. 'All right, what is it then? Where's the fire, man? Come on, spit it out.'

Frenssen was suddenly tongue-tied as he realized that all he had thought to say was based simply on his own vague suspicions. There was nothing really hard and fast in the whole damned business. 'Well, you see, sir,' he began, suddenly flushing scarlet like an embarrassed schoolkid caught with his dong in his hand in the shithouse, 'it's — it's —'

'The stubble-hoppers?' Christian suggested.

'Yessir.'

'Well, what about them, Frenssen?' Harsch demanded.

'I don't like the look of them, sir,' Frenssen answered lamely, wishing the earth would open up and swallow him up.

'You're not supposed to go and ask them if they'd like to *dance* with you, man,' Harsch rasped. 'What in three devils' name do you mean, you don't like the *look* of them?'

'Well, sir,' Frenssen tried again, they're funny. That big one with the scar on his face, sir, he don't say "sir" to his superior officer —'

'Well, that is not exactly a capital crime, Frenssen,' Harsch interrupted him severely. 'You'll have to do better than that.'

But Frenssen no longer needed to. Suddenly a voice was shouting at them from the shore. 'Fetch me across, please. I have something to say to you — *urgently!*' Even before they swung round, Christian recognized that clipped precise voice, now tinged with a trace of fear.

It was Colonel Kirsch, bare-headed and without weapons, his face no longer autocratic, but haunted and somehow suddenly sunken, as if he had come to the end of his tether, his nerves finally shattered. Again he waved to them and called over his request, crying this time, 'Quick — before it is too late!'

'I'll fetch him, sir,' Frenssen blurted out and dashed for the dinghy before anyone could stop him. A moment later he was paddling furiously for the shore.

Christian too reacted instinctively. Somehow he knew that there was something seriously wrong. Cupping his hands to his mouth he yelled, 'All you men in the water, back to the boat immediately. Do you hear me — *back here at once!*' His tone must have been convincing. The young ratings ceased their skylarking at once and even the Moses forgot his previous modesty. He dropped his soap into the shallows and naked as he was started to swim for the boat to join the mad scramble to get aboard.

'What in tarnation's name is going on, Number One?' Harsch cried in bewilderment, as the deck was abruptly flooded with wet, naked young men seeking their towels and uniforms. 'Is this a madhouse or something?'

'I don't know about that, sir,' Christian replied quickly, not taking his eyes off the shore and Colonel Kirsch, 'but we can't be too careful. Something tells me the shit has hit the fan.'

Harsch frowned but said nothing. Frenssen started to paddle back to the U-70 bearing Kirsch with him, and the half-dried excited sailors started to take up their duty stations. Somehow they had caught Christian's sense of urgency and without being commanded to do so, they hurried down the ladder to their positions, while from below the engineer called, 'Where's the fire, sir? What am I to do?'

'Nothing for the moment, Engineer,' Harsch ordered. 'Just stand by, please. There seems to be some kind of emergency.'

A moment later Frenssen was hauling Kirsch aboard effortlessly, reaching him up from the dinghy as if he were a mere babe in arms, with the latter already beginning to explain even before he reached the waiting officers.

'*Von Seydlitz!*' he blurted out, looking from one face to the other. 'Have you ever heard of the Von Seydlitz Committee, gentlemen?' There was a wet sheen over those cold blue Prussian eyes and Christian felt, with a growing sensation of fear, that Kirsch might break down at any moment and begin to cry. God in heaven, what had he done?

Harsch looked puzzled so Christian stepped in. 'General von Seydlitz was captured at Stalingrad last January, wasn't he, *Herr Oberst*?' he prompted.

'Yes, he, Field Marshal Paulus and all the rest of the big shots,' Kirsch said with sudden bitterness. 'They let Hitler talk them into hanging on there until it was too late, sacrificing us by the thousand to the enemy — all for nothing.' He lifted up a hand to touch his face and Christian saw that it trembled.

'But you — you said that you had been fighting and retreating all the time,' Harsch objected in bewilderment. 'You said nothing about Stalingrad and the surrender.'

Kirsch ignored the comment. 'There were a lot of us officers who thought, like Seydlitz at the time, that we had been betrayed by the High Command, who hadn't the slightest idea of the horrors of the siege in Stalingrad. Most of the others simply accepted their fate — that they would die as overworked starved *plenny* in the Russian prisoner of war camps. But von Seydlitz didn't. He — naturally with Russian help for propaganda reasons —' Kirsch laughed bitterly, but there was no mirth in the sound '— formed the Seydlitz Committee to actively fight against Hitler and the High Command. I joined.' He hung his head momentarily, as if in sudden abject shame.

'You mean you became a — a *traitor*?' Harsch snapped.

'Yes,' Kirsch said quietly, raising his head and looking at the two of them straight in the face, glad to have got that off his chest at last. 'I betrayed my country and the Army and Führer to which I had sworn an oath of loyalty. A renegade and a traitor, gentlemen.'

'But why are you ... free now?' Harsch asked, completely bewildered. 'I mean you have soldiers, you are armed... You said that the Russians were a day's march away... Oh, no, you mean...' His flow of words died away.

'Yes, the whole bunch of those rogues up there are renegades. All of us, we've accepted the Russians' salt,' Kirsch answered bitterly, face twisted in a mocking smile. 'We're all members of the so-called German Liberation Army, armed and fed by the Russians, our former enemies.'

'But I still don't understand,' Harsch persisted, while Christian's mind raced furiously. 'What role do you play? Why are you here?'

'We act as a reconnaissance unit for the Russians,' Kirsch answered simply. 'Wearing German uniforms like this and being former members of the *Wehrmacht*, it is easy for us to infiltrate the German line. Where we find the weak spots the Red Army follows.' He shrugged. 'A kind of Trojan Horse, if you wish.' He stopped short and looked at them, as if he half expected them to burst into angry invective, to revile his treachery, perhaps even strike him. But nothing of the sort happened. The two of them were too shocked by his revelations. Instead Christian asked quietly, his mind still absorbing this startling information, 'But why us? We have nothing to do with the fighting front and you stubble-hoppers. We're the U-boat Arm. We just chanced to be here at this time.'

'My dear Lieutenant,' Kirsch said, with a faint trace of his old autocratic Prussian style. 'You underestimate yourself. Don't you realize that there is a price on your heads. You have sunk the pride of the Soviet Black Sea Fleet —'

'You know about that?'

Kirsch nodded swiftly. 'Oh, yes, *we* know about that. Old Leather Face — that's what the Russians call Stalin — is deeply insulted. High Command ordered that you must be captured and brought to Moscow in chains, every single one of you. Stalin wants to see you personally, before he has the lot of you — shot!' Kirsch grated out the last word savagely, as if he had suddenly realized just how much of a Judas he was.

Christian gasped. 'Shot?' he echoed.

Kirsch nodded solemnly. 'We were sent specifically to find and detain you. That big brute of a sergeant-major managed to dodge your man last night and get away to report your position back to HQ. He's our political commissar and the real leader, you know. I'm just a convenient figure-head.'

'You mean, the Russians know the present position of the U-70?' Harsch asked urgently.

'They do. Our task is to keep you here until they arrive in force and take you prisoner. Last night, however, listening to your young men talk and chat up there on the height, I realized exactly what I had betrayed. Not just the big shots and the Führer, but these eager, confident youngsters who are still risking their lives for a cause I thought discredited, perhaps even totally lost...' His voice broke momentarily. 'Then I knew I could no longer be a party to this intrigue. I had to tell you what was afoot.'

'Thank you,' Christian began, but Harsch cut him off with a barked, 'Then, my God, we haven't a moment to lose! We've got to get the hell out of here, while there is still time.' He sprang to the voice tube, 'Engineer ... where the hell are you, man...? Yes, start up the engines at once. Hurry, man, it's a matter of life and death. *Los*!'

Below the diesels started to whine. Harsch, in a flurry of almost panic-stricken energy, cried, '*Leinen los*. Get those lines over the side, you deckies. Move sharply now. *Leinen los*! Give a hand there, Moses. Just don't stand there —'

'But, sir,' Christian broke in as the engines reached an ear-splitting pitch and the young ratings hurriedly began to pull

in the lines, 'what about the perimeter?' He beckoned wildly to the top of the cliff. 'We've still got Frenssen's men up there, sir!'

Harsch looked at him as if he couldn't believe the evidence of his own ears. 'The boat comes first, Jungblut, you *must* know that. The —'

The engines burst into sudden throbbing vital life and drowned the rest of the sentence.

Christian caught hold of the skipper before he could issue any further orders down the voice tube. 'There are ten men up there, ten young men, *Herr Kapitänleutnant*' he said icily, keeping his voice low and controlled. 'We cannot simply abandon them just like that. You've heard what their fate will be if they are taken alive. Torture first possibly, but very definitely death. *Herr Kapitänleutnant*, are you prepared to stand there and virtually sentence them to death? There isn't one of them older than twenty, sir?'

On the deck, the men hauling in the dripping ropes stopped their work. They had heard Christian's impassioned outburst and now they gazed in tense expectancy at the two ashen-faced officers confronting one another on the bridge.

'Can you live with that on your conscience, *Herr Kapitänleutnant*?' Christian persisted icily when Harsch didn't speak. '*Can you?*'

For a moment he thought Harsch was going to strike him for his eyes were bulging out of his face like those of a man demented. Then the skipper recovered himself. 'I am in command of this boat, *Leutnant*, and I alone make the decisions aboard here. The U-70 comes first.'

'No, sir, you can't,' the youthful voice came from below. It was the Moses, his face a mixture of pain and naked hatred. 'You can't let —'

'Both engines,' Harsch cried savagely into the voice pipe, 'slow ahead.'

'Both engines — slow ahead, sir,' the engineer's disembodied voice came floating up from below and with a slight jerk the U-70 started to move.

The Moses began to cry and Kirsch leapt forward to where the dinghy rocked at the side of the boat. '*Herr Kapitänleutnant*, let me try then, please.'

'Try what?' Harsch snapped, face rigid and white.

'Try to bring back your boys. I'm sure those ruffians of mine won't harm me, while the Sergeant-Major is absent. You've got to let me try. It will be one way I can atone for what I...' He faltered and didn't end the sentence.

'Do what you like,' Harsch snapped, dismissing the broken Army officer. 'Time is running out. We must sacrifice the few to save the many — and the boat.'

Christian felt the hatred and resentment well up inside him dangerously as Kirsch clambered into the dinghy and Frenssen handed him the paddles. Perhaps Harsch's first desire *was* to save the rest of the crew and the U-70, but somehow he doubted it. He wanted to save himself more — and bask in the glory that would be his if he succeeded in getting the boat back to the Reich. Instinctively he knew that was the skipper's real aim; and the men seemed to know it too, for as Kirsch began to pull away, his frail craft rocking more wildly now as the U-70 started to gather speed, there came a low but ominous murmuring and muttering from those ratings still on the deck. Angry sullen looks were flung at the captain, as he stood there proudly on the bridge, surveying his little kingdom, apparently unaware of the smouldering resentment his decision was causing.

Christian flung a wild glance at Kirsch, who was now scrambling up the cliff, heading for the perimeter. If he could warn the ten ratings up there now, there'd be still time. All of them could swim, and once they were in the water, even Harsch wouldn't dare abandon them before the eyes of their comrades. He'd have a damned mutiny on his hands if he did. He clenched his fists and willed the renegade colonel to pull it off.

Kirsch was almost up. Christian saw him haul himself over the ridge with the assistance of one of the stunted firs. For a moment he stood, his thin chest heaving, clearly outlined against the bright-red ball of the ascending sun, perhaps catching his breath, then he cupped his hands to his mouth. Obviously he was going to shout a warning to the still unsuspecting sailors up there. A single shot rang out, like a dry twig being snapped underfoot.

For an instant nothing changed. Kirsch still stood, hands cupped to his mouth. Then, abruptly, his whole skinny frame started to shake, the vibrations increasing as if he had suddenly been taken ill with a violent tropical fever. A shrill scream rang from his throat and he fell backwards, to go tumbling and falling down the cliff in a wild flurry of sand. He sprawled at the bottom, limp and silent, the golden sand already beginning to stain scarlet with his blood.

Christian groaned and stared wildly at the top of the cliff. Nothing. No movement, no sound, no people. Those ten teenage ratings' fate was sealed. Christian could have broken down and wept.

Harsch, his face set and hard, revealing nothing, brought the U-70 round and set course for the open sea, his gaze already taking in the dark smudge of smoke on the burning blue horizon. The Moses continued to sob like a broken-hearted child.

CHAPTER 7

'Up periscope!' Harsch barked, completely ignoring the mood of the crew. They were no longer the enthusiastic, if green, young men who had run out of Varna with such high hopes three weeks before. These men were bitter and virtually mutinous, their young faces already worn with experience and resentful at the way life was treating them. As the skipper bent to peer through the instrument, Christian told himself he had to be completely without feelings. He seemed to have forgotten altogether what he had done to those young men of the perimeter such a short time before. Was that what it took to become a U-boat ace? Had Prien, Kretschmar and all the rest of the great aces, now long dead or captured, become like this in order to achieve their tremendous victories? He didn't know. But he did know *he* wouldn't want to become such an unfeeling, emotionless monster, who would sacrifice everything and anybody in order to gain victory. He shook his head. No, the lives of these young men entrusted to him and the skipper were more important than all the 'kills'.

Seemingly unaware of the mood of his number one and the crew, *Kapitänleutnant* Harsch spun the periscope round the three hundred and sixty degree arc swiftly just to check that there was no enemy craft to the rear of the U-70. Then he switched to his immediate front and turned on the amplifier.

Immediately the Soviet destroyer called by the renegades sprung into the centre of the bright circle of calibrated glass, stark, black, and immensely powerful as it hurried to the cove at thirty knots, its sharp, beak-like prow cleaving the waves in a bright, white, bubbling wash. Automatically Harsch noted her armament, twin 75mm cannon fore and aft and the torpedo tubes midships. She was of the Kuznetsov class, displacement roughly two thousand-odd tons. A nice plump pigeon, he told himself, hurrying straight into the trap and not suspecting a damned thing.

As was customary with U-boat skippers, he sang out the details of what he had sighted and chortled, 'The Russian thinks we're still at anchor, I'm sure. Hasn't a clue we've already put to sea.'

But if he expected any reaction from his crew, Harsch was disappointed. They remained sullen and silent, save for Christian, who said, 'Are you going to attack, sir?'

Harsch took his eyes off the periscope for a moment and said in a voice full of wonder at such a question, 'Why of course I'm going to attack, Number One. That's what we're paid for, isn't it? Besides, the Russian is a sitting duck. It'll be as easy as falling off a bloody log.'

Christian forced himself to remain calm. He knew now that only he could protect the greenbeaks from Harsch's overweening ambition. In his desire for glory, Harsch was heading for destruction and Christian was going to make sure he didn't destroy his crew in the process. 'You realize, sir,' he said coldly, unemotionally, 'that if we attack that destroyer the Russian skipper will alert the whole Black Sea Fleet to our presence?' Suddenly unable to contain himself any longer, he blurted out, 'Christ Almighty, we'll be trapped in the piss-pot and the Russians will be shitting right on top of us!'

Harsch took his gaze off the tube and straightened slowly, his face set and ominous. 'I advise you to watch your tongue, *Leutnant zur See* Jungblut,' he said sharply, his tone overly formal. 'I do not want to hear that kind of language from any officer under my command, whatever his rank or position.

Please take note of that. And you,' he addressed himself to a white-faced broken Moses, 'stop that damned snivelling! If you don't, I'll order *Obermaat* Frenssen to have you arrested immediately. Now stop!' Harsch looked challengingly at his men, almost as if he was daring them to protest.

The men dropped their gazes and the Moses stopped his weeping. Harsch laughed cynically and in triumph. 'Well you dogs,' he cried, 'do you want to live for ever? Let's get on with it. We're going to attack and be damned. Bearing…'

It was, as the skipper had boasted, 'as easy as falling off a log'. They had rigged for silent running, with the hydrophone operators adjusting their dials, reporting back to the captain in whispers, while the steady beat of the unsuspecting destroyer's screws grew louder and louder. At the very last moment, when the Russians could not possibly escape the trap, Harsch had ordered a 'fan' of three torpedoes fired. They had broken the destroyer's back and it had turned turtle almost immediately, with no time for the crew to abandon ship.

As Harsch savoured his latest victory, the U-70 nosed its way past its silent victim. The still sea was disturbed by the occasional bubble of trapped air rising to explode obscenely. Gently the U-70's prow ploughed through the debris and the dead. The bodies bobbed up and down on the submarine's swell, borne by their life-belts, as if they might remain thus for ever, but a silent, moody Christian standing next to the skipper on the conning tower knew otherwise. Soon the seagulls — those damned white scavengers of the sea — would find them. They'd peck out the eyes first and then the nose and ears would follow. They'd strip the dead men's faces to the bones beneath and then finally they'd burst the life-belts to get at the flesh of the body itself. Christian shuddered at the thought.

Behind him Frenssen said sombrely, not taking his eyes off the Russian dead, 'Goes to sea all yer grown life, watching yer mates die one by one and thinking it'll never happen to you. But it does in the end. *It does!*' He spat sadly over the side.

Harsch was not troubled by such sombre thoughts; he appeared not even to see the dead, bobbing up and down everywhere in the U-70's wash. '*Kolossal!*' he exclaimed in delight. '*Kolossal, Number One!* Why our tonnage must be better than Prien's by now, what? The *Stalin* had a displacement of thirty-five thousand tons. And now this destroyer with another two thousand-odd… Tremendous.' He slapped his thigh in sheer rapture, completely unaware, or so it seemed, of the mood of the men round him. '*Who will ever know if we're sunk?*' Christian asked himself, for even Harsch dared not break radio silence to report his latest 'kill'. The Russians would be on to them like a shot. Suddenly he felt unutterably weary, sick of Harsch, this constant slaughter, the whole damned war. When would it ever end?

With difficulty he pulled himself together. He knew that the fate of the U-70 depended upon him. 'What are your orders, sir?' he asked, trying to shake Harsch out of his mood of euphoria and face up to the reality of the situation.

'What was that?' Harsch asked, not taking his eyes off the slowly sinking hulk of the Russian destroyer.

Christian repeated his question.

Harsch shook his head like a man waking up from a heavy sleep. 'Yes, of course,' he said, voice normal and reasonable once more. 'The alarm has obviously been given by now.' He rubbed his unshaven chin. 'We must take measures to get out of the Black Sea immediately. Two things, Number One. How far is it now to the entrance to the Bosporus? And how far is it to the start of Turkish territorial waters?'

Christian's heart leapt at the skipper's second question. It meant he hadn't been totally blinded by thoughts of adding yet another 'kill' to his record; he had been thinking about the future of the U-70. 'It's about a hundred sea miles,' he answered quickly, 'and we should be within Turkish territorial waters by this afternoon, sir.'

Harsch did a quick calculation. 'So we could be at the Black Sea entrance to the Bosporus by nightfall,' he said. 'And the strait itself is about thirty kilometres long. Submerged it would take us some two hours to clear it, Number One.'

'Exactly, sir. So you intend to use Turkish territorial waters, sir?'

'Yes.' Harsch favoured him with a tight smile. 'I know the Turks are neutral and we're violating international agreements and all that shit, but it's our necks that are at risk, not those of the damned stiff shirts in the Berlin Foreign Office. Let them, the diplomats, fight about it afterwards.'

'I couldn't agree with you more, sir,' Christian said eagerly, now he realized the skipper was thinking straight again. 'But we do run the risk of being arrested if the Turks discover us in their waters, sir.'

Harsch dismissed the suggestion with a careless wave of his hand. 'They've got to catch us first, Number One, haven't they?'

'Yes, sir. Of course, sir.'

'Right, well, let's get on with it,' Harsch said briskly. Behind them the rump of the sinking Russian destroyer disappeared on the horizon, and the sea was empty again, a vast still deep blue. For the moment it seemed they were the only people still left alive in a crazy war-torn world. 'We'll stay on the surface as long as we can. We must save the electric batteries for the run through Turkish coastal waters and the Bosporus. Double all look-outs. Take her down at the first sight of any trouble.' He yawned suddenly and said thickly, 'I'm going hit my ear and get a bit of sleep. It was a long night.' He yawned again. 'You have the conn, Number One.'

Casually he touched his cap in reply to Christian's salute and disappeared down the ladder into the interior of the submarine, yawning loudly. As the only one in the whole boat who had a cabin, tiny as it was, he'd probably get a good four hours' sleep, more than anyone did, however exhausted, for the whole length of a typical fighting patrol.

Frenssen waited till he had gone before remarking, 'Well, what do you think, sir? Is he a knight of luck?'

'Knight of luck?' Christian laughed softly at the old German expression, knowing full well what Frenssen meant. Like all the old hares in the U-boat Arm he was very superstitious. No boat ever set off on patrol before the whole crew had pissed on its hull to bring good luck. Cross-eyed men and blonde women, however pretty, were never allowed on board in port because they brought bad luck, every submariner knew that. Now Frenssen was wondering out loud whether Harsch was a lucky skipper. Among the U-boat crews luck counted for more than professionalism or even skill. Both Prien and Kretschmar had been skilled and professional; but both had bought it in the end because they had lacked that other essential element — luck.

'At first I wouldn't have thought it, Frenssen,' Christian said slowly, as the U-70 ploughed on through the sparkling, waveless sea. 'I mean all those years without sinking much, except that celebrated locomotive of his. Then suddenly the *Stalin* and after that Varna and the bay back there. I would have given odds on that he wouldn't get away with it.' He shrugged eloquently. 'But he did, didn't he?'

Frenssen nodded his head slowly, as if in agreement.

'If we can make it safely to the Bosporus, it'll be plain sailing afterwards. I have a feeling that even if the Turks spot us there in their own waters, they're going to turn a blind eye, as long as they know the Russians don't know they've spotted us. They hate the Russians with a passion and I'm sure they're not very happy with the fact that they are now going to occupy another border with them, that of Bulgaria.'

'I know nothing of politics, sir,' Frenssen growled. 'I just wanted to know if you think the Old Man is lucky. Now I'm beginning to think you're right. To my way of thinking he does everything wrong, lands us in the shit time and time agen, yet he comes out of it smelling of frigging roses.'

'I don't think I'd let him hear you speak of him in that manner, you big rogue,' Christian said mildly. 'Anyway we're not out of the, er, shit, as you put it in your own inimical manner, just yet, Frenssen. This day is going to be a damned long one.'

Frenssen said nothing. But the remark seemed to destroy his sudden good mood and he relapsed into a heavy brooding silence, staring out at the limitless expanse of the sea, brow furrowed, as if he were doing a lot of thinking.

The afternoon passed in burning slowness and the watch had to fight against falling asleep as they searched the horizon for the first sign of danger.

But there was nothing. The Red Fleet seemed to have abandoned their search for the U-70. Not even spotter aircraft appeared in the brilliant, hard-blue sky. The fact puzzled Christian. After sending that special team from the von Seydlitz Army to try to capture them, why had the Soviet authorities seemingly given up the hunt?

As the afternoon started to give way to the evening and the power of the sun decreased, with a cooling light breeze now blowing across the sea, Christian told himself that they probably hadn't given up the chase. They had guessed that the U-70 would attempt to flee the Black Sea through the Bosporus and would be waiting for the fugitive submarine at the entrance to the stretch of water that linked Asia and Europe. Why range all over the Black Sea when they could wait without fuss for the German boat to put its head in the noose? He frowned thoughtfully. In essence they were sailing straight into a trap.

'Penny for them, sir?' Frenssen broke into his reverie, as the watch changed and a fresh crew of look-outs began to file by and on to the deck, bringing with them that typical nauseating odour of the submarine's interior; a mixture of unwashed bodies and diesel oil. Even after all his years in the U-boat Arm, Christian still could not get used to it.

Christian told the big petty officer his thoughts, adding, 'Perhaps we're really living in a fool's paradise, believing the Russians are going to let us get away with the sinking of the *Stalin*. You can bet your life that that old bastard in Moscow will make a few heads roll in the Soviet Black Sea Fleet if they allow us to escape — and the Russian admirals know it.'

Frenssen nodded his agreement and fell silent too, for a while, as though oppressed by the problem. His narrowed eyes looked speculatively at the lieutenant from time to time. Jungblut was young, only a few years older than the crew, but his handsome face under the cropped blond hair was tough and determined, the bright blue eyes firm and purposeful.

Even now Jungblut radiated assurance and confidence. He had the look of a fighter about him. Whatever happened he would go down fighting to the last. Suddenly the big chief petty officer was overcome by a feeling that everything was going to be all right. They'd get through safely whatever the Russians attempted. 'Sir,' he said, with renewed confidence.

'Yes, Frenssen?'

'Well, sir, we're German aren't we, and everybody knows that one German is worth ten Russians any day. 1 mean the Russians are real slope-heads.' He tapped his temple contemptuously with a finger like a hairy pork sausage. 'Nothing up there but red porridge, not brainy like us Germans.'

In spite of his mood, Christian laughed softly. 'All right, Herr Professor Frenssen, piss or get off the pot. Get on with it!'

'Well, they know as well as we do we're going to the Bosporus. They think we're going to let ourselves be served up to them on a silver platter — like a plate of sauerkraut and sausage! But they're expecting the U-70, that's all they're looking for. One battered old German submarine.'

'And that's what they are going to get,' Christian said promptly, wondering what Frenssen was getting at, 'unless the U-70 miraculously grows wings and we begin to fly.' He laughed bitterly.

'No, no, you don't understand me, sir,' Frenssen protested hurriedly. 'What if there wasn't just the U-70 trying to enter the Bosporus, but two of us?'

'*Two!*'

'Yessir. What if there was a kind of — what do yer call them? — a decoy.' He snapped his finger and thumb together excitedly. 'That's it — a decoy!'

'How do you mean, a decoy, Frenssen?' Christian asked swiftly, realizing with mounting excitement that the big petty officer might have come up with a sort of solution, one that could possibly save the U-70 from her inevitable fate. 'Spit it out, man. *Dalli, dalli!*'

Frenssen took his time as if he were formulating his ideas in words as he went along. 'Soon we'll be inside Turkish coastal waters — anyway that's what you told the skipper earlier on.'

Christian nodded swiftly.

'Well, I can't see the old Ali Baba's having troops or police in every tinpot coastal village. I mean, everybody knows they're a couple of million years behind the time — it's all that fucking with them six or seven wives they've all got —'

'*Frenssen!*' Christian interrupted firmly. 'Please, no lecture on Turkish society! Please, get on with it.'

'So assuming we can find one of their villages without protection and providing there's the odd fishing boat anchored there, what say if we launch a boarding party —'

'Aircraft off the port bow!' came the cry from the deck lookout.

Instantly Christian flung up his binoculars, knowing even as he did so that the only aircraft flying over the Black Sea now had to be Russian.

He identified the radial engine immediately. It was one of the ancient 'sewing machines', as the sailors called the slow-moving Russian spotter plane, and it was coming their way. He hit the button. The klaxon started screaming its urgent warning. Frantically the deck crew raced for the conning tower. At three second intervals, as the drill for emergencies of this kind prescribed, they slid down the ladder, hit the deck below in a bundle and then darted out of the way before the next man came whizzing down at full speed.

Christian timed them and cried to Frenssen, 'All right, you next.'

'Sir!' Frenssen flung himself down the ladder, sliding down the guide rails, crying wildly, 'Make way for an admiral. Make way for an admiral down there!'

Christian took one last look at the 'sewing machine', and then as Harsch cried, 'Prepare to dive,' he too slid down into the fetid interior, feeling a lot more confident than he had done for many a day. They'd escape from the Black Sea yet...

CHAPTER 8

A brisk wind blew across the entrance to the little fishing port, whipping up the dark water into little spurts of white. Now and then they were blown across the deck of the silent submarine lying low in the water. Faintly the waiting men could hear the wail of Turkish music coming from the rundown place, with here and there a faint, yellow light visible.

Harsch sucked his teeth thoughtfully and lowered his night glasses. 'Nothing!' he declared. 'No sign of military or naval craft. Just that couple of big fishing boats, though they look as if they might have been built at the time of Noah's Ark — they're that ancient!'

'The main thing, sir, is that we can nobble one,' Christian said, 'and that it lasts long enough to sail through the Bosporus.'

'Agreed,' Harsch said slowly, as if still not convinced that Frenssen's scheme would work. 'All right' — his voice suddenly became firm and determined — 'let's go over it again. You go into the place together. Frenssen's party splits off then and cuts any kind of telephone wires they can spot — if a dump like that possesses a telephone. We don't want anyone warning the Turkish authorities in Istanbul what has happened. You, Jungblut,' he addressed Christian, 'will in the meantime have seized the larger of the two fishing craft. Of course, all hell will be let loose once you start the engines. That's where you come in again, Frenssen.'

'Sir.'

'You give *Leutnant* Jungblut covering fire — if necessary — to the very last moment before going aboard the craft.

93

Thereafter, we take over and afford any cover you might need from the U-70. Is that clear?'

'Yes, sir,' Frenssen and Christian snapped as one.

'Good, then all that remains is for me to say — good luck to both of you.'

'Thank you, sir,' Christian said and saluted. 'All right then, Frenssen, let's get started.'

Five minutes later the two teams of five men had each slipped over the side almost noiselessly into the still warm water and were swimming effortlessly towards the fishing village; while behind them the submarine disappeared in a swirl of water until only the dark wedge of its periscope was visible. If they failed, Christian, swimming at the head of his team, knew, Harsch would have no scruples. He would abandon them to their fate as he had abandoned the perimeter group to the renegades. He dismissed the thought, telling himself they were not going to fail and concentrated on finding his way through the bobbing, tinkling buoys which marked the channel leading towards the anchorage, where the two ancient fishing boats were moored.

After they had been swimming some five minutes the water became calmer as they penetrated deeper into the little natural harbour. The sound of Turkish music from one of the ramshackle wooden houses facing the front was getting louder too and Christian judged it might be a coffee house, where the men of the village would sit and drink coffee and play cards of an evening; the only form of entertainment the village possessed. It, and possibly the local police station, if there was one, would be the most likely places to have a telephone. He hoped that Frenssen had thought the same.

The Frenssen group emerged from the water first. Swiftly he and his dripping men doubled along the jetty, which stank of fish, garlic, and Turkish tobacco, heading for the sound of the music, sticking to the shadows cast by the overhanging wooden balconies of the shabby houses. Frenssen had reasoned as Christian that if there were a telephone line in the place, it would be at the cafe.

Suddenly Frenssen came to a dead stop and pressed himself against the wall, hardly daring to breathe. A knife of yellow light had sliced into the glowing darkness. Behind him the others did the same. There was someone there! Had he seen them? Frenssen doubled his fist round his terrible 'Hamburg Equalizer' — his brass knuckles.

Abruptly the figure in the doorway farted loudly, gave a sigh of relief and began to spray hot urine onto the cobbles. A moment later the door closed and the light vanished.

'Phew!' Frenssen breathed. 'What a mob! Pissing out of their own doorways. Nearly splashed me boots, too!' Then he forgot the crudities of Turkish village life and commanded in a hoarse whisper, 'Round the corner. If there's wire anywhere, it's there.'

He was right. Moments later one of his group had sawn through the solitary cable and they were moving on the tips of their toes through the dark streets searching for further telephone wires.

Two hundred metres away, Christian was now carefully edging himself over the wooden stern of the larger fishing boat, struggling around the large carbide-powered lantern at the back, which was used at night to attract the fish. Gently the boat rocked in the swell, its ancient timbers creaking. But that was the only sound. The boat was empty, it seemed. 'All right,' he whispered to the white blobs that were faces in the water below, 'you can come aboard now. But I'll have the eggs off any man who makes the slightest sound — with a blunt razor too!'

Someone chuckled softly and then they too were clambering over the gunwale into the boat, which stank of rancid fish and hard, unremitting labour. Christian moved forward at a half-crouch, taking care not to stumble over the crates and piles of rope which had been left carelessly everywhere on the deck. 'You, Martens,' he whispered, 'get down into the engine room. You go with him Moses. See if you can work the engines, but don't start up until I give the signal.'

The two of them nodded their understanding and clambered down the hatch. 'You two,' he addressed his remaining men, 'up onto the bridge. Wait for me there. I'll check the cabin.' He indicated the squat silhouette which backed onto the bridge. 'All right, off you go now.'

Silently they moved off while Christian made his way cautiously, ears pricked to pick up the slightest sound from the front. But there was nothing save the monotonous wail of a Turkish singer from the cafe. Frenssen had obviously not been detected. Everything was running smoothly, he told himself, knowing that all hell might well be let loose once they started the engines and the locals were alerted…

The sound was vague and low, but tense and worked up as he was Christian caught it immediately. His heart started to beat like a trip-hammer. His muscles tensed. There was somebody there — behind him!

He attempted to swing round, club raised. Too late! A brawny if fleshy arm wound itself round his neck. He gasped with shock, his nostrils suddenly assailed by the stink of sweat and cheap cologne. The arm tightened its grip and he felt himself pressed against the soft cushion of an enormous bosom, unrestrained by corset or brassiere. *His assailant was a woman*!

'*Çok güzel*,' she breathed with pleasure and squeezed even harder, as if she were a professional wrestler going to floor an opponent. Red and silver stars started to explode in front of Christian's eyes. He choked and wriggled furiously, trying in vain to get his breath. Instinctively, he jabbed his elbow into the big woman's chest. She yelped with pain and relaxed her grip a little. Christian didn't need a second invitation. He jabbed hard again and in the same instant her grip slackened even more, he slipped down and out of her hold.

He swung round. He gasped. The woman towered above him and was broad with it. Her hair was loose and hanging grey and matted to shoulders like those of an ox. Her great body was clad in a tent-like dress or gown, under which her huge breasts trembled like jelly. She was barefoot.

For one long second the two of them faced each other, both obviously surprised at the other's appearance. The Turkish woman recovered first. She lunged forward and caught him by the genitals. She chuckled with delight, and then twisted them hard, very hard!

Christian nearly passed out with the sheer agony of it and only just prevented himself from crying out loud. Christ, he told himself, as she exerted all her strength, grinning at him in the glowing darkness, cruelly, sadistically ripping at the soft flesh, she's gonna pull my frigging eggs off. Hardly knowing he was doing so, he brought his heel down on her naked foot.

She yelped with pain and let go, but she was ready for more action almost immediately, chopping a hand like a small steam shovel down and knocking the club out of his suddenly nerveless fingers. Then she launched herself forward, hands outstretched, grabbing for his throat yet once more.

He dodged the hands — just in time. He thrust out his two forefingers and the woman ran straight into them. They hooked inside her nostrils and went deep inside. Christian, hating himself for doing so, but knowing it had to be done, ripped outwards with all his strength. The woman screamed thickly. His fingers were suddenly wet with hot blood. In vain she tried to bring up her fat dimpled knee to connect with his genitals. He dodged the blow easily and exerted more pressure. Her whole moon-like face contorted with absolute agony. The blood streamed down right to his elbow as she tried to shake herself loose, and dripped to the deck.

Suddenly he slipped, his feet going from beneath him. The woman reeled back, shaking her head, splattering blood everywhere, moaning and cursing, the front of her tent-like gown splattered scarlet now. But she still had plenty of fighting spirit left. Staggering to the wooden bulkhead, she ripped the fire axe fastened there from its clips and swung a tremendous blow at Christian who was trying to get back on his feet. In the very last moment, he rolled to one side and the blade smashed into the rotten wood of the deck.

The woman grunted like an enraged bull and ripped the axe up again, high above her head, her breasts rippling under the loose material of her gown. This time Christian didn't have a chance. Her eyes gleamed crazily. The axe began to descend. Christian screwed his eyes tightly closed.

The Moses hesitated for a fleeting second, taking in the scene in a flash. With a grunt he thrust the knife deep into her back. She arched. There was a terrible sucking noise from somewhere down inside her. He plunged deeper, suddenly furious with her for not dying straight away. *'Croak, you bitch!'* he cursed through gritted teeth, *'Why won't you frigging well croak?'*

The axe tumbled to the deck from suddenly nerveless fingers. The woman began to sag, her breath coming in short, sharp gasps. He let go of her and sprang back, horrified at what he had just done, eyes wild and wide with terror. Slowly, very slowly, she started to sink to the deck like a barrage balloon being carefully deflated.

It was just then that the first burst of Schmeisser fire from the waterfront told Christian, pinned down by the dead woman's enormous bulk, that Frenssen had run into trouble...

The bottle of *raki* had started the trouble. They had just cut the second and last telephone wire, which ran from a pokey, evil-smelling hovel, and were on their way back to the waterfront when Frenssen had spotted the tumble-down shop. The goods behind the dirty window were poor and uninviting — a few rusting tins, a sack or two of rice and some shrivelled fruit — save for the bottle of pure white liquid that formed its centrepiece. Frenssen had seen it, stopped, nostrils quivering as if he could almost *smell* the alcohol. It was now forty-eight hours since he had drained the last of his precious flatman and he had been unable to resist the temptation. Whipping off his tunic, he had wound it round his right arm and hand and lunged forward with his 'Hamburg Equalizer'. The window shattered immediately and he had grabbed the precious *raki* in the very same instant that a yellow light flashed on above and someone cried out in sudden alarm.

In a flash all had been noise, confusion, and angry shouts, as if the whole village had been waiting all the time to be alerted like this. 'For chrissake!' Frenssen had shouted in disgust. 'It's only a bottle of frigging sauce, after all. And then he had bellowed, 'Come on, lads, take yer hind legs in yer hands and let's hoof it!'

As they raced down the waterfront towards the second fishing boat, blasts of shotgun fire were coming from all sides and someone up ahead was standing in the middle of the dusty road, one arm behind his back, the arm holding the pistol straight out, firing at them as if he were back on some peacetime range. Frenssen guessed, as he ripped off quick bursts to left and right, it could only be a cop.

Again the lone man fired. Next to Frenssen one of the greenbeaks staggered to a stop and went down on one knee. 'Sorry, *Obermaat*' he said apologetically, 'but I think I stopped one — in the thigh.'

Frenssen shook his head as if sorely tried. 'Stupid sod!' he said. 'Trust you young piss-pansies to get hit at a time like this.' He grunted and ripped off a quick burst to his front, swaying from the hip like a western gun-fighter. The man with the pistol screamed shrilly and went reeling back, his face suddenly trickling down onto his chest like red molten wax. 'Come on then, let dear old Petty Officer Frenssen give you a piggy-back.' Effortlessly he swung the wounded rating over his shoulder. They ran on, with Frenssen telling himself that Lieutenant Jungblut would have already heard the shooting. He'd start the engines at any moment. All he had to do was to get these piss-pansies to the stolen craft and ensure that the Ali Baba's didn't get too close before they could shove off.

Now he could see the fishing boat and hear the first dull sluggish whine as one of the boarding party tried to turn the engine over. 'Hey, you in front,' he gasped, as another blast of shotgun fire started pellets singing and howling off the cobbles all around them, 'get to them lines and cast them off — smartish. You,' he slapped the wounded boy's rump, 'in a minute I'm going to let you down. Do you think you can crawl to the boat? I've got to look after things here.'

'Yes, *Obermaat,*' the other replied dutifully. 'I can't feel a thing at the moment.'

'You will,' Frenssen said dourly. 'All right, lad, here we go.' He lowered him to the cobbles and then swung round, Schmeisser blazing at his hips at the spurts of angry flame coming, or so it seemed, from every damned house that lined the waterfront.

As the members of Frenssen's party came struggling aboard, followed by the Turks' fire, with the engines still stubbornly refusing to start, Christian, waiting anxiously on the little bridge, noted sudden jets of blue flame coming from the right and became aware of the stink of escaping petrol.

All at once Christian realized what the Turks were doing. 'Frenssen,' he yelled in alarm. 'Frenssen — to your right!'

'What is it, sir?' the big petty officer cried back above the ugly snap and crack of the small-arms fire. 'What gives?'

'They're using Molotov cocktails. This old tub'll burn like dry tinder if —'

The first primitive bomb — an empty bottle of *raki* filled with petrol and lit by a rag fuse — came sailing through the air to explode against the side of the fishing boat in a sudden whoosh. In an instant the wooden bulkhead was dripping flame and Moses, recovered from his shock, was hastily throwing buckets of sea-water at the sudden blaze.

'Got you, sir!' Frenssen yelled and directed an angry burst of 9mm slugs in the direction of the fire-bombers, crying, 'Stick that up yer dirty arse, Ali Baba!'

There was a shrill scream of pain and the sound of somebody dropping heavily to the cobbles, but at the same time yet another fire-bomb came sailing through the air to smack into the big lantern at the stern. It roared into a sheet of blinding white incandescent flame immediately as the carbide caught fire. In a flash night was transformed into day and the snipers in the houses along the front concentrated their fire on Moses, as he picked up the axe the big woman had intended to use on Christian and raced for the burning lantern.

Slugs and pellets whined off the brass rails and ploughed up angry slivers of wood from the deck all around him, as he hacked away at the lantern's mounting, his face flushed brick-red with the heat, his hair and eyebrows already beginning to singe. Ahead of him, Frenssen slapped home another magazine and scythed a long enraged burst the length of the houses.

One of the bomb-throwers cursed savagely as the bottle he was holding was hit and shattered. The curse turned to a frenzied howl of absolute unreasoning agony as the liquid burst into flames, immediately transforming him into a writhing twisting human torch. He staggered towards the water, but failed to make it, felled by the flames, and lay on the cobbles, still twitching weakly as that fierce cruel fire consumed him.

The Moses struck home once more. With a rending sound, the lantern tore loose and dropped to splash in the water below with a tremendous hiss. At the same moment, the engines below burst into noisy life. 'Come on, Frenssen!' Christian yelled from the bridge, 'run for it, man, we're off!' One of the ratings standing half out the engine room hatch looked expectantly at Christian on the bridge, for there was no signals telegraph. 'Take her away, leading hand!' cried Christian above the racket.

'Yessir,' the man replied eagerly and in his turn he cried to those working the engine below, 'The skipper sez — *take her away!*'

As the old fishing boat creaked and groaned, Frenssen began to run for it, ignoring the slugs kicking up ugly little spurts of blue flame all around his flying feet. A Turk stepped out of the shadow of some packing cases and attempted to bar his way. Frenssen's 'Hamburg Equalizer' flashed. The Turk went reeling back scattering packing cases, spitting out his teeth. The fishing boat was beginning to move. Frenssen made one last desperate effort, as yelling Turks began to emerge from the rickety wooden houses everywhere, intent on revenge. He hurled himself into the air desperately. His big body slammed into the stern of the departing boat, his hands frantically seeking — and finding — a hold. For one long moment he simply hung there, being trailed through the water, slugs slapping into the wooden stern all about, showering him with a rain of splinters; then helpful hands hauled him onto the wet deck where he lay panting hectically like a stranded fish until a familiar voice said, 'Now come on, you big horned ox. Let's have none of your malingering. On your feet and start earning your pay.'

Wearily Frenssen sat up and stared at Christian. 'Earn my pay, sir?' he gasped. 'Great crap on the Christmas tree, after this little lot I thinking I deserve *a frigging bonus.*'

CHAPTER 9

Christian eyed the sea without any pleasure. On the horizon, those grey shapes spaced out at regular intervals had to be the Soviet Black Sea Fleet. The Turkish Navy was hopelessly out of date; they were too modern to be Turkish vessels. As an afterthought, he took off his naval cap and put on the battered cloth hat they had found in the cabin. With his dirty uniform and the hat, he might pass muster as the skipper of a Turkish fishing smack if he were stopped. He prayed that the Russians wouldn't be able to speak Turkish.

Frenssen, standing next to him on the rickety wooden bridge, asked, 'Is it them, sir?'

Christian nodded glumly. ''Fraid so. I knew we couldn't stay lucky all the time.'

'Don't despair, sir.' Frenssen attempted to cheer him up. 'You know what they say — weeds never snuff it? Our luck will hold out.'

Christian wasn't quite convinced, but he knew there was no other way out. They'd have to run the gauntlet of the Russian ships before they could reach the comparative safety of Turkish coastal waters around the entrance to the Bosporus. He dismissed that unpleasant prospect for a moment and concentrated on the U-70. Its operators would have already picked up the prop noise of the enemy ships. Harsch would know what lay ahead. Now it all depended on his ability to position the U-70 directly under the old fishing boat. With a bit of luck — '*A helluva lot of luck, Christian*!', a cynical little voice at the back of his head corrected him sharply — the noise of both their screws would merge sufficiently to fool the Soviet operators listening for the first sounds of the elusive submarine. It meant that he and Harsch had to maintain a kind of mental telepathy in order to match the course, speed and manoeuvres of one another's craft. One slip, one minor error of judgement, and the U-70 would be at the mercy of the Russian ships; and in the shallow waters of the entrance to the Bosporus there would be no escape for the submarine.

Thus they proceeded, with the U-70 some twenty fathoms beneath the fishing boat's rotting keel, the tension mounting all the time, growing ever closer to the Russian ships. Frenssen, normally solidly imperturbable, obviously felt the tension too. He wiped a dirty, unshaven face, glazed with sweat, and said, 'I don't like this frigging tippy-toe shit, sir! Gets right on my frigging tits.' Suddenly he remembered the bottle of *raki* and his gloom vanished. He licked his cracked lips in anticipation and reached for his back pocket where he had placed it. 'Fancy a snort, sir, something to knock down behind yer back collar stud and —'

He stopped short abruptly, a look of absolute, total horror on his face and brought up his hand slowly to show Christian. It was wet and covered with glass splinters. 'Did — did you ever see the frigging like, sir?' he whispered, voice hoarse with shock. 'Them frigging Ali Babas have gone and shot up my one and only bottle of throat-juice.' He beat the bridge with the clenched fist in impotent rage at this further example of man's inhumanity to man.

Christian laughed softly and concentrated on the Russians. Already what looked like a destroyer to his front was signalling to her nearest neighbour, the Aldis lamp flicking off and on urgently. And Christian knew why. They had spotted the fishing boat and were either communicating the information to the other ship or were asking a superior's permission to stop and check her out. 'All right, Frenssen,' he said urgently, 'knock off the fooling. We've been spotted…'

Ten minutes later the pinnace bearing the blood-red flag of the Soviet Union pulled up alongside the fishing boat and for the very first time in two years of war with the Russians, Christian saw enemy troops at close quarters. Even in the midst of the terribly dangerous situation in which they found themselves, he was surprised at how ordinary they looked.

They were as young as his own ratings, blond, open-faced boys for the most part, very smart and efficient-looking in their striped jerseys, with the ribbons of their caps fluttering, in the faint breeze.

The officer in charge was a different matter. He was big and broad, clad in a leather coat which creaked when he moved, and his high-cheeked Slavic face was set in what appeared to be a permanent look of suspicion. As Christian ordered the fishing boat to stop, praying fervently that Harsch would be doing the same, the Russian naval officer flashed a hard, mean look the length of the rickety vessel before slowly opening his mouth to reveal a set of gleaming stainless steel false teeth. '*Kapitan*?' he queried, looking at Christian standing behind the wheel on the open bridge.

'*Da, da,*' Christian said hurriedly inwardly thanking God fervently that the Russian officer obviously did not speak Turkish.

The Russian grunted and held out a big hand while the helmsman held the pinnace steady in the choppy sea. '*Dokumenta*?' he demanded.

Christian felt an icy finger of fear trace its way down the small of his back. The Russian word was close enough to the German one for him to recognize its meaning. The Russian wanted the ship's papers! He continued to smile inanely, while his mind raced furiously. What the hell was he going to do? He wouldn't recognize a set of Turkish ship's papers if they were presented to him on a silver platter, tied up by a red ribbon.

He made a show of not understanding, smiling furiously all the while. Behind him Frenssen clicked off the safety on his Schmeisser under the cover of the bulkhead. '*Nix, nix dokumenta,*' he said finally in a voice that was decidedly shaky.

The officer's broad hard face took on a look of menace. He snapped something to his sailors and they raised their rifles threateningly, while his own hand felt to the big pistol strapped to his belt. '*Davai,*' he barked relentlessly. '*Dokumente*'

Christian didn't know the meaning of '*davai,*' but its intent was clear enough; produce those damned ship's papers smartly — or there would be trouble, serious trouble! For a moment his nerve broke. He froze, unable to think, act, do anything, while the Russian officer stared across at him, lips parted to reveal those terrible steel teeth.

Abruptly, almost as if in a dream, he became aware of the Moses walking across the deck below towards the Russian pinnace. In one hand he bore a large tin of Turkish cigarettes he had just found in the engine room; in the other, he carried something infinitely more precious to him. It was his normally well-hidden collection of well-thumbed photographs, bought from a middle-aged, knowing Frenchman at a street corner in Brest at the end of his recruit training.

While a mesmerized Christian watched him uncomprehendingly, he solemnly placed first the cigarettes in the Russian officer's big hand and then the photographs, muttering the word '*dokumenta,*' as he did so. Then he straightened up and waited, face proud and eager.

For what seemed an age, the Russian stared at the photographs, his eyes getting larger all the time, little drops of saliva beginning to trickle from the sides of his mouth and dribble down his chin. Finally he exploded into a tremendous '*Boshe moi!*' followed by a wave and the word '*horosho*'. Hastily he waved again and neatly pocketed the photographs, eyes glistening, the tremendous stainless steel teeth set in an approximation of a smile. '*Horosho,*' he cried once more when Christian did not react. '*Davai!*'

'Move it, sir. For chrissake move it!' Frenssen hissed. 'Before he changes his frigging mind!'

Christian shook his head and shouted an order to the engine room. The fishing boat started to move in the same moment that the pinnace's engine roared into life again. As the fishing boat chugged by the Russian officer straightened to attention and raised his hand to his cap. 'Holy strawsack,' Frenssen breathed in awe, 'the Russian prick is actually saluting us! *What the hellus did the Moses give him?*'

A minute later, an embarrassed brick-red Moses told them.

Frenssen guffawed out loud. 'You mean —' he gasped, 'you gave him a lot of dirty pictures? I allus knew them Russians were a lot of frigging wankers with hairy palms!' Again he laughed, throwing back his head, his relief obvious.

But their relief didn't last long. Moments later the urgent shrilling of a ship's whistle, followed by the ear-splitting shriek of klaxons told Christian things had gone wrong. Harsch had *not* stopped when the fishing smack had been forced to halt by the pinnace. He had gone sailing on and had been spotted. Now the Russian vessels, ignoring the humble fishing boat in their midst, were racing back and forth, smoke pouring from their funnels, the men already running towards the depth charge projectors, desperately attempting to detect the U-70 before she could escape into Turkish territorial waters.

Christian bit his lip as the first salvo of drum-like depth charges, each containing half a ton of high explosive, went sailing into the air. They had failed after all...

'*Verdamnte Scheisse!*' Harsch cursed, as the boat rocked with the impact of the exploding depth charges. Momentarily the lights went out. A man screamed hysterically and Harsch bellowed as the emergency lighting flashed on, 'Stop that noise there. I will not have —' He grabbed for a stanchion to prevent himself from falling as another salvo set the U-70 rocking and swaying violently.

Harsch pulled himself together, shaking off the paralysing shock of the terrible impact. Swiftly he took stock of his situation, as the skeleton crew stared at each other with wide fearful eyes in the faint yellow gloom. Obviously their trick had failed at the very last moment. Something had happened to Jungblut and the fishing boat. Now he was on his own in a few fathoms of water with the Russians right overhead. It could be only a matter of minutes before they planted one of those damned lethal eggs of theirs right on top of him. He had to do something — and fast.

He did a quick calculation. The U-70 could be only a matter of one or two miles from Turkish territorial waters. He visualized the map of the area in his mind, telling himself that the Russian ships would be dangerously crowded together in the narrow straits as they attacked the U-70.

Frighteningly the boat lurched and reeled yet again under the shattering blows of exploding depth charges close by. Hastily Harsch grabbed for support as crockery and glasses came raining down in the tiny galley and the cook screamed with pain as a pan struck him full in the face. There was the ominous sound of water rushing in. The U-70's plates had been buckled. She was taking in water. Harsch knew he had only minutes left.

Suddenly, surprisingly, a picture of the 'Big Lion' lecturing his U-boat skippers just before the war in Mürwik flashed into his mind. Lean, erect, cold-eyed he had stood before them that fine August day, with the sunbeams rippling on the calm water of the fjord outside, and said, 'I'm talking to you, gentlemen, as an old U-boat skipper myself today. So I feel justified in passing onto you this piece of advice. In a desperate situation, don't just accept the inevitable. *Fight back*! When my boat was trapped by the Tommies in the Adriatic back in 'eighteen, with no hope of being saved, I surfaced and took them completely by surprise. They'd expected me to lie on my back like a beaten dog and just let it happen to me. I might well have got away with it too but there were just too many of the buck-teethed Tommy buggers. I went into the bag, with my crew. But it's worth a try. *Never accept the inevitable*!'

With shocking clarity Harsch knew what he was to do. Sink or swim, it was the only way. 'Torpedo mate,' he called above the sound of the in-rushing water.

'Sir?'

'Prepare tubes one to four!'

Someone gasped, but Harsch pretended not to hear. Instead he barked as his handful of sailors stared at him wide-eyed, 'Up periscope!'

The boat reeled under the impact of a fresh batch of depth charges. Dials fractured and glass flew everywhere. The sound of the water rushing in grew louder. The pings of the enemy asdic searching for them tapped the outer hull like pecks from a gigantic bird's beak.

Harsch waited impatiently till the tube was ready. He bent his head to it and swung it in a one hundred and eighty degree arc.

In front of the long low shoreline of Turkey there were Soviet destroyers everywhere, milling around, racing back and forth with a white bone in their teeth, trailing vast streams of black smoke behind them. It was as he had guessed, the Russians were crowded into the narrow entrance to the Bosporus.

'Tubes one to four ready, sir!' the torpedo mate yelled.

Harsch's plan was to fire them in a wild fan with no intention of aiming at individual ships. All he wanted to do was to create a panic and so gain sufficient time to run for the safety of Turkish waters. He was assuming that the Russians would not dare violate Turkish sovereignty. They didn't want to force the anti-Russian but neutral country into Germany's arms. Hastily he rapped out firing directions, aimed at spreading the torpedoes in a sixty-degree arc.

Clearly bewildered, the mate repeated his orders, swiftly carried out the fittings before shouting, 'Ready to fire, sir!'

Harsch waited a moment till the boat ceased rocking after the latest batch of depth charges and then he roared, carried away by the wild, unreasoning bloodlust of battle, 'Fire *one* ... *two* ... *three* ... *four*!' As the boat lurched and shuddered with the release of each of the heavy torpedoes, he yelled, 'Take her up, Engineer!'

'What did you say, sir?' the officer cried aghast.

'Take her up! We're four knots faster with the diesels than we are with the electric motors and we need every last little bit of speed we can get out of her. *Now take her up*!'

Harsch waited tensely as the compressed air hissed and the water rushed out of the tanks. It would be a race with death, he knew, but he hoped the surprise of his sudden appearance would unsettle the Russians, already being surprised by the wide wild fan of his tin fish.

Seconds later the U-70 broke the surface and Harsch yelled crazily, 'Both full ahead, engineer. *Here we go!*'

Up top, Christian and Frenssen watched open-mouthed and shocked into a stupefied silence by the spectacle presenting itself to them. A mere sea mile away the world seemed to have gone crazy. The Russian destroyers and small craft, which a moment before had seemed about to destroy the trapped submarine with their depth charges, were now scattering wildly in utter confusion as the torpedoes fanned out in a wide arc. Obviously, Christian told himself, they had not been aimed at any particular target. Harsch had fired them to confuse the Russians. But to what purpose?

He had his answer a moment later. In the same instant that one of the wild torpedoes struck home with a great rending crash and a thirty-metre long blow torch hissed the length of a stricken Russian destroyer, consuming everything before it, the U-70 came popping out of the sea at a crazy angle, her diesels already pulsating all out.

The Russians saw her at once. But the daring move took them completely by surprise. It seemed to take their gunners an age before they started to open fire. When they did their aim was erratic and their shells wildly off target. Great spurts of whirling white water shot into the sky again and again and obscured the fleeing submarine, but each time she emerged from the shower of water unscathed.

Standing on the bridge Christian clenched his fists till his knuckles went white and his palms hurt, willing her to get through, telling himself she deserved to do so after all she had been through. Next to him Frenssen chanted a furious litany of obscenities, repeating over and over again, 'Come on, you son of a bitch, *make it!*'

On the sinking burning destroyer the Russian sailors were insane human torches, thrashing at their uniforms in a vain attempt to beat out the flames that ripped at them, tore at them, turning their flesh into a black bubbling pulp, the shrinking charred meat arching their backs into taut bows, skeleton arms flung out in a convulsive crucifixion.

Christian and Frenssen had no eyes for the dying, tortured Russian sailors. Their gaze was fixed exclusively on the death ride of the U-70, as it survived near-disaster time and time again, her superstructure ripped and scarred a bright silver with the shrapnel, her periscope bent, the shot-down radio mast trailing a wake of crackling blue electric sparks in the water, reeling drunkenly from side to side as the huge spouts of water buffeted and drenched her.

As if in response to some unspoken command, the shelling ceased, leaving behind it a loud echoing silence which seemed to go on for ever and ever. Christian breathed a fervent sigh of relief and relaxed at last. Next to him, Frenssen ripped open his flies and pulled out his penis, crying, 'Christ, if I don't do it here and now, I'll piss meself. Great buckets of bloody ordure, I don't want to live through anything like that agen.' He seized his organ and let go a great stream of hot steaming urine over the side.

Christian knew what he meant. He felt totally shattered, every last drop of energy drained from him, as if someone had opened a secret tap. The U-70 had done it! She had reached Turkish territorial waters safely. They were finished with the Black Sea. They would see the Russians no more. With a voice that he hardly recognized as his own, he croaked, 'All right engine room. Forward both. We're going into the Bosporus...'

BOOK TWO: THE END OF THE U-70

CHAPTER 1

The shrieking sirens of the motorcycle outriders set the skinny, dusty dogs scurrying for cover and frightened Arab women clutched their naked brown children possessively as the glittering cortège swung round a bend in the shimmering white road.

In front came the scout cars, paintwork gleaming, their rears filled with heavily armed troops, the machine-gunners in the cabs tensed, helmeted and expectant. Behind them came the half-tracks, tracks clattering furiously, the tall antennas of their radios whipping silver in the bright sunshine. Then *he* came.

The general stood bolt upright in his command car like a Roman emperor in a chariot. He was wearing his 'war face number one', the one he practised so assiduously in the privacy of his own quarters, a formidable, narrow-eyed scowl, his jaw jutting against the web strap of his highly polished, lacquered helmet with the two oversize stars of a major-general. From time to time he lashed his riding crop against the side of his elegant gleaming boot, as if he would dearly love to thrash to one side this dirty mob of 'A-rabs', as he called them contemptuously.

But there was no time for that. The motorcyclists in the lead were already slowing down as the remote camp in which the final conference was to be held loomed up in front of them; a square of desert, fenced off with triple layers of concertina wire, stork-legged watch-towers at each corner, in which squatted watchful machine-gunners and sharpshooters, and in its centre a huddle of prefabricated wooden huts surrounded by staff cars.

'Turn out the guard!' Over the roar of the motors, the general could hear someone shouting urgently. 'General officer approaching!' He smiled sternly and tugged at his belt with its twin ivory-handled six-shooters until they sat exactly right. He wanted these feather merchants of base troops to see what a real American fighting man looked like.

His staff car came to a halt exactly outside the guardroom. He took his time, staring down imperiously at the dozen men of the guard standing rigidly to attention in the hot sunshine, rifles raised in salute. His eyes narrowed to slits and slowly, very slowly, he began to smile, exhibiting his dingy, sawn-off teeth frighteningly. 'You, sergeant of the guard!' He pointed his riding crop at the pudgy guard commander, whose moon face was glazed with sweat.

'Sir?' The sergeant advanced hesitantly. His Adam's apple shot up and down his fat neck as if on an express lift.

'Do you feel a draught?' the general asked softly, too softly for a man of his hair-trigger temper.

'A draught, sir?' the perplexed sergeant stuttered in bewilderment. 'Why no, sir.'

'Then you goddam should!' the general exploded in sudden, red-faced rage, pointing his stick at the harassed sergeant. 'Don't you damn well realize that your collar button is undone? In the name of God Almighty' — he raised his gaze as if appealing to the Deity himself — 'what kind of goddam army is this when a man salutes a general officer *half-naked*! I will not tolerate any sonuvabitch who runs around like that. Now shape up, mister, or I'll bust you down to buck private — just like that!' He slapped the stanchion in front of him with his riding crop and made the unhappy sergeant jump. 'All right, driver, take this thing away. I just can't stand looking at that fat sad sack a moment longer. Move!'

Hastily the driver, who knew his master only too well, moved. Behind the cortège, the guard still stood to attention, even when the cavalcade disappeared round the corner, until finally the pudgy sergeant whispered out of the side of his mouth. 'Holy cow, I nearly creamed my goddam skivvies just now. Who the Sam Hill was *that* bastard?'

A tall rangy private first class, who had the leathery look of an old soldier about him, chuckled softly and said, 'Don't yer know, sarge, you've just been privileged?'

'Privileged to do what, Murphy?' the NCO snarled. 'You mean *privileged* to have my ass busted by that two-star prick.'

Murphy's grin deepened. 'For your information, sarge, that two-star prick is nobody else but old Georgie Patton!'

The sergeant gasped and dropped his rifle into the sand. 'You mean that was — was old Blood an' Guts Patton! Oh, my fucking Christ.' He swayed alarmingly, as if he might faint, his face drained of all colour...

All the top brass were there — Eisenhower, Montgomery, Alexander, Cunningham, Tedder — a glittering mixture of all three services, the 'pen pushers', as Patton called them contemptuously, dressed in sparkling Class A uniforms, the fighting generals in combat dress, uniforms dull, even dowdy, bare of decorations and insignia. For a while they mingled, drinking coffee out of paper cups. 'Don't they serve a real white man's drink like bourbon at these things?' Patton had snorted, but Eisenhower had only laughed. He had continued puffing nervously at yet another Lucky Strike, of which he chain-smoked over sixty a day. Finally he strode up to the head of the room and nodded to the full colonel acting as an orderly at this top secret meeting, and who was the lowest-ranking officer here on this hot June day. 'OK, Jenkins,' he snapped, stubbing out his cigarette and lighting another one almost immediately, 'haul ass!'

Jenkins duly 'hauled ass'. He pulled the cord and the heavy black velvet curtain, which had shrouded the map covering the whole wall there, swished back. Dramatically their target was revealed to them, that pear-shaped blob of land at the bottom of the Italian peninsula — Sicily.

In spite of the dramatic gesture none of them there were surprised, or even impressed. They had been planning this operation for weeks now, ever since the Germans had been defeated in North Africa. They knew the details of the attack backwards.

Eisenhower, however, his usually smiling face grim, tried to inject some enthusiasm into the briefing by saying, 'Gentlemen — Sicily! The start of our way back into Europe. The first step on the Allied march to Rome.'

His remark kindled no enthusiasm. Grandiose words were wasted on these hard-bitten professional soldiers. Even Montgomery, who had more reason than most of them there to want to avenge the defeat of Dunkirk, where the British had been kicked out of Europe so ignominiously three long years before, showed no emotion. Instead he continued to stroke his long beaky nose, set in a bright-eyed, bird-like face, as if he were pondering some problem or other.

'You all know the main details off by heart by now,' Eisenhower said, breaking into his famous big smile, as he realized that the drama of the new invasion escaped them. 'We shall go in with two armies, yours Monty and your Seventh, Georgie.' He indicated Patton, who had kept on his elegant gloves in spite of the heat, sitting bolt upright as if he were on parade. In front of his fellow general officers Patton was determined to maintain his fierce war-like posture. 'Our ultimate objective is Messina and the Straits across to Italy proper. However' — he paused to light yet another Lucky Strike — 'before we get there we can anticipate some hard and bitter fighting. We must, gentlemen, be prepared for a real killing match.'

'Don't worry, Ike,' Montgomery's high-pitched voice broke in, 'my chaps of the Eighth Army have seen off the Hun before. We'll do it again. We'll knock 'em for six.'

Patton didn't know what 'knocking 'em for six' meant. But he did know the 'little fart', as he called Montgomery contemptuously, was up to his old tricks, pushing forward his Eighth Army ahead of his own newly created Seventh US Army. Hastily he said, 'You don't need to worry about the fighting quality of the troops. My boys are raring to go, just like Monty's here. Besides, you didn't call us here, Ike, to give us a pep talk, did you?'

Ike smiled a little ruefully. He had known George Patton for nearly thirty years now. He never changed. After all those years he had never learned to respect his superiors, even one as tolerant and as easy going as he was. 'All right, Georgie,' he said, 'all right. Give your Supreme Commander a chance to pretend to be important, willya?'

There was a titter of laughter in the room and even Montgomery allowed himself a careful, wintry smile.

'No, I *didn't* call you here today, gentlemen, to give you a pep talk. My reason for summoning you to this place was to give you an express warning about security. My headquarters in Algiers is, as you know, a hotbed of espionage and loose talk. That's why we came here. There are German spies and sympathizers all over the place — and we simply cannot allow them to know two things.' He ticked them off on his nicotine-stained fingers, the nails chewed down to the quick. General

Eisenhower had been living off his nerves for nearly a year now. '*One*, the place of landing by your Eighth, Monty, and your Seventh Army, Georgie. There are 400,000 combat-ready German troops in Sicily. Now they are engaged in guarding the total shoreline of the island. If, however, they knew our landing sites they could concentrate in advance and there would be a massacre.' He looked hard at them and they returned his look, even Patton. All of them knew just how heavily outnumbered the assault force would be if the enemy were able to concentrate beforehand.

'*Two*,' Eisenhower went on, 'all efforts to make the enemy believe that we are intending to land in some other place on the European mainland must be kept up. They must not be able to suspect it's Sicily, although they know we are concentrating an invasion fleet here in North Africa. As far as I am concerned they can think we're gonna land in Greece or Yugoslavia, even Sardinia and southern France, but *not* Sicily.'

Eisenhower let his words sink in. There was total silence in the hot fetid briefing room, broken only by the soft whirring of the large overhead fan, which seemed merely to shift the hot air around, and the tread of the heavily armed sentries who were everywhere outside.

'From this moment on, all of you present here' — the supreme commander looked round the circle of solemn faces intently — 'are to be classified as *bigots*, the latest special security classification created for this operation.'

'*Bigots*!' Patton snorted, as always wanting to be first in, in order to attract attention to himself. 'Jesus, I've been a bigot all my life, Ike. I hate black people. I hate the Jewish! I hate Lim—'

'Georgie!' Eisenhower cut in sharply. 'Now that's enough of that!'

'Sorry,' Patton said suddenly crestfallen, knowing he had put his foot in it once again and knowing too that Ike wouldn't hesitate to sack anyone, including an army commander, who threatened to rock the fragile Anglo-American alliance. 'Just got carried away.'

Eisenhower shot him a hard look. 'You'll get carried away once too often one of these days, Georgie, and cut your throat with your own mouth. Now then, let's get with this damned business...'

An hour later the newly initiated 'bigots' emerged from the briefing room to enter their waiting cars, shielding their eyes against the blinding African sun. The escorts formed up, scores of heavily armed soldiers and MPs, as if the German *Wehrmacht* was massed in force outside in the desert, just waiting to launch an attack. In spite of Eisenhower's rebuke, Patton, as volatile as ever, had regained his high good humour, and slapped his crop against the side of his gleaming riding boot. He took out a big cigar, bit the end of it, and lit it with a flourish, as his command car drew up.

Colonel Koch, his chief of intelligence, followed him in and as they started, said, 'It's the Limeys, General. They've got the intelligence appreciation all screwed up. The way I figure they've got about half that number of Germans and Italians on the island, sir.' He contorted his flabby, pale face scornfully. 'The British have always been nervous Nellys.'

Patton nodded his encouragement. It was the kind of talk he liked; anything which fed his inflated ego. 'Go on, Koch,' he said.

'Well, sir, the Italians are spread out all over the place, static divisions, with no guns, no transport and *no guts*! A couple of rounds of artillery fire and they'll leg it. No sir, it's the Germans we've got to worry about. There are two divisions of 'em. They're short on tanks, but they are strictly hot mustard, sir!'

Patton grunted and took his baleful gaze off a soldier who was actually walking around in the presence of all this top brass without a necktie. By Christ, he told himself angrily, any soldier who did that in *his* army, even in a combat zone, risked facing thirty days in the stockade. You had to have strict discipline and dress decorum. All this democratic crap was ruining the US Army, making the men soft, a bunch of frigging canteen commandos. 'So you think all this bigot guff is strictly bullshit, Koch?' he snapped, suddenly angered.

'Yes, sir!' his chief of intelligence answered. 'If you'll forgive my French, the Supreme Commander is seeing goddam Germans beneath the goddam bed!' His fat jowls trembled with righteous indignation. 'It's a whole load of baloney!'

Patton, his anger forgotten as speedily as it had come, chuckled at the look on Koch's face. His chief of intelligence always took it as a personal insult when his own appreciations weren't accepted. He was as touchy as a broad in the change of life. 'Don't worry, Koch,' he said soothingly. 'Whether there are 400,000 or 200,000 Italians on the island, my Seventh'll go through them like crap through a goose. We'll leave that little fart Montgomery on the coast with his ass in a sling. Yessir!'

Half an hour later the little cavalcade approached one of the trim white French colonial villages which covered the area around Bouzareah, where Patton had set up his headquarters for the invasion of Sicily. As usual the ragged Arabs who inhabited the tumble-down huts and lean-to's made out of beaten flat petrol tins greeted them in stony silence. They hated the Americans. They thought they had come to North Africa to bolster up French colonial rule. Only the barefoot kids showed any enthusiasm. Immediately they started to beg, holding out skinny, sore-covered brown hands, demanding 'cigarettes for Papa', or offered 'sister, nice and clean, white lips inside, sir, just like French lady, plenty jig-jig —'

The French civilians were different. They turned out in full force yet again, waving flags and cheering as if they were viewing the gleaming immaculate Patton column for the very first time. Immediately the main street was crowded with men, women and children, the old men busy adjusting their medals and throwing Patton shaky military salutes, the women blowing kisses or leaning provocatively out of upstairs windows, revealing their charms to full advantage to the wide-eyed, admiring staff officers below.

Patton loved it of course. Immediately he put on his 'hail-the-conqueror' face, another one of the looks which he practised in front of his mirror at night. Like visiting royalty he waved his gloved hand to left and right, bowing stiffly at regular intervals. More than once he nudged a sour-faced Koch, who disapproved of such things, and whispered out of the side of his mouth. 'Will ya get a load of the tits on that broad up there, Koch! Holy cow, just look at the size of them!'

Opposite the neat, white-painted *mairie,* which now sported not only the *tricouleur,* but also Old Glory these days, the cheering mob thickened. Patton's command car was forced to a walking pace, with the driver angrily hooting his horn at civilians attempting to step in front of it. Flowers came sailing through the air to land in the general's lap. Happily Patton quipped to Koch, 'Only hope they don't start throwing bottles of goddam wine. Here, take the flowers, Koch, or people'll start thinking I'm a goddam fruit!'

Sims, the driver, suddenly braked hard to avoid a small child waving an American flag and wearing a cut-down version of a combat suit. 'Probably stolen from one of our goddam supply depots,' Koch told himself angrily, as the red-faced driver shook his fist at the laughing child, who had now been grabbed by his mother, a statuesque female with a massive bosom of the kind Patton admired.

Pushing by the nearest outrider, she advanced on the general and placed a tremendous kiss on both his cheeks, crying as she did so, '*Bon voyage, mon gènèral, pour Sicile!*' Then she was being pushed back into the crowd, followed by proud smiling child, and the cavalcade was moving once more, Koch's mind racing as it did so. His French was pretty rusty, but he had made out the last word well enough. '*Sicile*' she had said, '*SICILY!*'

'Jesus H. Christ,' he breathed to himself, as the convoy started to pick up speed once more and headed back into the desert, 'if a French peasant like that knows where we're going, how long is it going to take the Germans to find out as well...'

CHAPTER 2

'*Kavala!*' Harsch announced, as they started to limp into the entrance to the little Eastern Greek port. 'Used mainly for shipping tobacco but it has German harbour facilities.'

'Yes,' Christian agreed, his nostrils twitching at the pungent odour of drying tobacco leaf coming from the land, relaxing at last. They had escaped from the Black Sea, had safely negotiated the Bosporus without any interference from the Turks. Now they were running into the first port after Turkey, which was safe in German hands. Even the guerrillas wouldn't bother them here; they were far away in the mountains. He held his pale face up to the warming rays of the morning sun. 'The men will be glad sir. They've had a hard time. They need a rest.'

'Possibly,' Harsch murmured, as though he wasn't quite convinced. 'At all events, we shall stay here until the crew is brought up to strength. I am not chancing the Med with the boat so seriously under strength, Number One.'

Christian frowned, as he suddenly remembered the men they had lost in their flight from Varna. His frown deepened as he thought of the task of writing to their next-of-kin while they were at Kavala. It was a duty Harsch would delegate to him, he knew. The skipper dreamed solely of glory. The price in men's lives for achieving that glory didn't interest him.

'Slow — both ahead!' Harsch snapped into the voice tube. The battered U-70 edged closer to the jetty, already thronged with curious *Kriegsmarine* sailors in summer whites and a handful of Greeks employed by the German Army of Occupation. 'Run up the Jolly Roger, Number One,' Harsch ordered a moment later, becoming aware of the spectators. 'Let's give them a show for their money.'

'Yes, sir,' Christian answered and nodded to the Moses.

Behind Harsch's back, Frenssen grimaced and pulled an invisible lavatory chain, while Moses ran up the black flag of the U-boat Arm, complete with skull and crossbones. Where once there had been just black, there were the white silhouettes of the ships they had sunk in the Varna operation, dominated by the large bulk of the *Stalin*. On the dock, the sailors started to cheer and Harsch puffed out his chest manfully.

Christian smiled. The skipper was going to savour this moment of glory. He had been waiting for this moment a long time — probably from the day he first joined the submarine service. Let him have his moment of triumph, for in the end, in spite of the poor young men who would never be returning to the Homeland, all had worked out well. Most of the U-70's crew had come back unharmed.

He observed a portly middle-aged officer clattering down the steps of the port office, hastily buckling on his ceremonial dirk. He would be the port commandant, Christian told himself, coming to congratulate the victorious U-boat ace. Harsch thought the same, for as the U-70 slowly came to rest amid the renewed cheering of the sailors, he snapped hastily, 'All the men up top, Number One. Form them up. At the double now. *Los!*'

Five minutes later, the informal ceremony commenced with the crew of the U-70 standing to attention, staring woodenly into the far distance, seeming not to notice the admiring gazes of the crowd, while the port commandant cleared his throat self-importantly and began his address to a delighted Harsch. 'Commander Harsch, and you brave crewmen, I salute you in the name of myself, the staff of Kavala Port, and' — His voice trembled with emotion suddenly and Christian could have sworn tears dimmed his eyes behind the gold-rimmed pince-nez for a moment — 'that of our beloved Führer — Adolf Hitler!' He threw up his right arm dramatically and cried, '*Sieg Heil*.'

There was a half-hearted response from the weary crew of the U-70 and the seagulls rose shrieking in alarm at the noise. Just behind the skipper, Frenssen farted disrespectfully, but, carried away by the emotions of his great moment, Harsch did not seem to hear. Instead he kept his gaze fixed on the pompous little base officer like a child waiting expectantly for a conjuror to produce the promised rabbit from his top hat.

The port commandant pulled a piece of paper from the double cuff of his sleeve and held it short-sightedly. 'This message was received by all port commandants along the Greek coast this morning,' he announced proudly, 'in expectation of you, my dear Captain, making landfall somewhere in Greece.'

Harsch inclined his head slightly, as if expressing his approval at such forethought.

'It comes from no lesser person than the Führer himself,' the port commandant intoned.

Harsch tensed.

'It reads,' he said, screwing up his eyes to see better, ' "In the name of the German Folk, it gives me the greatest of pleasure to award Lieutenant-Commander Harsch, in recognition of his great victory in the Black Sea against our implacable foes" ' — Christian shook his head. Hitler might be a great commander, but his prose was dreadful. Could he *never* get to the point? — ' "the godless Russian Bolsheviks, in that he sank the Soviet battleship *Stalin*" ' — the little Port Commandant gasped for breath and then cried out the last phrase — ' "*the Knight's Cross of the Iron Cross!*" ' He smiled winningly at Harsch and, clicking to attention, raised his flabby hand to his gold-braided cap in salute.

Harsch flushed with pleasure, eyes gleaming with fanatical triumph, as Christian heard himself saying, 'Congratulations, sir, you deserve it,' and the crew, roused from their weariness by the engineer officer, were crying half-heartedly, '*Hoch...* *Hoch... Hoch!*'

Thereafter, events speeded up. A guard of soldiers, still buttoning on their equipment, were rushed up to the dock on the double to guard the battered U-70. The crew were whipped away in a small fleet of *Volkswagens,* each one of them clutching a posy of flowers somewhat stupidly, for showers — the first in three weeks — and food, while Harsch was invited to be the special guest for breakfast of the port commandant himself. Now that the arrival of the U-70 in Kavala had been reported to Mürwik, the telegrams of congratulation were beginning to flood in from the Reich — from the 'Big Lion', Harsch's old comrades, former skippers of the U-70, even one from Göring himself — and the port commandant was eager to bask in this reflected glory. Overnight, it seemed, Kavala, this remote Greek backwater, had become the centre of the world, and the fat little officer wanted to enjoy it while it lasted.

Christian declined the port commandant's offer to be included. For a little while, at least, he wanted to be away from his fellow men, even Frenssen, good sort that he was. He was sick of the sight and smell of men. All he wanted to do now was to wallow in the luxury of a slow hot bath and then perhaps find a woman, a body rounded, soft, bulging even, gentle, different from the hard, lean angular curves of young men. Undoubtedly there would be the customary piss-up compulsory for all members of the crew this evening. There always was, especially after a fighting patrol had been as successful as this one. But for the rest of the day he did not want to see a single other man from the crew of the U-70.

Slowly, savouring the smells and sights of the seafront, clutching his briefcase, he wandered along the jetty. Everywhere streams of sailors and soldiers were pushing their way through the swarthy Greeks, who tried to sell them everything and anything from the piles and piles of luscious fruit and grapes heaped up in the backs of their donkey carts to the women lounging in the shade, made-up faces pouting in fake concupiscence. Twice he was approached by touts, but he turned them away gently, unlike the soldiers. They found it great sport to aim kicks with their heavy, cruelly nailed boots at the skinny behinds of these pimps, crying, 'Get off, you greasy whore-master! Piss in the wind, man, with yer rotten putrid women!'

Five minutes later he had found a hotel, in reality a couple of sleazy rooms above a *taverna*, where the grizzled old men sat over their coffee and glasses of water, playing cards noisily, or simply sat staring into space, fingering their worry beads. After the tightness of the submarine, the big bare room, dominated by a sagging brass bedstead underneath the usual ikon, seemed enormous. He opened the window to let in the air from the sea and slumped on the bed, savouring the space, feeling the stiffness vanished from his tense limbs. Unwashed, unshaven, probably a little lousy, too, to judge from the sudden stirrings underneath his shirt, he was suddenly happy…

Frenssen was happy too. Just like *Leutnant* Jungblut, he wanted to escape from his fellow men. Face red and gleaming after a shower and the first shave for three weeks, he bellowed happily at the young men wreathed in steam, giggling and flicking towels at each other's wet naked rumps like silly schoolboys, 'It's no use, you bunch o' piss-pansies! No use flashing yer arses at me. I've gone right off yer, *even you Moses*! He tugged on his boots with a grunt and straightened up to fasten the Knight's Cross around his brawny throat. He was one of the handful of petty officers in the whole of the U-boat Arm who possessed that high decoration. 'It's women I want now, not the other… Hot steaming juicy women !' He laughed uproariously and planted his little blue side hat squarely on the top of his cropped head. 'Shipmates,' he said with a little bow, 'I bid you adieu. For love beckons *Obermaat* Frenssen.'

'Yer,' one of the old hares growled surlily, 'and a nice dose o' clap as well, I'll be bound.'

'Proper charmer, Lutz, aren't yer just,' Frenssen answered easily, and without rancour. 'Not for me though. With me it's strictly — *love!*' With that he was gone, sauntering out jauntily into the bright sunshine to savour the life of the port, ogling the peasant girls with bright scarves around their heads leading ox-carts to the wine cellars, giving the pimps threatening looks, which made them stop their importuning immediately. 'It's gonna be roses, frigging roses all the way,' he told himself happily. 'A handsome man like Frau Frenssen's well set-up son — why I'll be beating them off wholesale!'

He plumped himself down outside one of the *tavernas* that lined the waterfront and an old woman hobbled out to serve him. 'Beer' — he mimed someone quaffing a glass of suds — 'and keep it coming till I say stop. Oh, yes, I want some grub as well. Fried eggs. You know?' He imitated the crowing of a chicken and flapped his big arms up and down several times. 'Got it.' He placed a wad of greasy occupation money on the dirty little table, then, as an afterthought, followed it with a gold twenty mark piece he had stolen somewhere or other. The old crone's rheumy eyes lit up at the sight of the coin. She grabbed it with a claw of a hand and bit it. Apparently satisfied it was genuine, she shuffled off, cackling to herself, leaving Frenssen to survey the field. 'Tits,' he whispered to himself, oblivious to the stares of the old Greek men sipping their muddy coffee and the occasional glances of burning, black-eyed hatred from the younger men passing, 'acres of tits, that's what Frau Frenssen's handsome son wants. Luscious female knockers, juicy great melons a sailor man can get his mitts on.' Almost unaware he was doing so, he accepted the first glass of *Fick's* beer from the old crone and downed it in one gulp. He wiped the froth from his suddenly scarlet lips and thrust the glass back at her with the command. 'More — at the double now!'

But if Christian and Frenssen preferred to spend their precious free hours away from the war, the newly decorated *Kapitänleutnant* Harsch was happier immersed in the middle of it once more, as he sat in the port commandant's office, drinking the ice-cold *ouzo* from the latter's 'special bottle' and smoking one of his excellent cigars.

'You see, my dear Commander,' the fat little base official related, his eyebrows gleaming with sweat, face red with alcohol, 'it is clear the Western Allies are massing in North Africa, now their superiority in men and material has forced Field Marshal Rommel to evacuate his men from there. Their target too is obvious. It is going to be somewhere along the Med coastline. Greece, Italy, Sardinia.' He shrugged expressively and Harsch told himself that the fat-bellied rear echelon stallion had been among the decadent Greeks too long, he was beginning to act like them. 'Since the day before yesterday the whole theatre has been placed on red alert. We are very much on our toes now for the first sign of the enemy attack.' He smiled proudly. 'But the High Command need not worry about the position in Kavala. We are ready to meet them if and when they come. To the last bullet and the last man! There will be no Stalingrad at Kavala, I can assure you of that.'

'Of course, of course,' Harsch agreed hastily, a faint idea beginning to stir slowly in his mind. 'Presumably when the Western Allies come, it will be a seaborne invasion?' he asked.

'I think so, according to the little information I possess. We are somewhat neglected with information from the top here, I don't know why. Well, as I was saying, according to my information, the Western Allies possess only two airborne divisions in the theatre. The bulk of the assault force will have to come by sea.' He paused and looked at Harsch's tough face. 'But why do you ask, *mein Lieber*?'

For a few moments, Harsch did not appear to hear the question. Instead he rolled the glass of white spirits between his big hands, his face thoughtful. From outside there came the drunken singing of the 'U-boat Man's Song'. The port commandant frowned. All these submariners had in their mind was women and drink when they came off patrol; he hoped there would be no trouble. He had a nice little sinecure here in this remote port, far from the shooting war. He had a thriving business going in rare ikons which were stolen for him from the local monasteries and shipped back for sale in the Reich. And Elena, his mistress, was very exciting. God knows how he would settle down to his wife Gerda again once he was posted back home.

'There will be plenty of splendid prizes, of course,' Harsch said suddenly, startling the other man a little.

'Prizes, *Herr Kapitänleutnant*? I don't quite follow you.'

'When this new invasion starts, there will be heaps of targets, prime targets,' Harsch explained slowly, almost as if he were trying to convince himself.

'Oh, I see what you mean,' the port commandant said. 'Yes, I suppose there will. They'll have to use a great deal of shipping in order to transport an assault force of that —' He broke off abruptly and then said in surprise. 'But you are not thinking of another patrol, my dear fellow, are you?' he asked hastily. 'I mean, it is highly commendable and worthy, but your boat — the state it is in. Besides, you are seriously under strength. What could you —' He stopped short, for he could see that the other man was not listening to him but to his own tunes of glory.

Harsch had won Germany's highest honour and could return honourably to the Reich to be fêted as a hero, without having to incur any further danger. He had, he knew, done more than was expected of him. But as he had survived trap after trap, even managing to escape the Russian Black Sea Fleet's attempt to block off the entrance to the Bosporus, he had come to believe he bore a charmed life and that he and his boat were indestructible. Why, he had told himself more than once in the last few hours, with a bit of luck he could become the U-boat Arm's greatest ace ever. A few more kills and he could even outshine Prien, who had sunk the *Royal Oak* back in 1939. What was the antiquated British battleship in comparison with the brand-new *Stalin*? Besides Prien was dead these two years. The time had come for a new super U-boat ace — *Otto Harsch*!'

His voice filled with renewed energy as he snapped, 'I would appreciate it, Captain, if you could expedite the dispatch of reinforcements from the Reich for the U-70. Or perhaps you might possibly have trained hands from the U-boat Arm here in Kavala?'

The port commandant shook his head. 'Apart from a handful of E-boat men who managed to escape overland from the Black Sea debâcle, Commander, most of my people are over-age dock workers, stevedores, welders and the like. They would be perfectly useless for your purpose. But, Commander,' he tried once again, 'can't you leave the business of tackling the Allied invasion fleet to the *Luftwaffe*, or the Italian Fleet?'

'The Italian Fleet!' Harsch sneered scornfully. 'Those spaghetti-eaters would fill their pants at the first sight of a Tommy craft! Look how they turned and ran at Matapan. No, Port Commandant, my mind is made up. As soon as we are re-supplied and I have my reinforcements, we sail to do battle, immediately the *Abwehr* lets us know that the Allied invasion fleet has sailed.' His eyes glittered. 'My God, the mere thought of those big fat troopers gives me goose pimples. *Himmelherrje*,' he cursed and brought his fist down hard on the table in front of him, making the other man jump, 'what — what a damned great slaughter it will be!'

CHAPTER 3

'*And now I'm frigging well gonna sing!*' the drunken, half-naked grey mouse declared, swaying alarmingly as she attempted to position herself next to the battered mess piano. '*J'attendrai* — that's Frog. And I'm gonna sing it in French whether you bloody Lords like it or not. So there!' With her last vestige of dignity she carefully slipped back her left breast into her bra, from which it had popped with the vehemence of her declaration.

'Show us yer tits!' someone suggested drunkenly and the navy pianist put out his cigarette in the glass of beer on the piano in front of him, put his hand up the grey mouse's skirt, and exclaimed in delight, 'Hairy, isn't it?'

The grey mouse looked down at him disdainfully, 'What d' yer frigging think — *feathers?* Now I'll sing...'

She started to sing drunkenly, but in the babble of loud voices, bouts of coarse drunken laughter, female shrieks and giggles, and the steady clink of glasses being slammed together in toast, no one could hear a word.

The traditional 'boat's piss-up', which always followed a fighting patrol was now in full swing, with the officers, petty officers, and ratings, all distinctions of rank abandoned for this one night, letting off steam at last. Two hours before Frenssen, as senior petty officer, already well-oiled and wearing a pair of frilly, red-laced knickers on his cropped head for obscure reasons known only to himself, had started the proceedings with a bellowed, '*It's liberty hall, lads!* Yer mother's drunk — and yer frigging father as well! So it's get in Uncle Otto and enjoy

yersens. There's plenty of sauce and suds. There's fart-soup' —
he meant pea-soup — 'and turds aplenty — *and there's girls*!'

The first of the grey mice had come bursting in, had
accepted a glass of Greek firewater from a beaming Frenssen,
gasped with shock and had spat it straight into the nearest vase
of flowers, which had immediately begun to wilt in protest. A
great roar of delight had gone up from the happy ratings and
the drinking and whoring had commenced.

They had gone through the lifeboat drill, a drunken crowd of
red-faced sailors, laughing and giggling, sitting in the spilled
beer and *ouzo*. They had practised parachute drill, jumping out
of the first floor window, using the grey mice's blouses as
parachutes, sailing in a shower of broken glass through the
cold frames in the garden below. They had bellowed all the old
songs about the 'nut-brown maidens' who would be 'mine,
mine!', how the 'icy wind blew over the Westerwald, hi-de hi-
do' and naturally they had marched 'against England' several
times, '*denn wir fahren gegen Enge-land, ahoy!*', to which Frenssen
had commented sardonically, 'That'll be the day!'

Now there were 'beer corpses' sprawled in the spilled beer,
slumped in corners, snoring heavily, heads down on the trestle
tables awash with *ouzo*, lying full length among the 'dead
soldiers' — the empty bottles they tossed carelessly to one
side. A hydroplane operator had undone his flies and was
staggering around with one of those dry fish which the Greeks
eat sticking out, crying thickly, 'Bet yer ain't never seen one
with fins on before!' A fat grey mouse was cradling a blond
young rating, who must have been half her age, thrusting an
enormous breast into his open mouth, sighing drunkenly,
'Come on now, don't be naughty, baby, have a suck at
mummy's titty!'

A bemused, happy Christian sat in the far corner watching the drunken orgy progress, the crazy antics of the crew, happy they were having this time out of war, however cruel and brutal their concept of pleasure was. He began to realize that someone was missing — *Kapitänleutnant* Harsch. This sort of thing, he knew, was not the kind of entertainment that particularly appealed to the skipper. Yet he must know it was the time-honoured tradition of the U-boat Arm that even the skipper appeared and let his hair down on these occasions. So why wasn't he here?

Frenssen, swaying dangerously, eyes red with drink, seemed to read Christian's mind. He pushed a young rating out of the way, crying, 'Begone, you asparagus Tarzan, there's plenty of women over there for perverted muff-merchants like you,' and staggered up to Christian. He threw him a tremendous drunken salute, whacking himself against the temple, and said thickly, 'Beg to report the skipper, Herr *shitting Kapitänleutant shitting* Harsch ain't made his *shitting* appearance yet.' He sat down abruptly next to Christian and belched.

'Frenssen, for God's sake, will you watch your tongue? If the skipper ever heard you talking like that, it'd be prison bars for you.' He held his fingers in front of his face to indicate what he meant.

'I don't give a wet wank for the skipper,' Frenssen said defiantly. 'Besides, you can say what you like at a boat's piss-up. It's allus been like that.' He looked at Christian in cross-eyed drunken confusion. 'And what about the Moses, eh? What about him, *Herr Leutnant?*'

In spite of the drink and the warm satisfied glow he still felt from the nubile, dark-eyed Greek girl he had enjoyed in the squeaky brass bed during the afternoon, Christian felt sudden apprehension, a feeling he was being forced into a situation which was distasteful to him, one in which he would have to make unpleasant decisions. 'What — what's that supposed to mean, Frenssen?' he asked carefully…

In the corner a young rating was being sick into an ashtray, his skinny shoulders heaving with the effort.

'Well, sir, you know?' Frenssen said, abruptly coy, even in all his drunkenness.

'Well, I know *what*?' Christian persisted, his veins feeling suddenly as if they were filled with ice-water. Abruptly he felt totally, completely sober, the noise, the drunks, the laughing, giggling half-naked grey mice forgotten. 'Go on, Frenssen, you've always had a damned big trap. Open it,' he persisted coldly, 'spit it out, man!'

'But it's difficult, sir. You see, I think that the skipper and the Moses —'

'*Kameraden des U-70s.*' The familiar harsh incisive voice cut through the noise. '*Darf ich um Ruhe bitten, Kameraden?*'

Christian looked up sharply as the noise died away, the music trailing away leaving the drunken grey mouse burbling on by herself. The drunken red faces turned slowly in the direction of the suddenly opened door.

Harsch stood there, legs planted firmly apart, hands on his hips, a look of triumph on his face. Behind him was the Moses, shoulders bent as if in pain, face ashen, gaze fixed on the floor. He did not seem to want to look at his happy drunken comrades, as though he felt out of things in this joyful confused throng of men and half-naked women.

Christian rose slowly to his feet and touched his hand to his forehead carefully, eyeing the two of them — the masterful officer and the downtrodden, seemingly hurt young rating — his brain racing. Something had happened — something terrible. He knew that instinctively. But what was it?

Harsch didn't give him an opportunity to consider the matter. Instead he said, '*Leutnant* Jungblut, would you please ask the, er, *ladies*' — there was no mistaking the note of contempt in his voice now — 'to leave the room. I want to talk to the crew privately. Thank you.' He turned his back as if it hurt him to see the drunken, half-naked women a moment longer.

'*Pfui*!' someone called in dismay. Another gave the skipper a raspberry. One called to the half-naked grey mice as they straggled out, clutching their uniforms to their impressive bosoms. 'Don't forget to keep yer legs crossed till we get back. I don't want to be working on wet decks, ha, ha, —' the chuckle ended in a grunt as a disgusted Frenssen reached out a big paw and pushed the speaker backwards over the trestle table. 'Piss in the wind, big mouth!' he snarled in disgust and, picking up a bottle of *Korn* poured a huge slug straight down his throat. He smelt trouble and the only way out he could see was to get blind to the world.

Five minutes later the 'beer corpses' had been slapped and tugged into some sort of attention and Harsch was standing on one of the tables among the litter of 'dead soldiers' staring down at the crew of the U-70, face burning with impatience.

A little wearily, reluctant to hear whatever the skipper had to say, Christian saluted and repeated the traditional regulation formula. 'Two officers, thirteen petty officers and thirty crew members of U-70 all present and correct, *sir*!'

Harsch returned Christian's salute with an impressive flourish and launched into his news immediately, his eyes gleaming fervently. 'Comrades, great news — *tremendous news*! Intelligence has reported that within the next few days the decadent Western Allies will make a vain effort to launch an attack on *Fortress Europe*, and that attack will come in — *by sea*!'

If Harsch had expected that his information would arouse any enthusiasm among the men he was sorely disappointed. There was no reaction whatsoever. The men looked blank and vague, save for a rating who had a woman's stocking soaked in vinegar wrapped around his forehead in an attempt to sooth a splitting headache. He groaned weakly and said, 'Can't nobody put me out of me frigging misery. Holy strawsack, I think the back of my frigging head is gonna fall off any minute!'

But Harsch was too tense, too excited, too full of new plans for further glory, to take any note of the mood of his crew. His whole being throbbed with electric energy. He had never felt like this. At last he had achieved both fulfilment and a realization of his true role in life. The way ahead was wide open and nothing was going to stop him achieving his destiny. 'The details are still vague, but I have been in contact with Berlin. Yes,' he emphasized, as if he believed that they might

doubt his ability to contact the capital of the Reich from this arsehole of the world, '*Berlin*! From there they informed me that, although they are not one hundred per cent certain all the indications are — from agents in Africa and other sources — that the island of Sicily just off the toe of Italy is to be the objective of the Western Allies.'

Christian frowned, a vague, nagging suspicion beginning to raise itself at the back of his mind. Harsch was up to something, something which boded no good for the surviving hands of the U-70, and somehow he, for he was the only other crew member who possessed any authority, had to put a stop to it.

'It will be only a matter of hours — say twenty-four at the most — before the *Abwehr* will be able to confirm it is really Sicily. If it is, any U-boat in position in the Med by the time the Allied convoys sail from the North African port will be presented with rich prizes, tremendous prizes. There will be troop transports, cruisers, aircraft carriers, even battleships. There'll be ships carrying generals, corps commanders, perhaps even army commanders!' He gasped for breath, eyes glistening like those of a demented man. 'In the whole history of sea warfare there has never been a target like this. With a bit of luck, a lone U-boat let loose among a great armada like that cannot help but succeed. There'll be kills by the dozen!' He stopped short, face red with emotion, chest heaving wildly, as if he had just run a great race.

His remarks were met by a stony silence. Even the man with the splitting headache had stopped moaning and was staring at the skipper in astonished silence, as if he could not believe the evidence of his own ears.

For what seemed a long time, no one moved, no one spoke. There was a heavy brooding silence, broken only by the skipper's own harsh hectic gasping for breath. His listeners remained rooted, beer mugs forgotten, petrified into a tableau of shocked, total silence.

In the end it was Christian who broke the spell. 'Do I understand,' he said slowly, taking care with his choice of words, trying to quell the burning anger which threatened to overcome him, 'that you think we should take part in some operation against this invasion fleet off Sicily?' Just in time, he remembered to add a 'sir' to his question.

'*Take part*, Number One!' Harsch yelled exuberantly, completely overlooking the mood of his crew. 'My God, man, it's a U-boat skipper's dream, the opportunity of a lifetime. Don't you see, the Tommies and their friends the Jewish-American plutocrats will have already sealed off the entrance to the Med at Gibraltar. That means none of our boats stationed at Brest will be able to get into the attack. You can forget the damned yellow Macaronis at Bari and La Spezia. They're probably already preparing to betray us the moment the Anglo-Americans land in Sicily.' Harsch leaned forward, eyes blazing crazy fire, willing the tall young handsome officer to be infected by his own tremendous enthusiasm for this daring new project. 'Don't you see, Number One, we will have the field to ourselves? No competition from other subs. No pack leader telling us what to do, grabbing the best prizes for himself. Not even the Big Lion in Mürwik breathing down our necks. We will be totally alone, in complete charge of the operation, and the glory we will achieve will be solely ours. *Heaven, arse and cloudburst!*' he cried fervently, staring up the ceiling, as if challenging the very gods themselves to stop him, 'we will make newspaper headlines all over the world. *God, we'll go down in history!*' He paused dramatically, fists clenched, body trembling with emotion.

But the tired young crew of the U-70 were not interested in going down in history. The angry murmuring started almost immediately. A young rating sprang to his feet, knocked over a beer glass and stood quivering with suppressed rage. Frenssen snorted, 'Fuck history, history's for corpses!' In the corner a group of old hares began stamping their heavy boots in defiant unison. The crew's sudden hatred was palpable. Christian could almost smell it.

Hastily he held up his hands for silence. The look of triumph started to vanish from Harsch's red face to be replaced first by one of bewilderment and then by slowly dawning rage. '*Herr Kapitänleutnant,*' Christian said slowly and very formally, 'I should like to draw your attention to a few things — *please,*' he added, when it appeared Harsch might interrupt him.

Harsch grunted something, but didn't object.

'*One*, the U-70 has achieved outstanding successes in the Black Sea for which you have been decorated. *Two*, we are seriously undermanned. *Three*, you'll admit it yourself, the U-70 is in poor shape. *Four*,' he hesitated momentarily, trying desperately to keep calm and not give way to the burning anger within himself, 'don't you think, sir, the crew has done enough?'

There was an immediate response from the men. As one, their boots began to stamp on the floor in agreement and someone cried angrily, '*Richtig, Herr Leutnant*, exactly right, sir!'

Without taking his eyes off Harsch, Christian snapped, 'Enough of that, lads. Let's keep it quiet, please. Well, sir, what do you say, *please*?'

'Back in nineteen-eighteen, *Leutnant zur See* Jungblut,' Harsch said in an equally formal tone, 'I was in Kiel when the mutiny of the High Sea Fleet took place. In the U-boat Arm, we were made of stronger stuff — our men did not mutiny. But as I was saying, I was there when the cowards, the reds, the weaklings rose in mutiny, not only against their Kaiser, but also their very own officers under whom they had served many years. The men went on a rampage through the streets. Senior officers, men who had grown grey in the service of their country, were abused, spat upon, had their decorations and epaulettes torn from their shoulders. I too suffered, though I prefer not to go into the details here. Suffice to say, I suffered.' He paused and looked sternly around the men, most of whom now appeared bewildered, as they wondered to what purpose they were being given this lecture on the most traumatic experience of the German Navy since its foundation — the Great Kiel Mutiny.

'But how did it start? I ask you that. Later it was said it was the work of agitators, professional revolutionaries.' He shrugged. 'Perhaps they did play some small part in the mutiny. I think, however, differently.' He leaned forward to make his point. 'In my opinion, it originated in the men losing faith in their cause, thinking that they were already defeated before they were, not being prepared to fight on when things looked black, to fight on — *and win*!' He reached out his hand and clenched his fist till the knuckles showed white. 'We *must* believe in Germany's sacred cause! We *must* believe that we as individuals do not count! We *must* believe in personal sacrifice if it is for the good of the community as a whole! We *must* fight on to the end, come what may! For we are volunteers all, the cream of the *Kriegsmarine*, who knew from the first day we joined the U-boat Arm that by the law of averages we are fated to die sooner or later.' There were tears in Harsch's eyes now and Christian felt for him, glory-hunter that he was.

But the crew did not respond to his impassioned appeal to their loyalty and dedication to the cause. Their faces remained obstinately set, this was 1943. On the land the *Wehrmacht* had lost the battles of El Alamein and Stalingrad. On the sea, they had been chased out of the Black Sea and even the greenest of them knew that the situation in the North Atlantic bordered on the catastrophic; a fresh U-boat was sunk virtually every second day. Volunteers they were, but at the same time they were intent on survival too. Above all, Harsch had promised they would be returned to the Reich after the victory over the *Stalin*. Now he was proposing new missions when all they wanted to do was to go home to mother. They had had enough.

Harsch frowned, face set, all passion spent. 'So be it,' he said in the end, with a gesture of dismissal. 'I have made my decision. You can get on with your drunken carousing as far as I am concerned. Enjoy it while you may.' He dropped listlessly from the table and looked to the door where the Moses had stood, but the youngest member had vanished. He shrugged, as if it did not matter much anymore, and went out, ignoring Christian's salute.

Thirty minutes later the engine room of the U-70 started to burn...

CHAPTER 4

Rear-Admiral Henry K. Hewitt was his usual deliberate, somewhat ponderous self, as he stuck out his hand and said, 'Well, George, here we go again, eh?'

Patton took the hand of the big bluff sailor with whom he had crossed swords more than once in this last year or so, and snapped, 'Well, I hope the Sam Hill the Navy doesn't make a goddam mess of this one like it did back in November with *Torch*. Thanks to the goddam US Navy I lost all my personal kit. Nearly lost my pistols, too.' He slapped his thighs. 'Didn't even have a toothbrush to clean my foul mouth with.' He gave the admiral a dingy-toothed grin and added, 'Glad to see you, Henry.'

Together the two senior commanders walked along the dock, which was ablaze with lights in spite of the fact that it was after blackout time. Sweating US Army stevedores were moving back and forth, carrying the supplies the invasion was going to need. Obediently, long lines of infantry, laden down with equipment like pack animals, each man's helmet marked with the chalked number of his embarkation serial, shuffled forward towards the gangways, where they were checked off by officious NCOs and officers armed with clipboards. Cranes and gantries rattled, puffed and huffed, emitting clouds of black smoke as tanks, trucks, heavy cannon were swung aboard the waiting transports. Heavily armed, white-helmeted military policemen, hard-eyed and laconic, patrolled up and down in pairs, watching and checking. All was controlled, hectic confusion.

'This one is going to make history, Henry,' Patton announced, automatically snapping off salutes to right and

left as he was recognized by the staff officers supervising the embarkation. 'No amphibious operation — not even the Marines in the Pacific — has been tried on so broad a front. Eight reinforced infantry divisions landing abreast. It's going to be a lulu! In my Second Corps alone — just to show you the complexity of the operation — there are one hundred and fifty one separate units involved, ranging from an infantry regiment right down to the shit-shovelling detail!' He grinned again and Hewitt shook his head. Old Blood and Guts was living up to his reputation for foul language. They would never have tolerated his kind of talk in the US Navy.

'In essence, we are eighty thousand red-blooded US fighting men, landing on three beaches covering a front of sixty-nine miles,' Patton continued, striding on rapidly, as if he had an urgent appointment, with Hewitt trying to keep up, 'carried there by three of your naval forces —' 'Yes,' a panting Hewitt managed to interrupt, 'code-named Joss, Dime and Cent.'

'I'm surely not going in in the "Cent",' Patton announced firmly as Hewitt took him by the arm and steered him to one of the transports, its decks clearly outlined by footlights, as if the German *Luftwaffe* didn't exist.

'No, George, it's the "Dime" for you, naturally. The top of the tree, and here's your transport, the SS *Monrovia*.' He extended his plump hand like a head waiter pointing out a table to a favoured client. 'She's a new ship, built early last year for the Delta Line, but we took her over and converted her into an assault transport.'

For a few moments Patton said nothing. He screwed up his eyes and surveyed the ship, evidently liking what he saw, for he said finally, 'Well, I don't expect I'll be on the sonovabitch long enough to find that the heads don't work and the mess stewards are all fruits,' he growled. 'Yeah, she looks okay to me. Are you sailing on her, Henry?'

'Yep. I'm taking personal charge of you, George. You're going to be my own personal guest on this one.'

Patton grabbed him by the arm and steered him firmly towards the gangway. 'If that's the case, Henry. Let's get aboard and have a shot.'

'But you know that the US Navy is dry, George!' Hewitt protested.

'Not when General George S. Patton Junior is aboard, it isn't,' Patton cried exuberantly, favouring the admiral with one of his dingy-toothed smiles. 'Now, where's the hooch?'

Twenty minutes later he sat bolt upright in the special leather armchair Hewitt had provided for him in his cabin, sipping his whisky reflectively. The fire had gone from his face. Nine months before he had commanded a totally green force, which had sailed all the way from the States to invade Morocco. But the opposition had been merely the French, whose heart had not been in the fight. They had surrendered easily.

Now his force was not so green. It contained the 1st and 3rd Divisions, which had seen action in North Africa. But the opposition was different to that in French Morocco. The Italians naturally didn't worry him, but the Germans did. As Monk had said, the Germans on the island of Sicily were strictly hot mustard and he worried how his men of the green 45th Infantry Division, which was going in in the first assault wave, would stand up to them.

The week before he had inspected the 45th Division in its assembly area for the assault. The men had looked fit and reasonably tough, but they were so obviously green and he had tried to give them more confidence in themselves with one of his pep talks, telling them in his squeaky, high-pitched voice; 'Battle is the most magnificent competition in which a human being can indulge. It brings out all that is best. It removes all that is base. All men are afraid in battle. The coward is the one who lets his fear overcome his sense of duty. Duty is the essence of manhood. Americans pride themselves on being he-men — and they *are* he-men.'

Now as he sat, sipping his drink, listening to the noises of the ship and the shuffle of men's feet outside on the deck as the GIs crowded onto the *Monrovia*, he wondered. How would those green American boys really make out in combat in four days' time? You could train and train them, and then train them some more, he reflected, but training was never like the real thing. He frowned and stared at the bare wall of the cabin.

The knock on the door startled him. Instantly he forgot his gloomy forebodings and put on his 'War Face Number Two', a staid but confident look, calculated to inspire trust in his subordinates. 'Well, for God's sake, come in!' He barked.

It was Codman, his personal aide. His handsome, well-bred Bostonian face looked worried. Patton saw that immediately. 'All right, Charles,' he snapped, 'park your butt and tell me where the goddam fire is.'

In spite of his bad news. Colonel Codman grinned. It was typical Patton. He could never say anything in the normal man's way. His words always had to be bold, dramatic, profane. 'Thank you, sir,' he said and 'parked his butt'.

'All right?'

'Well, it's from Admiral Hewitt. He has just received a signal from the met people in Malta.'

'Yeah. What do the met people say?'

'Bad things, General,' Codman replied, wondering how Patton would take his news. He had a hair-trigger temper. It didn't take much for him to fly off the handle. 'You see, sir, they signal that a storm is impending. There is a, er, Boreas on the way from Greece. It —'

'What in Sam Hill's name is a frigging Boreas?' Patton interrupted the colonel, pointing his big expensive cigar at the other man like an offensive weapon.

'The Admiral informs me, sir, that it is a north wind which originates in the Alps,' Codman explained hastily. 'When it hits the Mediterranean, it usually whips up a full-scale gale —'

He broke off abruptly when he saw the look on his boss's face. Outside the porthole someone was saying, 'Will ya just take a look at it, Joe. It's the usual goddam frigging snafu — situation normal, *all fucked up!*'

His companion laughed hollowly and Patton nodded his grizzled head in agreement with the unknown GI's comment. 'Have you spoken with Commander Steere, the ship's meteorologist, Charles?'

'Yessir. That's the first thing I did after Admiral Hewitt told me the bad news.'

'And?' Patton snorted hastily. 'What did Houdini say?'

'Well, sir. Houdini, as you call him, sir, working on his own figures, calculates that the Boreas will last for three days. It will be pretty violent while it lasts. But he thinks it will moderate on the day of the invasion and he feels that the weather will be fine by H-Hour, General.'

Patton sniffed. '*Thinks! Feels!*' Patton mused. 'Nothing very definite, except that the invasion fleet's gonna have one hell of a storm.' He took a puff at his cigar and did a quick calculation of his own. 'Today is July 6th. We sail for two days and start concentrating on July 8th. Then we all set course south of Malta for Sicily. By the evening of the 9th, we should be out of the protection of the air umbrella over Malta and heading for the assault beaches to land at zero two forty-five — H-Hour. That means if Houdini isn't right we'll be on the Italian radar screens trying to land eighty thousand guys in the middle of a great storm. Am I correct in my thinking there, Charles?'

Codman nodded but said nothing, but he felt for his boss. He was already under tremendous strain as it was. He was nearly sixty and the oldest combat general in the United States Army. He should have been long retired but he was going to decide not only the fate of the Allies' first attack on *Festung Europa*, but also the individual fates of eighty thousand young American soldiers. Now he had this new problem thrust upon him. Once the assault force was beyond the cover of the air umbrella over and around Malta it would be up to Patton to decide whether the attack should go in or not. It was a terrible problem.

For what seemed a long time, Patton did not speak. He sat, puffing at his big cigar contemplatively, staring into space.

From outside came the rattle of lines and hawsers. The ship's engines started to throb and the bulkhead creaked. Codman told himself that it wouldn't be long now. He felt the old thrill, the same one he had experienced in the first war when he had gone overseas as a shave-tail lieutenant in the Air Corps, with the band playing 'Over There' and the crowds cheering on the pier. Soon they'd be going into action again and although he was a middle-aged colonel now, who could have been the father of that callow boy who had gone to France in 1917, he felt a mounting excitement.

Suddenly Patton stirred. 'All right, Charles,' he said with an air of finality. 'I'm going to dismiss the matter right from my mind. It's in the hands of the gods for the time being. I shall start worrying about your goddam — what's the goddam thing called?'

'*Boreas*, General.'

''Kay. Well, I shall start worrying about the Boreas on the evening of the third day.' He forced a wintry smile. 'Now Charles, off you go to the mess and have yourself a stiff drink. We all probably need one in view of what's to come.' He winked suddenly. 'And they tell me there are some mighty pretty female nurses aboard.'

Colonel Codman blushed a little.

Patton chuckled, 'Yeah, I know, Charles, you're married — to a pretty little woman as well. But forget the marriage ring, Charles. We're going to war. Getting away from the wife and having fun with other women — that's half the fun. Do you know, I swear sometimes that's why guys go to war. Now enjoy yourself, Charles.'

Codman mumbled something and went out hurriedly. But after he had gone, Patton's smile vanished and he became deadly serious once more, a worried frown furrowing his high brow. Suddenly he stabbed out his cigar in the ashtray, finished his drink with one gulp and went down on one knee, holding the chair for support.

Reverently he bent his greying head. Outside there was the metallic clatter and rumble of the anchor cable being raised.

But Patton didn't hear, His mind was with his God, for in spite of his immorality and profanity, the general was a religious man. 'Oh, Lord God of the Hosts,' he prayed. 'I know I am destined to achieve some great thing. What, I don't yet know. Thy divine hand will guide me, I know, and Thy will be done. But, Almighty and most merciful Father, I humbly beseech Thee, of Thy great goodness, to restrain this immoderate storm which threatens to engulf us. Graciously hearken to me, Thine soldier who calls upon Thee, that, armed with Thy power, we may advance to victory and crush the oppression and wickedness of our enemies and establish Thy justice among men and nations. Amen.'

The ship shuddered violently and started to move. With a little grunt Patton rose from his knee and sat back in his chair, feeling quite pleased with himself. If God was on the side of the right and the good — Patton's side — the goddam Boreas was taken care of. He poured himself another large whisky.

Outside the ship's siren shrilled. Soldiers cried excitedly. There came the sound of cheering. That would be the dock crews sending them off. 'And the frigging condemned man ate a hearty breakfast,' the same disgruntled voice as before said in front of his porthole. '*Them* mothers ain't going like we is!'

Patton grinned. As long as his soldiers grumbled, there was nothing wrong with his new Seventh Army. He took a deep drink of his whisky.

Slowly the SS *Monrovia* moved out into the sound. They were on their way. The die was cast. He was returning to Europe to fight once more, after an absence of a quarter of a century, and he was returning as the commander of America's first fully fledged army in Europe in World War Two. After a lifetime of waiting, his hour of destiny had arrived at last...

CHAPTER 5

'Ordinary Seaman Hinze,' the port commander barked, peering over the edge of his pince-nez, 'how do you plead?'

The Moses, standing to attention at the back of the storeroom serving as a courtroom did not react. It was as if he had been used so long to the traditional name of 'Moses' that he had forgotten his real name. Frenssen, armed with a pistol and wearing a helmet that seemed too small for his massive cropped head, dug the boy in the side and whispered, 'Answer him, lad.'

The Moses, looking pale but tearfully defiant, for he had been crying most of the time since Harsch had had him arrested for 'wilful sabotage and weakening of military potential', said, 'I don't know... I just wanted to go home... sir... We all did.'

There was a murmur of agreement from the men of the U-70, packed in the back of the hot stuffy room, sitting on packing cases or on the floor, while the boat's officers and those from the port authority, all wearing dress uniform, were seated on chairs borrowed from the nearest *taverna*. Someone said thickly from the back of the men, 'Why pick on the poor little shit? He's only seventeen — just.'

Angrily the port commandant, seated at the blanket-covered trestle table, decorated solely by an unsheathed dirk, snapped, 'I will have no further talk, Master-at-Arms. See to it, please.'

The master-at-arms, helmeted and armed just like Frenssen, and just as big, turned his rat-like gaze on the men of the U-70. 'You heard,' he said in a voice thickened with drink and cheap cigars, 'you heard what the Port Commandant said. Any more noise and there'll be trouble!'

Frenssen could see that the other chief petty officer, who, to judge from his beer belly and bloodshot eyes, had come through the war pretty easily so far, looked a bad bastard. Perhaps that was how the poor weak fool of a Moses had got the black eye he was now sporting, and the swollen cheek. They had worked him over in the cells after he had been arrested.

'The fact that you wanted to go home has nothing to do with the matter at hand,' the port commandant lectured the prisoner severely. 'This is a court-martial and you just enter a proper plea.' He looked at Christian. '*Leutnant* Jungblut, you are the prisoner's friend. What plea does he enter?'

Christian hesitated. Everyone knew that the Moses had started the fire in the U-70's engine room the previous evening. In a flood of tears he had confessed to it at once. The question was how was he, Christian, going to ensure that the court-martial understood that there were special circumstances attached to the crime, which it certainly was. God, why had he been picked to help the kid? He knew next to nothing about Navy law.

'Well, Lieutenant?' the port commandant rasped impatiently. 'What is it to be?'

Christian looked at the Moses, who was now crying again, the tears rolling unhindered down his wan cheeks. 'Guilty, sir, but with diminished responsibility.'

The port commandant made an entry in the big ledger in front of him and murmured, 'Well, that's better. All right, *Kapitänleutnant* Harsch, you have the word.'

Harsch stood up and grasped his ceremonial dirk firmly as if he needed the support of its hard comfort. Swiftly he stated the facts, without once looking at the Moses, detailing how the fire had been discovered while the crew of the U-70 had been enjoying their party; how it was discovered that one of the crew, namely Seaman Hinze was missing; and how, when he was found hidden in some packing cases on the jetty, his uniform was singed and he smelled of petrol, which was what had been used to start the fire in the engine room. He paused and for the first time looked at a miserable Moses.

Next to the prisoner Frenssen urged, 'Look up, man. Face him out — for chrissake!' Frenssen glared fiercely at the skipper, who could see him whispering, as if challenging Harsch to say something.

But Harsch didn't need to. The Moses remained silent, his his head hanging, as if he were animated by some deeper shame than the charge of sabotage and could not face looking at the captain.

'After his arrest,' Harsch continued, 'he admitted immediately that he had started the fire in the engine room.'

'How serious was the sabotage, *Herr Kapitänleutnant?*' the port commandant asked, though he knew already, but as he always maintained, '*There has to be order.*'

'Serious enough to delay our sailing by another twenty-four hours,' Harsch answered darkly, 'though by now most of the essential repairs have been carried out. Now all we need to do is to clear up the mess and get the boat ready for sailing.'

'Thank you.' The port commandant looked at Christian and Harsch sat down, face revealing nothing, though every now and again he shot a furtive glance in the direction of the prisoner.

Christian cleared his throat and at the same time wished the earth would open up and swallow him up. Why should that poor boy's life be placed in his hands? 'The prisoner has admitted, sir, that he did set fire to the engine room, though it must be stated it was not a very serious fire, sir. We managed to put it out in a matter —'

'Sabotage is sabotage, Lieutenant,' the port commandant interrupted firmly, 'whatever its degree. Please continue.'

Christian flushed and told himself he hadn't a chance with a little pompous prick like the port commandant in charge. 'The prisoner, as I have said, sir, then admitted his guilt. But I think there are one or two things about him which have to be taken into account to explain an act which he now bitterly regrets,' he lied glibly for he had been unable to get a word

out of the Moses about his crime, save the same old statement, 'I just wanted to go home. We all did'.

Hurriedly he blurted out the details of the Moses' young life; how he had volunteered from the naval section of the Hitler Youth for the U-boat Arm; how he had become the youngest member of the crew at seventeen, with a bare six month's training behind him; and how he had proved his courage amply during the escape from the Black Sea. 'The men were, *are*, tired, sir,' he said, looking boldly at Harsch. 'The Moses, like the rest of them, has been through too much. He, and they, clung to the one thing that kept, *keeps* them going — the promise of going home. Unfortunately that promise cannot be kept ... and' — he ended lamely — 'he snapped... He did what he did...' Christian bowed to the port commandant. 'That's it, sir.'

'Thank you, Lieutenant,' the other officer said and made a note in his ledger. 'Then I think we will clear the court —'

'Not just yet!' It was Harsch, rising to his feet, face suddenly red and angry. 'This whole matter is being trivialized. *A young volunteer, full of enthusiasm for Germany's cause!*' he sneered, using Christian's words to describe the prisoner. 'In this war there have been *many* young volunteers, full of enthusiasm for

Germany's cause. From homes throughout the Reich — and not only privileged homes like that of Hinze either. But when the going got tough, they didn't take the law into their own hands because they wanted to go *home* — his face contorted into a sneer — 'or because they were *tired*.' He hammered home the words ruthlessly. 'No, they knuckled under and fought, on land and sea, fought on when there was no hope for them, no chance they would ever return home.' He glared at Christian, eyes full of unconcealed hate, as if he had suddenly discovered that the handsome young second-in-command had been his deadly enemy all along. '*They fought on to the very end*.' He gasped for breath, chest heaving mightily. 'There can be no excuse, sir' — He addressed the port commandant, who was red and flustered himself at this surprising outburst — 'no excuse whatsoever. Ordinary Seaman Hinze deliberately sabotaged one of our boats in order not to have to fight any more. The man is nothing more than *a craven coward*.'

Slowly the Moses raised his head as if to say something, his face wet with tears, his bottom lip trembling.

Harsch didn't give him a chance. He flung out his right hand passionately and pointed a finger that trembled with emotion at the Moses. 'There can be no other sentence,' he cried, head twisted to one side, face purple with effort, speech thick and guttural, 'than one of death. Ordinary Seaman Hinze has forfeited his right to live, for not only has he betrayed his country, he has betrayed his comrades as well.' Suddenly, startlingly, Harsch sat down and gazed at the palms of his hands.

For what seemed a long time no single sound broke the heavy, brooding silence of the hot tight room until finally the port Commandant said in strangely hushed voice, 'The court will rise, please.'

'What do you think, sir?' Frenssen asked, as the two of them lounged in the noonday shade, lazily puffing at cigarettes, watching the Greeks go by as they headed back to their shabby little houses to eat their frugal midday meal. Over at the port commandant's office, after a brassy blare of military music, a hard bombastic voice was declaring, '*Die Grossdeutsche Wehrmacht gibt bekannt!*' It was the usual midday communiqué from Radio Berlin.

'You mean the Moses?'

Frenssen nodded.

Miserably Christian flipped his cigarette end into the dust. He had made an awful balls-up of being the 'prisoner's friend'. Who needed enemies with friends like him? 'Oh, he won't escape punishment,' he said. 'However young and foolish he is, he must take the responsibility for a serious act of sabotage. That's for certain.'

'Torgau military prison?' Frenssen queried, looking at a young Greek

woman passing, bearing an earthenware pitcher of wine on her head, her loose fine breasts rippling under the material of her sleeveless blouse, great jet-black tufts of hair revealed at her armpits.

'Possibly. Perhaps even a punishment battalion at the front, with no leave ever again. The infantry, so they tell me, is crying out for bodies. The Russian front eats them up…' He let the words trail away, trying not to even think of the third possibility. It was too dreadful to contemplate.

Frenssen tugged the end of his red nose. 'The *Jungs* don't like this one bit, sir, you know.' He indicated the crew of the U-70 squatting opposite in the shade of a great pile of rations intended for the U-70. They were glum and morose, barely speaking, most of them puffing silently at cigarettes, each man wrapped up in a cocoon of his own gloomy thoughts.

'So?'

'They blame the skipper, sir,' Frenssen persisted, 'and rightly so. Couldn't he have just waited with his announcement of all that invasion fleet shit and how we was going to tackle the Amis and the Tommies? I'm surprised that not more of them didn't blow their stack. Besides, the skipper and the Moses —'

'I don't want to hear any more of that kind of talk, *Obermaat Frenssen*!' Christian interrupted him harshly. 'You'll do him — *and yourself* — no good talking about such things.'

But Frenssen was not going to be stopped. 'But it's obvious, sir,' he blurted out angrily, his face suddenly red with rage. 'The skipper wants to be rid of the Moses. He knows too much. The skipper wants to go home to the Reich to be fêted as a hero with a clean sheet, with no shit attached to his heels, with —' He stopped short. The ugly brute of a master-at-arms was pushing the Moses through the door opposite, his hands manacled behind his back, his face lathered in sweat and set in a look of absolute total despair. 'They're gonna start up again. They've made their decision, sir,' he said hastily.

Swiftly Christian adjusted his cap and tugged at his tunic, as the port commandant, followed by Harsch, the Moses, and the rest started to file across the yard, the port commandant patting his red, somewhat fleshy lips, as if he had just eaten a good meal and didn't want any traces of food on his mouth to reveal that fact.

Hastily Christian barked, '*Hab acht!*'

Lazily, almost contemptuously, the crew came to an approximation of the position of attention, as Christian saluted and Harsch passed. Their eyes met momentarily and then

Christian knew, with total instant clarity, that now Harsch was his implacable enemy.

'All right,' he said finally, breaking out of the spell the knowledge had cast over him, 'Inside with the lot of you again.' He looked at Frenssen. The latter looked grim and murmured, '*fingers crossed, Herr Leutnant.*' Then they too followed the rest of the subdued U-boat men into the makeshift court.

The close heat of the room hit them like a blow across the face. After the shade they were all instantly bathed in sweat again. At the blanket-covered table, the port commandant was already mopping his streaming brow and tugging at his wilting stiff collar. Only the Moses seemed unaffected by the sudden heat in the tight, airless room. Flanked by Frenssen, he sat on the wooden-backed chair, face pale and sunken, looking almost as if he were chilled.

'Ordinary Seaman Hinze,' the brutal-looking master-at-arms commanded, the sweat streaming down his ugly face, 'you will rise and face the court.'

With infinite weariness the Moses rose to his feet and swayed as if he might faint. Hastily Frenssen reached out a hand to support him, but the Moses shook his head and a little crestfallen Frenssen let his hand drop.

The port commandant took his time. Perhaps he was enjoying this moment of drama in his humdrum provincial existence in this remote Greek backwater. For his part, Harsch was nervous, even impatient. He kept looking at his watch, as if he wanted the matter over and done with so that

he could get on with his bold dreams of glory. Christian bit his bottom lip with worry. Only the Moses seemed unaffected by the mounting tension.

The port commandant adjusted his pince-nez fussily and began to read from the single sheet of paper in front of him, which had obviously been prepared during the break. 'Ordinary Seaman Hinze, you are arraigned on the charge of violating Paragraph 65 of German Military Law,' he said in a dry-as-dust manner. 'That is, you have committed sabotage on property of the Third Reich while on active service in the face of the enemy. You have pleaded guilty to this grave charge and the Prisoner's Friend has submitted diminished responsibility.'

Christian clenched his sweating fists until it was painful. Here it came!

'After some consideration, Hinze,' the port commandant said severely, peering over the top of his pince-nez at the young sailor, 'I find that you were fully aware of what you were doing when you committed the crime in question, despite your age. As *Kapitänleutnant* Harsch has rightly pointed out, other young men of the same age as yourself have fought to the last, without questioning their orders or demanding the right to return to the Homeland.' He paused and stared sternly at the Moses.

He showed absolutely no emotion whatsoever. He seemed to be on another planet, a million kilometres away from the earth.

Slowly, the port commandant reached out a pudgy dimpled hand for the dirk resting on the blanket in front of him. Quite deliberately he began to turn it, so that the hilt no longer faced the prisoner and the pointed blade was directed towards him.

There was a collective gasp from the young seamen and suddenly Christian found his heart was beginning to thump frantically. He knew the significance of the turning of the dirk. That ancient naval custom dating back to the foundation of the old Prussian Navy meant one thing only — the Moses had lost the case! What would the sentence be?

Solemnly the port commandant rose to his feet and the master-at-arms barked, 'Court will rise!'

There was a quick shuffle of feet, the scraping of chairs and officers and men rose hastily, standing to attention, the sweat streaming down their strained faces in glistening rivulets. Christian felt his uniform clinging to him unpleasantly. He waited.

The port commandant took his time obviously savouring these last moments of the drama in which he was the star. Still the prisoner remained completely apathetic, as if the whole business had absolutely nothing to do with him. He cleared his throat self-importantly, aware that he was the focus of all their gazes, then he began to read the sentence. 'Ordinary Seaman Hinze is sentenced to lose his rating, to be dishonourably discharged from the service of the Greater German *Wehrmacht*, to forfeit all pay and special allowances due or to become due to him..

'Come on, come on, you unfeeling pompous bastard!' a shrill, angry little voice at the back of Christian's brain cried urgently. *'Out with it, in God's name!'*

'...and to be shot to death with musketry —'

The rest of the port commandant's words were lost in a sudden outburst of noise, angry shouts, cries of rage, threats from outraged men of the U-70, as the full impact of the fat officer's words hit them. Only two men remained unmoved and aloof from the angered noisy reaction. They were Harsch and the Moses. For a moment their eyes met, the one's full of triumph, the other's sad and resigned. The bull-like master-at-arms was tugging at his pistol holster and crying above the shouting, 'Stop that noise in here. Stop that noise in here — *at once*. You, *Obermaat!*' he bellowed at a bemused Frenssen, 'get that frigging traitor out of here — at the double, man. *Los!*'

For a long moment it seemed that Frenssen might refuse. Then he grabbed the Moses' arm and whispered something to him urgently. The Moses shook his head and gently released Frenssen's grip from his skinny arm. Head erect he left, leaving the courtroom in chaos, the red-faced port commandant yelling for order and the master-at-arms, pistol in hand, shrilling his whistle for reinforcements...

CHAPTER 6

They were going to shoot the Moses near the cliffs to the east of Kavala. Harsch had attempted to insist, in the presence of the port commandant, that men from the U-70 should carry out the execution. But Christian had objected violently, reminding the skipper he would soon have to sail with these men. Their present mood was bad enough, but if they were forced to shoot their own comrade… He shrugged and left the rest of the sentence unsaid. The port commandant had intervened hastily and, as he outranked Harsch, ordered the shooting to be carried out by twelve of his own sailors under the command of the master-at-arms. The outbreak in the court had unsettled him and he wanted no further trouble from these rebellious young U-boat men. Indeed, he would be glad when they were gone and he could return to his comfortable backwater existence, his willing Greek mistress and the profitable trade in black market ikons.

With bad grace, Harsch had agreed, telling himself that once he had the crew of the U-70 safely back in the Reich, there would be charges. In particular, he would see what he could do about getting Jungblut court-martialled. The man was a veteran, a decorated war hero, but what would his word count against that of the man who had sunk the *Stalin*? It was all too clear where his number one's sympathies lay — with the crew! Jungblut was no better than all those damned liberals and parlour pinks from the middle classes who had made the Kiel Mutiny of 1918 possible. The men needed a firm hand, not this soft pandering to their whims and moods. Jungblut was simply too soft!

Now it was dawn. The sky above the cliffs was a tremulous delicate pink and the birds were still silent. Kavala itself was just beginning to wake, with the first blue smoke of the kitchen fires ascending into the lightening sky. It was going to be a perfect July day. The air was already warm, with hardly a breath of wind. It would be very hot.

At the execution site, the port commandant's middle-aged sailors were already busy, stripped to the waist, hammering in the post to which they would tie him, erecting the 'baffle board' so that stray bullets would not be deflected and strike a spectator, clearing the stones so that the ground on which the firing squad would stand would be fairly even. The port commandant's carpenters had also devised the other piece of apparatus required by *Wehrmacht* regulations for such occasions, the braceboard and straps. If the Moses collapsed, he would be strapped into the board and frog-marched to the post where he would meet his end. In the event it proved that the Moses would be the bravest of them all that beautiful morning in July.

At seven, with the cocks still crowing in Kavala, the firing squad drove up in a navy truck. They were all middle-aged sailors, some of them wearing the decorations of the Old War, and they were all embarrassed, trying to avoid the hostile sullen looks of the crew of the U-70 which had been paraded by Harsch to view the execution of their shipmate. Clumsily they descended from the trucks, holding their rifles awkwardly, as if they wished the weapons with which they were soon going to shoot a fellow human being would disappear. The master-at-arms beckoned them over, to where he stood with the port commandant and Harsch, and began distributing clips of ammunition. The petty officer in charge, looking a little helpless, took the black hood and the white cardboard heart from the big chief petty officer.

Down below the bells from the churches began to jingle and boom. They were summoning the old women, wrapped in black, to attend the first service of the day. It was then that the truck bearing the Moses arrived from the port. He was bareheaded, with a blanket around his skinny shoulders, his wrists manacled, with two ropes attached to his body leading back to the two naval MPs who were his guards.

Low animal-like groans and moans went up from the men of the U-70 when they saw their shipmate and the master-at-arms shot the submariners a threatening angry look. The Moses smiled wanly at his old comrades, but he was already lost in a far world, his lips moving in the act of contrition. Vaguely a mesmerized Christian heard the words as he was led by. 'Oh, my God, I am heartily sorry for having offended Thee and I detest all my sins... Mother of Mercy, pray for us... Most Sacred Heart of Jesus...' In the hour of his death, the youngster had abandoned the new creed of national socialism and had returned to the religion of his childhood.

The master-at-arms's brutal voice cut into the prayer as he bellowed at the top of his voice, sending the nesting birds rising from the cliff in angry squawking protest, 'As officer in charge of the execution I am required by military law to read out the following...' As if to prolong the young man's agony, the chief petty officer read out the charge against the Moses yet again and then the sentence, before bellowing, 'Ordinary Seaman Hinze, do you have a statement to make before the order directing your execution is carried out?'

The Moses looked at him calmly, then at Harsch, who shrank visibly as his calm clear gaze was directed at him. He looked again at the big brutal chief petty officer and said softly, 'No.'

The big petty officer stepped back and nodded to the other one in charge of the firing squad. Gently the latter led the Moses to the firing post, while his crewmates watched with bated breath. The blood-red ball of the sun now appeared and hung on the lip of the cliffs, as if it were hesitating to ascend higher and illuminate the dread scene below.

With the assistance of the two MPs, he tied the Moses' ankles to the post and then did the same with his skinny young shoulders, fixing the straps to a spike at the back of the pole to prevent him from slumping. Now he presented a clear upright target to the nervous uneasy men of the firing squad; and all the while the Moses held the same calm clear look on his young pale face, his eyes revealing no emotion that a tense, breathless Christian could discern.

The two MPs stepped back and reluctantly the petty officer asked the Moses to bend his head. He did so obediently and hastily the petty officer passed the black hood over his head. The Moses' face was blotted out for ever. It was only then that the petty officer pinned the white heart on the prisoner's chest.

Now there was absolute silence. The bells had ceased in Kavala and the birds had settled again. No one seemed to be breathing. All eyes were fixed on the hooded man tied to the post, who might well have been dead already, for he made no movement and a watching Christian, tensed for the first orders to the waiting firing squad, could not detect any movement of his chest.

'*Squad.*'

Christian jumped, startled, as the first command rang out.

'Squad — *ready!*'

Awkwardly, the middle-aged sailors raised their rifles, fixing their gaze exclusively on the young man about to die, not daring to look at the suddenly horrified faces of his shipmates.

'Squad — *aim!*' The command cut into Christian like a sharp knife. He bit his bottom lip until the blood came. God, when would this horror be over?

The petty officer in charge of the firing squad hesitated momentarily, then he cried, '*SQUAD... FIRE!*'

The volley cracked out, the middle-aged riflemen reeling back here and there with the impact. The Moses jerked hard. He strained at his bonds frantically. Frenssen gasped. For a moment or so it seemed to him the frail, tortured youth would burst free. But that wasn't to be. As scarlet patches appeared suddenly all over his upper body, his head fell to his chest limply.

Sickened and horrified, Christian forced himself not to look away, as the little naval doctor hurried forward and the echo of that final volley ran around the circle of surrounding hills.

He placed the stethoscope against the Moses' chest, ignoring the blood jetting from a severed artery in a flood of bright scarlet.

Impatiently, Harsch, the only one there who seemed totally unaffected by this ritual slaughter, cried, 'Stand away, doctor! We don't want anyone getting *accidentally* killed!'

Even the master-at-arms, who was passing out a fresh bullet to each of the firing squad, had paled and was subdued. The riflemen slipped the new slug in their breeches.

The doctor looked up angrily at Harsch and said, 'Give him another volley if you like it so much, *Herr Kapitänleutnant*, but it will be a waste of ammunition... He's passed on.' Bitterly he folded his stethoscope. 'Ordinary Seaman Hinze, I can inform you officially, is *dead*.' With his head bowed he trailed back to his place with the officers.

For what seemed a long time, no one moved. They all stared at the dead sailor hanging suspended in his straps, the blood dripping down his torn, burnt shirt, the only sound the incongruous braying of an ass somewhere down in Kavala.

Harsch looked at the port commandant, but he was sunk in his own thoughts, as if he were realizing for the first time what he had done. The court-martial he had thought of as a mere matter of routine had resulted in someone's life being taken. The sailor he had sentenced was now dead and he was responsible for having made the decision.

Harsch's lips curled in contempt at such weakness. He turned to an ashen-faced Christian and snapped, 'Number One, take over. March the men back to the boat.' When Christian did not appear to hear or understand, he repeated his order, barking icily, 'Or are you going to join this mutinous rabble too, *Herr Leutnant*?'

Christian pulled himself together with a visible effort and saluted, 'Yessir. I understand, sir.' He turned to Frenssen, who was just as shaken as he was. '*Obermaat* fall the men in.'

Five minutes later they were marching away down the slope back into Kavala, while at the site of the execution, others began to cut the Moses down, prior to slipping the body into a mattress cover. The dead man would be buried in an unmarked grave outside Kavala, probably to be dug up and desecrated by the local Greeks once the Germans occupiers had left.

As they marched back towards the waterfront where lay the U-70, their mood sombre, ignoring the curious looks of the Greeks, who had obviously heard the volley of rifle-fire, Christian realized for the first time he was fighting for a cause that was unjust. The war had gone on for so long he had forgotten the reason why it was being fought. It seemed at this moment as if his whole life had been spent fighting. Why had Germany gone to war? '*Not to shoot kids who simply want to go home, no sir!*' a harsh incisive voice within him snapped. 'There's got to be something wrong with a system that shoots seventeen-year-old boys. There has!'

It was then that Lieutenant Christian Jungblut swore a great oath to himself, though an outside observer would have thought from the look on his handsome young face that his mind was completely blank and that he was drained of all emotions. But he wasn't. He swore with every fibre of his being that he would get what was left of the U-70's crew back home, come what may. He owed it to the memory of the dead Moses. If Harsch tried to interfere and risked their young lives with his damned stupid dreams of personal glory, then he wouldn't hesitate.

'*Hesitate to do what?*' that hard little voice within him rasped.

Christian's face hardened. His jaw set. His eyes were suddenly full of menace. 'Don't you know?' he answered the hard little voice. 'He killed the Moses, even if he didn't actually pull the trigger.'

'Well, come on, piss or get off the pot!' the voice taunted him. 'Say your piece and have done with it.'

The marching men swung round the bend in the road and there was the battered old submarine, its hull still blackened with the smoke from the engine room fire, which the dead Moses had started in his futile attempt to ensure that they would all go home safely. In essence the dead boy had sacrificed his life for his shipmates.

'Oh, for chrissake,' the voice insisted. 'Don't *fucking* well indulge yourself in *your fucking* maudlin sentimentality! I've asked you a *fucking* question. What will you do?'

'I'll kill him,' Christian snarled. '*Kill him, just like he killed the Moses*'

CHAPTER 7

The Boreas hit the great convoy heading for Sicily on Friday. Up to then the voyage had been calm and peaceful, but during the dog watch that morning the wind had suddenly started to freshen, growing in intensity by the second. Rapidly the tremendous wind rushing down from the Alps strengthened. Soon the ships were tossing up and down the angry grey-green white-capped rollers. Valiantly they steamed on, trying to punch their way through the gigantic waves, as the storm buffeted them mercilessly.

Men went down by the score, the hundred, the thousand as sea-sickness overcame them. The heads were blocked by hundreds of choking, vomiting, green-faced soldiers, British, American, Canadian, as the 2,500 ships of the huge convoy headed by Malta and turned south-west towards their target, Sicily. Loose gear rolled back and forth as the ships wallowed in the troughs like drunken sows. Here and there Mills bombs broke out of their cases and rolled to and fro like lethal steel baseballs. The rigging went, as did the radio masts, sprawling across the crowded decks in a flurry of angry blue and red sparks.

Soldiers bearing mess tins went in search of food only to retreat when they saw what the sloppy begrimed British cooks were offering them; greasy bacon and sausages swimming in a pool of cooling fat. 'Only Limeys would play a damn fool, rotten trick like that on a dying man!' they complained and retreated below, where in the fetid nauseating atmosphere hundreds of men lay sprawled green and groaning in their hammocks. 'You could 'ave had a nice pair o' juicy kippers, if you'd have liked,' the cooks called after them mockingly. '*Bleeding Yanks!*'

Patton was unaffected by the weather. He had a cast-iron stomach. While his much younger staff officers went down with sea-sickness one after another, he stuck to his cigars and whisky, his gaze fixed constantly on the crazily heaving sea through the porthole. Already he had received a signal from a worried Washington, enquiring whether the attack was on or off.

Promptly he had signalled back, 'I shall land in the eye of the hurricane.' But that proud boast had been overtaken by the weather. Now the convoy *was* battling a hurricane, with the wind howling and tearing at the rigging of the SS *Monrovia*, buffeting the big trooper with hammer blows that sent her reeling from side to side.

But the weather was not the only problem Patton had to contend with. Although they were still within Malta air space, the weather would prevent the British fighters based there from taking off if the convoy was attacked, though of course it would stop the Germans fielding their own planes as well. But it *was* ideal weather for a submarine attack. How would the ships protect themselves from enemy U-boats if there were no planes to guide them? There simply were not enough destroyers and frigates to cover such a huge convoy.

Patton took another reflective sip of his whisky, while outside on the dipping deck one of his staff officers clung grimly to the rail and tried unsuccessfully to vomit against the howling screeching wind. If the Germans did attack with their submarines and struck lucky by torpedoing the SS *Monrovia*, for example, the whole invasion would be threatened. If he and Hewitt went to the bottom of the Med, the brains of the operation would be gone and he had absolutely no faith in the ability of his subordinate commanders to execute the attack on their own.

He frowned. Then that little fart of a Limey, Montgomery, would go it alone and grab all the kudos of a successful first invasion of Nazi-occupied Europe. 'No, sir!' he snorted angrily to no one in particular. 'That little prick has hogged the headlines ever since El Alamein. Now it's time we Americans grabbed a little bit of the limelight.' He puffed at his cigar with sudden ferocity at the thought of his dead body resting at the bottom of the sea, while a victorious Montgomery, bathed in the hot Sicilian sun, enjoyed the cheers of a triumphant crowd somewhere or other. 'I'm just not going to let them damn well sink the *Monrovia*!'

Abruptly animated by a surge of renewed confidence, Patton stubbed out his cigar, drained the rest of his whisky, grabbed his lacquered helmet and headed for the door. He would go onto the bridge with Admiral Hewitt and take charge himself — if he could. Come what may, he'd see the convoy through to the Sicilian beaches, just to spite Montgomery. The little fart wasn't going to make this another British El Alamein. He grinned his dingy-toothed smile as he flung open the door and was struck by the full force of that terrible wind. 'Just you watch my frigging smoke, Sir Montgomery,' he yelled defiantly at the crazy, heaving sea. '*Here comes George S. Patton Junior!*'

It was then that the *Monrovia's* klaxons started to sound their dread warning, followed an instant later by the urgent jingling of the alarm bells, as the tannoy system crackled into hasty metallic life, and an unreal voice cried, '*Now hear this. Now hear this. This is a submarine alert. Now hear this… This is a submarine…*'

'*God in heaven!*' Harsch breathed in awe. 'I've — I've never seen so many ships in my whole life!' He staggered back from the periscope and allowed Christian to take over. Hastily Christian switched on the amplifier and pressed his right eye closer to the periscope. To his front, shrouded with flying spray and spume, the whole green heaving horizon was filled with enemy craft; ugly wallowing troop transports, clumsy stub-nosed assault ships, great grey menacing cruisers, with destroyers and frigates scuttling back and forth like angry sheepdogs trying to keep the flock from straying, bouncing in and out of the huge waves, staggering as if they were striking solid brick walls. He whistled softly and then straightened up, saying, 'It's the target of a lifetime, sir, I agree. Even a one-eyed drunk couldn't miss among that lot up there, sir.'

Harsch remained as sober-minded and sombre as ever, though there was no mistaking the fanatical gleam of excitement in his eyes. 'I'm glad you agree, Number One,' he said sardonically. 'And I have no intention of missing either, I can assure you of that. Down periscope!'

While Christian waited for Harsch to explain his plan of attack, he did a quick calculation. They had four torpedoes left and enough fuel to get them to Bari in southern Italy, once they had made their strike. It would be nip-and-tuck. There would be little fuel available for any extensive evasion action. Fortunately the storm raging above would make the U-70 safe from the prying eyes of the crew of one of those damned Tommy Sunderlands. As he saw it, it was a matter of making a quick safe strike somewhere on the edge of the great convoy and then running like hell for the safety of Italian coastal waters and Bari.

But when Harsch finally spoke, he seemed to have other ideas. 'Listen, listen all of you men.' He addressed the crew directly, instead of through his second-in-command, which Christian knew was meant as a deliberate snub. Not that he minded. He knew his reputation stood high with the rank-and-file. Instinctively they had guessed that if anyone could protect them from the skipper's excesses, it would be him. 'I'm speaking to you directly, because I want each and every one of you to be aware of the vital nature of our mission.' He let his words sink in, but if Harsch had expected some enthusiasm from his men, he was sorely disappointed. Their unwashed and bearded faces showed only defensive expectancy. 'We are not merely going to sink tonnage this time,' Harsch continued, barely able to contain his mounting excitement, Christian could see. 'We are going to sink the key ships.'

'*Key ships?*' Christian butted in. 'How do you mean, sir?'

Harsch did not seem to hear. He kept his gaze fixed firmly on the crew's faces, yellow blobs in the dim green fetid interior of the submarine, the only sound the soft whirr of the electric motors. 'It is my intention to penetrate the outer defences of the convoy and attempt to seek out the command ships. We have four torpedoes left. That should be sufficient to knock out those vessels. Can't you see,' he cried out in exasperation at the lack of fervour in the crew's faces, 'it is a golden opportunity! An opportunity to paralyse the enemy's attempt at invasion before it even starts. Instead of simply striking off the outer limbs, *we smite the head!*'

Frenssen waited till the skipper had stopped speaking, aware now that Harsch no longer paid any attention to Lieutenant Jungblut, and asked, 'But sir, how are we to penetrate the destroyer screen in the first place? They've probably got us on the asdic already. Once we get close enough to present a threat, they'll be on to us like a ton o' bricks. The surface'll be *shitting* depth charges!'

There was a mumble of agreement from the others and someone safely concealed in the shadows towards the rear said, 'Ay, that's telling him, *Obermaat*!'

Surprisingly enough Harsch did not seem angered by Frenssen's pointed question and the reaction of the crew. Indeed he seized upon the chief petty officer's question eagerly. 'Easy!' he said. 'That storm up there is a godsend for us. It grounds the enemy aircraft and has reduced visibility to virtually zero. Now all we need to do to take the U-70 out of asdic range is to surface.' He smiled frantically at the crew, willing them to approve of his mad scheme.

'*Surface*!' Frenssen stuttered, completely bewildered by the skipper's statement. 'You mean, sir, go up … with that lot everywhere up there?' He grabbed his throat, his face suddenly flushing a brick-red, as if he were being choked. 'You can't mean that, sir.'

'I can — and I do,' Harsch barked triumphantly. 'That's the beauty of this storm. Once we start the diesels on the surface they lose us. All we have to do is sail right in through the destroyer screen and pick out targets at leisure. It will be the kill of a lifetime, man!'

Standing to Harsch's right, Christian could see from the look on his face that there was no stopping him. The skipper's mind was made up and there was no changing it, save for outright mutiny. Indeed there was some merit in his plan. Visual observation from the air was impossible in the storm raging topside. It would be exceedingly difficult too for the naval look-outs on the surface craft to spot the U-70's low silhouette in the water under those conditions. But using the diesels to battle the storm would use up the boat's precious fuel at a tremendous rate. That was the catch. They might well sink an important ship, one of those 'key ships' the skipper had mentioned, but find themselves afterwards drifting helplessly, out of fuel.

'Well, Number One,' Harsch turned finally to him, as if he had suddenly remembered his presence, 'have you any objections?' There was no mistaking the sneer and Christian felt himself flush a little to be talked to thus in the presence of the crew.

But he contained himself and said calmly. 'No sir, I think your plan is good and might well succeed. The only problem, as I see it, is that of fuel.'

'Let that be my worry, Number One,' Harsch snapped after Christian had explained what his fears were. 'We got away with the sinking of the *Stalin* and managed to escape from the Black Sea with the whole of the Russian fleet looking for us, when everyone — including several men present here at this moment — thought we didn't have a snowball's chance in hell! Now we're going to do it again.' He glanced severely at Christian. 'All right, Number One, take it.' He elbowed aside the crewmen nearest to him and pulled his pistol belt off the hook on the bulkhead. As Christian issued his orders, he strapped the belt on and slapped the butt of the pistol significantly. 'Just so everybody has the right idea,' he snapped, looking around at the circle of faces. 'Now hear this. I shall personally *shoot* the first man I think is neglecting his duties or who shows the first sign of cowardice. *Los*! Get about your duties.' As the compressed air started to hiss out of the tanks and the U-70 began to rise slowly, Harsch gave a worried Christian a wintry smile. But his eyes remained menacing. Christian shuddered in spite of himself.

Because of the huge waves pounding the tiny U-boat, the bridge watch were lashed to the rail with a leather safety-belt. Surprisingly enough it was easier for the U-70 to ride the storm than for the huge hulks of the troopers they vaguely glimpsed through the murk all around. The force of the sea breaking over her was terrific. Nevertheless the U-70 shot through the wild, white water like an arrow, with little pitching or rolling, as the waves went over her like they would over a breakwater.

Still, the effect of the storm was horrific for the men chained to the bridge. They were continually swamped by tons of cold grey-green water. It blinded them and penetrated everywhere, soaking them to the skin, filling their seaboots, even though the old hares had punched holes in the soles of theirs to let the water run out. Time and time again Christian, legs spread apart, muscles crying out with the red-hot pain of trying to balance, felt his belt would be snapped by the tremendous force of the waves and he would be carried overboard to be lost for ever. But the steel-reinforced belt, which dug painfully into his ribs, held; and for a brief second or two he would be able to peer through his binoculars before the next wave came roaring and hissing like some savage primeval monster determined to exterminate these puny little mortals.

If Harsch felt the cold, the blows, the numbing bone-shaking pounding of the waves, he did not show it. Every time Christian emerged, eyes stinging with salt-water, gasping and spluttering for air, he would be standing there, legs braced, glasses held to his eyes, as if it was a point of honour with him not to lower them for one single second.

Once Frenssen ventured upside, bellowing against the howling wind, 'Coffee and rum, gentlemen,' but Harsch had cried angrily, 'Rum? Have you got all your cups in your cupboard, *Obermaat*? There'll be no spirits drunk on this bridge. Why, it'd cut our reaction time down —' Just before the next wave submerged them, he had swept out his hand and sent the tray on which Frenssen was carrying the steaming mugs of coffee flying. Frenssen had disappeared down below, cursing furiously to himself.

Now they were fighting their way down the outer lane of the great convoy, which seemed to be formed in a square of five files, each one many kilometres in length. Behind them they left the protective screen of destroyers, though they did spot a lone destroyer scurrying before the storm in this lane, which made Christian think there must be other fighting craft in between the lanes. But although they were passing within five hundred metres of the troopers, while Harsch selected his 'key targets', no look-out on the enemy ships spotted them. Harsch's plan, or so it seemed, was working famously.

It was just about the time to change watches so that the men on the bridge could stagger below, where they would have to be helped out of their soaked leather jackets and oilskins, when Harsch muttered something and, bracing himself against yet another wave, began focusing his glasses furiously.

Hastily Christian followed the direction of his gaze, eyes stinging with sea-water. As he blinked and spluttered he inwardly cursed the storm, the captain, the whole bloody war. Dimly through the streaming glass he glimpsed the huge hulk of a battleship steaming stolidly on some two kilometres away, seemingly totally unaware of the U-boat.

A couple of tons of green boiling water smashed over the bridge again and for a few moments Christian fought to stay on his feet numbed again by its savage force. Next to him Harsch shook his head and spluttered, 'Did you see her?'

'Yes sir. I think it's a Tommy. One of the old *Queen Elizabeth* class they built in the last war.'

'Agreed,' Harsch said eagerly, peering down at the rangefinder. 'It's probably the *Warspite*. She's reported in the Med.' He wiped the moisture from his face, eyes red-rimmed but brimming with excitement. 'My God, Number One, think of it, twenty-five thousand tons of her. Two enemy battleships sunk on the same patrol! Nobody has ever done that before. And they haven't seen us.'

'No, sir,' Christian agreed warily, feeling none of the other man's excitement, as he considered the risk. 'I don't think they have.'

But Harsch was no longer listening. Instead he was bending to the voice tube, ignoring yet another watery onslaught, crying above the howl of the wind, 'Stand by to fire a spread of two.' They were going to attack…

CHAPTER 8

'All set, sir,' the disembodied voice of the torpedo mate came floating up the tube, as the storm lashed the bridge, deluging the tense, anxious men with water.

Hastily Christian read out the range and bearing.

Harsch repeated the figures. The great grey hulk of the *Warspite* grew ever larger so that it seemed to fill the whole, madly tossing and heaving horizon. Taking one last look, he lowered his binoculars and cried, '*Fire one! Fire two!*'

There was the sudden hiss of compressed air. Bubbles burst on the surface. The U-boat lurched as it was lightened by a couple of tons of steel leaving it and then there was a flurry of wild white water as the two torpedoes fanned out and raced towards their target.

Hurriedly Harsch and Christian flung up their glasses, the storm forgotten as they counted off the seconds until the torpedoes struck their target.

Suddenly, however, Harsch's great dream of sinking two battleships on one fighting patrol vanished totally. Out of nowhere the lean shape of a destroyer with a bone in her teeth came racing out of the green gloom, knife-like prow slicing the waves as it rushed towards the U-70. Christian groaned and Harsch slammed his fist down on a stanchion with rage. '*Verdammte Scheisse*, the damned thing's coming right in between the *Warspite* and the damned tin fish, Number One!'

It was just then that the skipper of the destroyer spotted the torpedoes heading straight for his ship. He sent the destroyer violently reeling to the right in a daring manoeuvre which had her superstructure almost touching the waves before she righted herself. Harmlessly the torpedoes flashed by her bow and disappeared into the storm.

There was a muted crack directly above the horrified men on the bridge of the U-70 and a star shell burst in a flash of brilliant, incandescent silver light. The gloom vanished and it was as bright as day. Almost immediately the destroyer opened fire. Midships, multiple pom-poms opened up on the U-70. Red, green, and yellow tracer ripped the length of the bow and pattered off the conning tower. A sailor yelped with pain and writhed in agony, held in place by his safety belt. Christian didn't wait for the skipper to react. He slammed the alarm button and as the klaxon started to shrill its warning, he cried urgently, '*Crash dive! Crash dive!*' Frenssen freed the wounded man and effortlessly dragged him inside, in the same instant that the bridge party started to tumble down the ladder in a flurry of confused wetness.

'*Sir!*' Christian yelled as another salvo of machine-gun fire pattered against the conning tower and the first shell plunged into the sea only metres away. 'We're diving, sir!'

'*Damn you, Jungblut!*' Harsch yelled, hand falling to his pistol holster. 'Who told you to give that order —' He howled with sudden pain, face abruptly white with shock, as he was slammed back against the side of the conning tower, his leather coat ripped and smouldering. 'I — I've … been hit!' he gasped. He touched his stomach with his hand. It came away a dripping scarlet.

'Quick, sir!' Christian cried, as another shell exploded nearby and sent shrapnel howling across the deck, clanging and clattering where it hit the hull. 'He thrust his arm under Harsch's and half-dragged, half carried him to the ladder. 'Frenssen,' he yelled. 'Quick! Get hold of the skipper. He's been hit!' He let go and Harsch fell heavily. Frenssen stretched out his arms and caught him effortlessly.

Christian threw one last glance at the scene around him. Shells were exploding all around the U-70 with a hellish, electric roar. The destroyer was racing towards the boat at full speed, the wash sweeping up in two white gleaming curls at her sharp prow. It was obvious what her skipper intended. He was going to ram the U-70! Christian flung himself down the ladder. An instant later, with the enemy asdic ping-pinging off the U-70's hull, he was taking the boat down at a crazy angle, throwing the rule book out of the window in his frantic attempt to escape destruction.

At one hundred fathoms they levelled out and immediately Christian shouted out a new course, racing against time. The depth charges would come at any moment. Slumped in the corner, holding his stomach, Harsch weakly murmured something. Christian ignored him. There was no time for discussion, they were in the centre of a great Allied convoy. In a matter of minutes the enemy would concentrate a half a dozen warships against the battered U-70. He wanted to try the trick they had used attempting to escape from the Black Sea; get under the rump of some unsuspecting enemy vessel and merge the sound of the U-70's motors with those of the other ship. It might fool the searchers, as long as he could sail the same course as the surface craft.

At the hydrophone, the nearest operator, white-faced, tense and sweating, pressed his headset tighter and called, 'They're almost on top of us now, sir. I can hear their screws loud and cl —'

The whole boat rocked violently as the first depth charge of the pattern exploded close by. The electric lighting flickered, went out, and returned. Glass tinkled. A couple of the dials burst. Further down the craft, plates buckled and there was the sudden rush of incoming water. Although he was as shocked and surprised as the greenest of his crew — you never got used to depth charges, no matter how many times you suffered their attack — Christian ordered in a calm, collected voice, 'Get those pumps working, you pumping crew. We're shipping water.'

'Come on, get the digit out of the orifice,' yelled Frenssen. 'You heard the CO. Get moving now!'

Another salvo burst close by. The U-70 lurched a good twenty metres backwards, propelled off her course. For one crazy moment, her screws thrashed the water purposelessly, the crew flew in all directions, banging into bulkheads, slithering helplessly the length of the suddenly crazily tilted deck.

'Stand by for depth charge attack!' Christian yelled desperately as the battered U-70 righted itself defiantly.

Again the boat rocked alarmingly as depth charges exploded on both sides of her. Metal whizzed through the air as valves smashed. The helmsman yelled, the compass had gone. Christian opened his mouth automatically to prevent his eardrums from being smashed, as the depth-charging continued. Dimly he took in the ashen, sweat-glazed faces of the crew, knowing full well what all of them were thinking, as their hands stretched out to touch their escape gear. He noted too the petty officer in the control room, his hand already on the flood valve to let in the compressed air they would need if they were to surface.

How long the bombing went on, Christian never could work out afterwards. It might have been a mere ten minutes, but to him it seemed ten long years, with the old boat fighting for survival every second, ploughing forward, doggedly attempting to get beneath the cover of the nearest Allied ship.

It seemed to Christian that their hunters had guessed their plan and were working full out to prevent them escaping in this manner. In all his three and a half years of active service at sea, he had never experienced a depth-charge attack of such intensity and devilish ferocity. Time and time again the U-70 was rocked and battered by the explosion of the half-ton charges, and flung metres through the water like a child's toy. The steel hull shrieked wildly under the almost unbearable pressure. Deck plates sprang upwards. The lights flickered off and on all the time.

And then the intensity of the attack began to ease off. The patterns of exploding depth charges grew fewer and fewer and Christian gave a sigh of relief, wiping the sweat from his forehead. They were getting close to the Allied troopships and the attacking destroyers were now running the risk of damaging their own ships. In a few minutes they'd stop attacking altogether and the U-70 would be safe, for the time being at least. But the destroyers would be waiting for them to emerge from their cover. There was no doubt about that.

There was the ripple of asdic running the length of the outer hull like a handful of pebbles being thrown at the metal, one last pattern of depth charges and then silence. They had done it! They were underneath the cover of one of the enemy ships!

Christian forced a grin, though he had never felt less like smiling. '*Na, Jungs,*' he croaked, 'we've done it!'

There was a murmur of relief from the ashen-faced, wild-eyed crew, and for a moment the harassed hydrophone operators rested slumped in their seats, their singlets black with sweat. Frenssen leaned weakly against the bulkhead, up to his ankles in the debris-littered water. "Bout frigging time, sir,' he said weakly. 'They really had us with our hooters in the shit that time!'

Christian was business-like again. 'Report!' he barked.

'All batteries from the electric motors leaking, sir...', 'Oxygen for two hours, sir...', 'Major plate buckling aft, sir.' Christian's face lengthened as the litany of woe continued from the petty officers at their stations, while the crew, almost at the end of their tether, listened in apathetic silence.

'Fuel?' he rasped.

The engineer officer did a rapid calculation. 'If we run on the straightest course possible, sir,' he reported, 'with a bit of luck and a tail wind, we should make it to Italy, sir.'

'Thank you.' Christian considered for a few minutes, the only sound the steady drip-drip of the water from the leaking plates and the soft moans coming from Harsch, while the men stared at him anxiously, knowing their fates lay in his hands.

Finally Christian spoke. 'For the time being,' he announced, 'we are safe down here, as long as we can keep roughly the same course as our guardian angel up there.' He laughed weakly, but no one else did. They didn't have the strength. 'But sooner or later, as you know, our oxygen will give out and we'll be forced to surface. It is my fervent hope that when we do, the storm above will still be raging. If it is, then we shall attempt to slip away and set the shortest course for the toe of Italy and Bari. With a bit of luck we'll do it, *Jungs.*' His voice lacked conviction, he knew, but it was the best he could do. All of them knew, even the youngest and most naïve greenbeak among them, that the destroyers would still be waiting for them when they surfaced — and if the storm had abated by then... Christian preferred not to follow that particular unpleasant thought to its logical conclusion.

'You are forgetting one thing, Number One.' Harsch opened his eyes slowly and spoke for the first time since he had had been wounded.

Startled, Christian turned to him, noting just how deathly pale the skipper was. He had been badly hit. 'And what is that, sir?'

'The torpedoes.'

'The torpedoes, sir?' Christian echoed somewhat stupidly.

Harsch looked up at him, eyes filled with pain, but with a flash of his old overriding arrogance. 'Are you still forgetting we have still two torpedoes left, Number One?'

Christian's mouth dropped open incredulously. Harsch was dying, he could see that. There was a pool of bright-red blood where he lay slumped. Perhaps if they had had a doctor on board, he might have been able to save the skipper, but they didn't. 'But, sir, we're fighting for our lives —'

'We are also fighting for our Fatherland,' Harsch interrupted him. 'Never forget that, Number One.'

'Yes, I know, sir. But, sir —'

'No buts, Number One. I am still the captain of the U-70 and I am the one who gives the orders here until I have no breath left to give them. When we re-surface, Number One, I expect you and every man here to obey me implicitly — or else.' Slowly, painfully, he looked around at their faces, pausing at each one and staring hard. Finally, when he had finished, he said. 'Then boys, we will attack.' His eyes closed, his head lolled to one side and he was unconscious.

Christian stared at the unconscious captain dumbfounded. He knew he should do something about tending the skipper's wound, but somehow he couldn't move. He became aware of the crew's expectant stare. He knew they wanted him to deal with Harsch once and for all. The execution of the Moses had been the final straw. He had lost their respect and loyalty for good. They wanted him to take over and take them back to the Reich. They had had enough of the horrors — and glories — of war. Just like the poor dead Moses, they simply wanted to go home!

'Let him croak, sir.' Frenssen broke the heavy silence in a hoarse whisper, as if he did not want to awaken the unconscious captain. 'He's gone crazy! We can't attack the state we're in — and in the middle of the Tommy fleet. It would be' — he groped for the right words — 'sheer suicide, sir!'

There was a mumble of agreement from the others, their wan, sunken faces, suddenly flushed a little. 'Christ Almighty,' someone exclaimed angrily, 'by the time he's done, he'll croak the lot of us, shipmates!'

Christian bit his bottom lip and said numbly, 'But he's the captain, *Jungs*. You can't have the crew deciding what should be done in a U-boat or there'd be anarchy.'

'We don't give a fuck about anarchy or anything else, sir!' Frenssen burst out enraged. 'We've done our bit, Ay, and *more* than our bit, I'm athinking! We've put our necks on the block time and time again. Well, I say, sir, that you should take over and get us back to Italianland sharpish! We've had a *frigging* enough!'

This time the crew were no longer afraid of restoring Harsch to consciousness. Their reaction was loud and vociferous. Frenssen had put their own thoughts into words.

'But that would be mutiny!' Christian objected sharply, holding up his hands for silence. 'The skipper's still alive, you know, and still in command until he decides to hand over to me, which I think is highly unlikely.'

Frenssen looked down at Harsch's unconscious body, huddled against the dripping bulkhead. 'Alive, yes, but only *just*. Besides, sir, we all know he's *meschugge*. Why else would he have poor Moses shot? Crazy as a coot! So, how can a crazy man command the U-70? No, sir,' he looked directly at Christian, challenging him to accept, 'there is only one person who is going to save the U-70 and that's *you* sir — and you frigging well know it.'

'Thank you for the vote of confidence, Frenssen, you big rogue,' Christian said slowly, weighing his words, 'but I simply can't do it. Wounded he is — gravely, I think. Crazy he may be too. But as long as *Kapitänleutnant* Harsch is still alive, he is commander of the U-70.' He turned his back on them, unable to bear the look of sudden defeat in their faded eyes any longer. It was as if he personally had condemned them to death...

CHAPTER 9

'Goddam storm,' Patton cursed as he struggled along the slick, dripping deck towards Admiral Hewitt's cabin for the ceremony. It was nearly midnight on 9 July 1943 and Harry Hewitt wanted to do the thing in proper style. But Patton thought, as yet another huge wave came pounding and pouring over the heaving bow of the SS *Monrovia*, if the storm continued, the ceremony would be pretty purposeless. 'What's the latest from Houdini, Charles?' he asked Codman, as they hauled themselves up the suddenly steeply tilting deck by means of the life-lines.

'Not so good, sir, frankly,' Colonel Codman said. 'He had the storm figured to abate by twenty-two hundred hours. But as you can see...' He shrugged and said no more.

'Let's have faith in him, Charles.' Patton ducked as a slurry of ice-cold green water came flying over the rail. 'Old Houdini has never been wrong before.'

'Yessir,' Codman said dutifully, though his voice lacked conviction.

They turned the corner and there, vaguely outlined by the little blue light, was the marine sentry guarding the admiral's day cabin. He clicked to attention when he saw the two officers and Patton acknowledged his crisp salute.

They knocked and went in.

The big bright cabin was filled with brass, both Navy and Army, and in spite of the storm, all of them were dressed in their Class A uniform, bright with decorations and badges of rank, their faces a little flushed, as if they might have been drinking somewhere or other, although the ship was officially 'dry.'

'George,' Admiral Hewitt said, stretching out his hand, as if meeting the general for the first time for many years.

Patton took the proffered hand and whispered loudly, 'Have you been having a little snort, too, Harry?' He winked. 'Naughty, naughty!'

Hewitt smiled. 'You will have your little joke, George, won't you, though.' His craggy lined face was suddenly gloomy. 'There's nothing very much to joke about at the moment with this goddamned storm.'

'I'm hoping for the best, Harry,' Patton said confidently. 'Houdini's promised good weather. The wind will moderate soon.'

'Hope you're right, George, I sure do.' With an effort, Admiral Hewitt forced a smile. 'Now General, it's up to you. The speech.'

Patton smiled back. 'I was wondering when you were going to ask, Admiral.' He cleared his throat and the chatter died away. The top brass stared at him expectantly. Patton took his time, his gaze fixed on the clock on the wall of the admiral's cabin. Patton always had an eye for the dramatic moment or the right timing. Now he wanted to ensure that the event occurred at a suitable time, worthy of recording in the history books; for Patton was determined to go down in history. He began. 'Gentlemen, it is now one minute past midnight 9/10 July 1943,' he proclaimed in his squeaky, high-pitched voice, 'and I have the honour and the privilege to activate — *the Seventh United Slates Army.*'

There was a polite outburst of applause and Patton smiled. He knew they would remember this moment aboard the wildly tossing trooper out in the Med, with battle to come on the morrow; and it was people like these high-ranking generals and admirals who would help to ensure his place in the history books. His face hardened and he gave them his 'man of destiny' look.

'Gentlemen,' he declared vigorously, 'this is the first army in history to be activated after midnight — and baptized in blood before daylight!'

'Hear, hear!' someone cried. Another admiral yelled, 'Give it to 'em, Georgie!'

Hewitt signalled hastily to his elegantly uniformed aide.

The man disappeared smartly and shouted something down the passage. Orders were barked. There was the sound of marching feet. Patton beamed as the colour party, the man bearing the new flag escorted by two immaculate riflemen, entered.

'Halt!' the officer in charge snapped.

Awkwardly the little party halted in front of an admiring Patton, for he recognized the flag, as Admiral Hewitt turned to him and said; 'George, a brand-new flag for a brand-new army!'

Patton began to weep.

But in spite of the tears, Hewitt could see the fire in Patton's eyes. He knew that in his imagination Patton was standing not on the plain steel deck of a trooper, being tossed by the waves, but on a remote peak — the peak of glory.

But the dramatics did not last very long. Suddenly there was a hurried knock on the door and a tousled-haired signals officer, cap tucked formally under his right arm as naval regulations prescribed entered at Hewitt's command. He reported excitedly, 'Sir, we've just picked up the coast of Sicily on the ship's radar!'

The news was greeted by an excited outburst of comment, but the officer was not finished yet. 'Sir, and there's something else, sir.'

'What is it, Jenkins?' Hewitt barked.

'The weather, sir,' the young man answered hurriedly, obviously wanting to get away from all these senior officers as quickly as possible.

'What about it?'

'Topside, they report that the wind is moderating. Houdini — beg pardon, sir,' the officer flushed purple at his slip, 'Lieutenant-Commander Steere has just said that within half an hour or so it will have eased away altogether.'

Patton let out a great yell and the man holding the Seventh Army's new flag almost dropped it with surprise. 'Goddammit to hell!' he cried. 'What do you say to that, gentlemen. For an old jerk like me, not bad.' He looked up at the steel ceiling as if he half-expected the Deity himself to be visible there. 'The old guy with the harp must have been listening to my prayers after all.'

The sally was greeted by a burst of laughter, the top brass obviously relieved at the change in the weather. Then Patton became business-like again. He flashed a look at his expensive wrist-watch and said; 'Gentlemen, in exactly two hours and thirty minutes we assault Adolf Hitler's Europe...'

Two miles away from the *Monrovia*, a sweating gasping Christian consulted his watch yet again. All around his men, slumped on their haunches or weakly in their seats, watched him apathetically, most of them lathered in sweat like himself and having difficulty in focusing their eyes. Christian knew why. Their oxygen supplies were running out rapidly. Air was getting scarcer by the minute. He shook his head and the hands of the wrist-watch floated vaguely into focus. It was thirty minutes after midnight. They had been below nearly two hours. Neither their electric motors nor their oxygen would last much longer. He would have to make his decision soon, while the men still had the strength to carry out his orders.

Slowly, very slowly, he turned his attention to Harsch. The skipper still lay slumped in the comer, squatting in his pool of sea-water and blood. But he was conscious again, his chest heaving rapidly as he fought for air. But his eyes were open and they were staring directly at an exhausted Christian, challenging him to make a decision.

Christian licked his parched cracked lips, his tongue feeling like dry leather. 'Sir,' he ventured.

Slowly Harsch nodded, while the crew creaked their heads round so that they could watch the interchange.

'Sir,' Christian repeated, wanting to be absolutely sure he had Harsch's attention, and, with a hand that trembled badly tried to wipe the sweat from his face. 'We're in bad shape and we are fast running out of oxygen.'

'I know,' Harsch said. His voice was weak, but under control and Christian noted dully that the skipper was no longer bleeding. 'I breathe air too, you know.'

'Of course, sir,' Christian replied.

'Can't you see, Number One? We've about had it.' Harsch spoke slowly, with many pauses, but all the same his words were determined. 'There is little more we can do. When our oxygen runs out, we can use the masks and turn off the electric motors. We might last another hour like that. But we lose the cover of the ship above us on the surface. They locate us and begin depth charging us once more.' He shrugged weakly. 'Or we surface tamely, and, knowing your attitude and that of the crew, Number One,' Harsch looked at Christian with some of his old hard determination, 'we give in.'

'You mean surrender, sir?' Christian gasped.

Harsh nodded and said, 'I do. The way you see it, there is no other alternative. If you don't surrender, the Tommies will blow us out of the water. We haven't a chance.' He paused and gasped. A thin trickle of bright red blood ran slowly down the side of his unshaven chin.

'What — what do you want us to do then, sir?' Christian asked.

Frenssen muttered something angrily, but caught himself in time. Instead he glared at Christian's pale glazed face, as if he didn't like the way the conversation was going — didn't like it one bit.

Harsch took his time, chest heaving shallowly. All around him, in the green fetid hell of the battered submarine, the exhausted young sailors, shirts black with sweat, craned forward to hear Harsch's answer to that question.

'What do I want to do?' Harsch echoed. 'I'll tell you. I want you to go out of this world like men … not like spineless cowards…' He coughed thickly. 'There is no hope for me now, I know that. There is no hope for all of us.'

At the back of the boat someone started to sob softly, as if the sailor had suddenly realized the truth of the skipper's words.

'We are doomed men, the lot of us. Why not then,' Harsch said, 'show the world what we Germans are made of … even in the moment of death? End on a note of glory?'

'You mean go into the attack, sir?' Christian said tonelessly, the note of resignation in his voice clear to all their listeners.

'Yes. Let us die bravely in battle so that the Fatherland will remember us as heroes —'

'*No!*' *Obermaat* Frenssen cried passionately, his big chest heaving with the effort. 'Rather a *live* coward than a *dead* hero!' He ignored Harsch's look of sudden burning anger and directed his gaze at an abruptly undecided Christian. 'There must be some other way out, sir? All right, so we'll have to surface soon. But there are at least four hours till first light — '

'I forbid you to talk like that, *Obermaat!*' Harsch snapped petulantly. 'I am in command here,' he coughed thickly, his ashen cheeks flushing a hectic red.

Frenssen continued to ignore him, fixing Christian with an angry burning gaze, willing the officer to find a way out of the trap they found themselves in. 'Surely there is some escape for us, sir? I don't want to surrender and spend the rest of the war in some Tommy cage, but I don't want to have my big turnip blown off in some stupid operation that won't change the course of the war one frigging little bit, either!' he declared hotly. 'You've got to take charge...'

His words faltered away to nothing and there was a collective gasp from the crew. Harsch had righted himself somehow and had drawn his pistol. Now its muzzle pointed directly at Frenssen's big heaving chest, the knuckles of Harsch's finger on the trigger white and bloodless as he took first pressure. And there was no doubt in Frenssen's mind; the skipper would shoot him down like a dog, without a moment's hesitation.

'That is enough, Frenssen!' Harsch hissed through gritted teeth. 'I will not have any more of that kind of seditious talk.One more word out of you — or any of you mutinous dogs for that matter — and I'll show you no mercy. I'll shoot — *to kill!*'

'But, sir,' Christian protested.

Harsch didn't take his mad eyes off Frenssen. Instead he said, 'I order you, Lieutenant Jungblut, to take the U-70 up.

Torpedo mate, prepare the last two tin fish... Well, go on, man, get on with it.'

'Yessir. Of course, sir.' The torpedo mate started to fiddle with his settings.

Outwardly Christian appeared mesmerized by the strange turn of events, but in reality his brain was racing. Both Harsch and Frenssen were right. They couldn't stay submerged much longer. They *had* to surface — and they had to do so soon if they were going to take advantage of the darkness. But could they — should they — attack, as Harsch wanted, in some last desperate suicidal assault on the great enemy fleet? The outcome could only be certain death for himself and the crew. My God, what was he going to do?

'Well, Number One, what is it going to be?' Harsch rasped, turning to Christian, pistol still grasped in his hand, murder in his red-rimmed eyes. 'Are you — are you going to take her up?'

Christian let his shoulders slump, as if in defeat. He wiped the sweat from his forehead and said wearily, 'Yes, sir ... I'm going to take her up.'

Frenssen moaned and took a step forward as if he might rush the dying captain.

Hastily Christian raised his hand to stop him and began issuing his orders. Slowly the battered U-70 started to rise for the very last time.

CHAPTER 10

A last hiss of escaping compressed air, the slither of water running rapidly from the hull, the whoosh and plop of the conning tower emerging from the sea and they had surfaced.

Still in a kind of a trance, though his brain was working at a frantic rate, Christian supported the skipper as he fought his way up the dripping ladder to the bridge, while behind them Frenssen still mumbled in impotent rage. The hatch swung open. The interior of the U-70 was flooded with the clean sea air and those who were staying down below gasped with relief, sucking in great mouthfuls of it.

Christian clambered out onto the bridge and did his customary three hundred and sixty degree survey. All around them in the gentle darkness were the silhouettes of the troopers, some of them already halted, as the crew worked on releasing the assault barges. For to port, clearly defined, was the dark smudge of Sicily, with the red pimple of the volcano, Mount Etna, emitting pinkish smoke. He told himself that it would not be too long before the invasion force started landing. Soon the fighting would commence. Weakly he raised his glasses and surveyed the ships all around him, as the U-70 wallowed low in the water, her diesels still switched off. Even in the midst of his present confusion, Christian had remembered to order the engineer not to turn them on. He wanted the U-70 to remain noiseless so that she wouldn't be detected until the very last moment.

'Look at that one, Number One,' Harsch said, voice very faint. 'You see that mass of radio masts. They can mean only one thing.'

'A command ship, sir,' Christian agreed, focusing his glasses on the big trooper some fifteen hundred metres away, her speed decreasing noticeably as she approached the already stationary transports preparing to unload the assault infantry. He identified the big ship for Harsh. 'A Delta class merchantman. Most of them were taken over by the Ami navy last year.'

Harsh didn't seem to hear. Instead he said, 'It is our obvious target, Number One. Take her out — cost what it may — and we can die happily, knowing that we have done something vitally important for Folk, Fatherland and Führer.' He trotted out the old formula with something of his old dash.

At his side Christian cringed. That word '*die*' had cut into his consciousness like a sharp knife. Suddenly he knew he didn't want to die even for 'Folk, Fatherland and Führer'. He wanted to live; he was too young to die. All of them were. 'But once we start up the engines to attack they'll be on to us like a shot,' he protested. 'I think I can see a way out for us — a chance of escaping from this mess safely. You see those troopers which are going to unload the in —'

'We attack, Number One,' Harsh interrupted him brutally. 'There will be no discussion of the matter.' He drew the pistol from his belt and placed it significantly on the bridge in front of him.

Miserably Christian set about preparing for the attack. He ordered both diesels started at once and raised to full speed. There was no time to warm them up. The generators were started too to recharge the electric batteries. Within minutes, he knew, they would be making enough noise on the enemy asdic to attract every destroyer in the whole damned Mediterranean into the attack. But even though he seemed resigned to his fate, he tried a last trick to put off the enemy.

Hurriedly he ordered a dozen gas-filled balloons to be released into the now moderate wind. They would appear as submarines on the enemy's radar and the Tommies would be amazed, he hoped, to find that there was not *one* U-boat in the area, but over a *dozen*! The thin wires hanging from each balloon acted as a submarine decoy.

Harsch did not appear to notice the decoys. His whole being, what was left of his dying strength, was concentrated exclusively on the big Delta class merchantman. As the U-70 moved into the attack, a look of what Christian could only describe to himself as sexual greed appeared on his face. He wanted that ship, as a man might lust for a woman in bed. The torpedoes he would soon fire would enter the ship like an excited, passionate man entering a woman. Angry with himself, Christian shook his head to drive away the crazy fanciful imagery. He had to concentrate on the harsh realities of the U-70's position. At any moment now, even if the enemy radar were temporarily fooled, a look-out on one of the ships all around them would spot the U-70 and then all hell would be let loose. *God Almighty, what in three devils' name was he going to do?*

General Patton dressed with care. As H-Hour approached he began to put on the uniform laid out for him in the cabin by his servant. First came the silk underwear, the perfectly pressed OD woollen shirt, the tight-fitting custom-made breeches that marked him as a cavalryman. The gleaming riding boots followed and then he was staring in the mirror as he knotted his tie firmly, tucking it in beneath the second button, as regulations prescribed — and Patton was a stickler for regulations. Woe betide the soldier in his army who went into combat without a tie!

He adorned his trim six feet two inches frame with a pair of outsize binoculars. His single pistol followed, placed in an open holster, ready for action, as if he might have to shoot his way ashore. Finally he placed his gleaming helmet, with its three outsize stars on the front, on his grizzled head and stared at himself in the mirror, posing with his 'War Face Number One', liking what he saw there. Most American generals, he told himself proudly, looked like seedy, middle-aged second-hand car salesmen running to fat. He looked like a real soldier, a fighting man.

He reached out for one of his usual huge expensive cigars, but before he could light it, there was an urgent knocking on his door. 'Come in,' he barked, and even as he did so, an excited flushed Codman was stumbling, crying in alarm, 'Message from Admiral Hewitt, sir! Enemy subs, sir. Subs everywhere. They've had half a dozen sightings on the radar in the last ten minutes.' Patton's confident 'War Face Number One' disappeared to be replaced by one of terrible alarm. 'A whole wolf-pack must have slipped through the escorts, sir!... It's terrible.'

'*Goddammit it to hell*!' Patton roared. 'Why the frig has this got to happen to me — just frigging now!' He slammed the lacquered helmet to the bunk in a fit of pique. 'Christ Almighty, if those subs get in among the transports when they start discharging the men, there'll be all hell to pay!' He controlled his rage with difficulty and then, picking up his helmet, he cried, as the klaxons started to shrill their warning through the *Monrovia*, 'Come on, Codman, let's root out the staff. I want anybody who can see up on the deck. The more look-outs we have, the goddam better. Wait a minute.' He flung open the door of the little steel cupboard that contained his personal gear and brought out a sub-machine-gun.

Codman gaped. 'But what's that for?'

'What do you frigging think, Charles?' Patton snorted. 'If I see any of the U-boat men on the surface, I'm gonna shoot the German ass off'n 'em! Now come on. Let's move!'

Five minutes later Patton and his staff officers were spread out over the upper deck of the *Monrovia*, viewing the total confusion and panic which reigned everywhere as the great invasion fleet slowed down and crawled at a snail's pace into the invasion anchorage.

On all sides flares — green, red, silver — shot into the night sky. At regular intervals the destroyers, racing back and forth urgently, fired star shells, turning night into day, flooding the heavens with cold silver light, while the look-outs peered through their binoculars in a vain attempt to spot one of the U-boat wolf-pack.

The enemy coastal batteries were beginning to react. All along the coast there were sudden flashes of cherry-red light like the glare from some enormous blast furnace and huge 15 inch shells tore the night apart with a great ripping sound as they plummeted down into the sea with a flurry of wild white water.

'Christ on a frigging crutch!' Patton cursed, chewing his big cigar from one side of his thin lips to the other, nervously fingering his tommy-gun. 'What a goddam mess! If we don't watch it, they're gonna clobber us.' He swung round on an equally anxious Admiral Hewitt. 'Harry, what's wrong with your gunners? Or are they having a goddam tea break — like those goddam Brits? Why aren't they giving answering fire, eh?'

'We were waiting for targets, George.' Hewitt tried to appease Patton who could see his dreams of glory vanishing rapidly if something drastic wasn't done soon.

'Sure as hell the frigging Italians won't invite you to frigging shell them,' Patton snarled.

'You know what I mean, George. We want trained observers ashore first to direct our fire accurately. It's no use popping off and wasting ammunition. That will serve no good purpose —' He stopped short, for he could see in the glowing darkness of yet another star shell that the general was not listening. Instead he was staring intently out to sea off the port quarter. 'What is it, George?' he snapped.

'I don't know for sure. My eyes aren't what they used to be,' Patton said, voice calm and controlled now, as it always was when he faced up to real danger. 'But I'm sure there's something out there … something low in the water. Let me show you where, Harry.' He raised the tommy-gun, tucked the butt neatly into his right shoulder and, without appearing to sight the weapon pressed the trigger. The tommy-gun erupted violently. White tracer zipped lethally across the dark heaving surface of the sea only to fall harmlessly into the water a couple of hundred yards away. 'Goddammit to hell,' Patton cursed furiously. 'The thing has no range! It's as frigging good to me — *as a pecker'd be for the frigging Pope in Rome!*'

The sudden burst of machine-gun fire snapped Christian out of the spell he had been under ever since Harsch had taken over. 'They've spotted us, skipper!' he cried urgently. 'Did you see that tracer — it was definitely aimed at us.'

'It's too late to worry about that now, Number One,' Harsch said thickly and bent to the voice tube. 'Stand by one and two,' he rasped, his breathing harsh and shallow.

'Standing by,' the disembodied voice of the torpedo mate came floating up the tube.

'For chrissake, sir!' Christian yelled, as a star shell exploded directly above them bathing the bridge in its cold merciless silver light. '*Let's make a run —*'

His words were drowned by a thunderous explosion that engulfed the whole bridge. A blinding blue flame seared along the deck. Controls shattered. Glass and metal splinters howled through the air, pinging off the superstructure. For a moment the deck glowed a dull scarlet. The boat reeled and heeled. With a scream of despair, one of the look-outs went over the side, to disappear in the suddenly boiling water.

'*Fire!*' Harsch screamed, hands fluttering to his ruined face, fingers already covered in blood. 'Fire one and two —'

As another shell hurtled towards them, the torpedo man cried desperately from below. 'They're locked, sir. That shell locked the ports. I can't fire!'

'Get ready to man the gun!' Harsch shrieked. 'We're going to take her down with us.' He laughed suddenly. It was an eerie crazy sound that made the hairs stand erect at the back of Christian's neck. 'We'll go down together ... *ha ha!*'

'Let me take over, sir,' Christian pleaded, as another shell slammed into the U-70, sending her periscope and radio tumbling to the deck in an angry shower of blue and red sparks.

Harsch pushed him away. 'Don't you dare touch me! Keep away,' he snarled thickly. For some reason he couldn't fathom his world had become a red wet darkness. He tried to raise his right arm to wipe his eyes. He couldn't. He no longer had a right arm.

'*Sir?*'

Harsch backed away, dying on his feet, blinded, but still in these last moments of his unhappy life craving glory. 'Where's the gun crew?' he choked, blood spilling from his mouth. 'Gun crew —'

Another shell slammed into the U-70. Oil started to spurt from her ruined plates and as the submarine began to settle lower in the water, her deck a shambles of broken superstructure and tangled wires. Frenssen shouted from below. 'Sir, we're badly hit. We won't survive much longer. She's shipping a devil of a lot of water, the poor old bitch.'

'All right, all right, Frenssen, I read you,' Christian yelled back angrily, mind in a turmoil, the crippled U-boat reeling again under the impact of a shell. 'See if you can stick a pudding into the main hole... For chrissake, give me thirty minutes and we'll do it.'

'Yessir.' There was sudden hope in Frenssen's voice. 'I'll fix the best frigging pudding the U-boat Arm has ever seen.' He vanished from sight, shouting swift orders as he went.

Hurriedly Christian turned back to the skipper, whose face was a mess of blood and pulped flesh, a purple suppurating hole where his right eye had been. He was dying on his feet, Christian could see that in the harsh merciless silver light of the star shells. It could be only a matter of moments. Yet he refused to go down. He was fighting off death to the very last. Despite the fact that he detested Harsch, had even hated him at times, now Christian could not but admire his dying courage. 'Skipper,' he said gently, 'we're sinking. Do you understand, sir? *We're sinking!*'

'Engage them with the deck gun, Number One,' Harsch croaked crazily, spitting out blood as he spoke. 'We've got to do it. Vital to the success ... war effort ... Germany expects us...'

'Sir,' Christian repeated, as from below began the sound of urgent hammering as Frenssen and his assistants worked frantically on the 'pudding', 'the U-70 is sinking. Can't you understand that?' He simply couldn't be angry with Harsch, in spite of the urgency of the situation. 'Our task now is to save the men ... that's all that is important, sir.'

'So little time left, Number One,' Harsch mumbled crazily, his knees beginning to sag beneath him at last. 'So little time.'

Christian thrust out a hand to support him and this time the captain did not push him away. Instead he submitted gratefully to the younger officer's grasp, as if he needed the comforting warmth of another human body. A strange rasping sound was coming from his gaping blood-filled mouth and Christian guessed his lungs were filling up. He was drowning in his own blood.

Another shell shrieked home. A great spinning slab of metal from the conning tower sailed in a crazy cartwheel through the air. One of the look-outs threw up his arms and pitched face-forward over the side. A searchlight stabbed the glowing gloom and circled the dying boat. Christian told himself they had only minutes to attempt an escape.

'I did sink the *Stalin*,' Harsch whispered. His lips trembled and the mouth moved and Christian cradled his head closer so that he could hear. 'Didn't I, Number One?'

'Yes, skipper, you did.'

Harsch gave a sigh, as if of relief. 'Jungblut,' he croaked.

'Sir?'

'Break ... break...' Blood was pouring from his gaping mouth. 'Break off the action,' he choked. Abruptly, startlingly, his head fell to one side, the light vanished from his eyes at last. *Kapitänleutnant* Otto Harsch, the glory-hunter, was dead.

Gently Christian lowered him to the debris-littered deck and then he shouted frantically into the tube. '*Reverse both! Reverse both! Dalli, dalli...*'

CHAPTER 11

The battered boat lurched under a shattering blow, which sounded like a gigantic club thrashing sheet of iron. 'Goddammit!' Christian cried in despair, as Frenssen worked desperately to squeeze the 'pudding', a roll of canvas filled with packing, into the hole to caulk it. 'Won't the swine ever let up?'

The interior of the U-70 was an unspeakable shambles. Below deck was a mess of smashed and twisted metal; the water was waist deep with a hundred and one personal items bobbing up and down in it. The pumps worked frantically at lowering its level. Not only was the hard-pressed boat under constant attack on the surface, but she was gradually sinking at the same time. If Frenssen couldn't get the 'pudding' in soon and stop the inrush of sea-water, there wouldn't be a hope in hell of carrying out his plan, Christian told himself.

Knowing that if anyone was going to do it, it would be Frenssen, he left him and his men to do it and splashed his way back to the conning tower, its exterior now a mass of ugly steel scars, where the shells had struck it. He stepped over the body of one of the bridge crew sprawled out among the litter, trying to avoid looking at it. The rating was minus his head, which now rested in the corner, complete with helmet, looking at him with wide-open eyes. He peeped over the side.

The nearest enemy destroyer was just under a kilometre away, racing towards them at full tilt, its forward turrets spitting fire that sent huge gouts of water plummeting upwards in the battered submarine's wake. Desperately Christian flung a glance to the transports, loading troops into the assault barges closer to the shore. They were about a kilometre away too. He did a quick calculation. The destroyer, he estimated, could continue firing at the U-70 without hitting its own troops for another ten minutes. If he could get the U-70 among the assault barges, he would be safe. If only he could coax some more speed out of the sinking boat!

Again a salvo from their pursuer's guns struck the sea only a hundred metres away from the U-70 and the bridge was deluged by a mass of sea-water. Christian clung on grimly as the bridge swayed and the helmeted head rolled back and forth like an abandoned football. In another minute the destroyer would have its guns zeroed in and the U-70 would not escape a second time. Impatiently he hammered his fist against the bulkhead and cried out loud, 'Come on, damn you, you son of a bitch. *Move faster!*'

Stubbornly, the U-70 refused, and the destroyer came ever closer. Desperately, Christian cupped his hands to his mouth and yelled below. 'Torpedo Mate, any luck with those damned tubes?'

A moment later his reply came floating back — and it was negative. There was no hope of turning about and facing up to the destroyer. Christian cursed and cast around frantically for some way out of the trap. A salvo ripped the sky apart above his head and plummeted into the sea just to their front. The bow heaved and disappeared for an instant under several tons of water. They had been well and truly straddled. The next salvo would land directly on the U-70.

Suddenly the U-70 gave a lurch. There was a muffled sound of cheering from below. Christian knew at once that Frenssen had fitted the 'pudding' as the U-70 started to pick up speed. He had stopped the water coming in and holding the submarine back. In that very same instant the next salvo from the pursuing destroyer came hurtling down — to land fifty metres *behind* the U-70. They had picked up those extra three knots just in damned time. Grimly he held on as the U-70 reeled and heeled yet again. But even as he rejoiced, Christian knew they couldn't survive much longer.

'Look-out,' he cried as the U-70 righted herself, 'what depth have you got?'

Expertly the look-out dropped his lead. Straining his eyes in the gloom and feeling the knotted line, he answered, 'Very shallow, sir… Seven fathoms, sir!'

Christian's mind raced. 'Good. Look-out, sing out at every fathom!'

'Sir!'

'Frenssen,' he cried into the interior of the boat, 'get the men up topside. Everybody in his life-belt and rescue gear. We're going to abandon ship. And Frenssen,' he added as a hasty afterthought, 'see everybody is armed. Knives, clubs, bayonets — anything easy to handle!'

'But sir —'

'No buts, you big horned ox. We've haven't time. At the double now!'

The men began to come up on deck clad in their life-jackets and bearing the wounded. The look-out continued singing out the depth, while all the time, with frightening, monotonous regularity, their pursuer pounded the battered old boat, submitting the U-70 to tremendous, gruelling punishment. Christian ordered the floats and dinghies to be readied for pushing over the side at a moment's notice. The depth grew progressively shallower. '*Five fathoms … four fathoms…*' the sweating anxious look-out flung his lead and yelled above the crump and roar of the gunfire '… *three fathoms…*'

'What's the drill, sir?' Frenssen shouted. He cradled a machine-pistol in his brawny arms, and the dull brass of the 'Hamburg Equalizer' gleamed on his right fist.

Christian, eyes wild and excited, cupped his hands about his mouth and yelled above the awesome racket, 'We've no hope of escaping now in the U-70. Let's use the old boat as a decoy, Frenssen —'

'*Decoy*, sir?'

'Yes. Let that damned destroyer think he's got us when we run aground, which will be soon —' He staggered suddenly, as the U-70's keel grazed some sandbank or other and she heeled to port momentarily. 'But we won't be aboard to be shot — or shoved into the bag.'

'But where will we frigging well be, sir?' Frenssen bellowed frantically.

'Where?' Christian echoed joyfully, his wild plan now clear in his mind. 'Look over there ... those landing barges —'

'Great crap on the Christmas tree!' Frenssen exploded. 'You can't mean it!'

'I damn well do, Frenssen! Now let's get those dinghies over the side for a start.'

Frenssen let out a whoop of joy, his relief all too obvious. He grasped the nearest dinghy and tossed it into the sea as if it were a toy. Immediately the others followed his example, ignoring the shrapnel, fist-sized, glowing, razor-sharp shell fragments scything through the air, knowing instinctively that Lieutenant Jungblut had some scheme to save them.

It was about then that the bows of the battered old U-70 simply heaved out of the water without any particular noise. '*Two and a half fathoms, sir!*' the look-out sang out. The submarine's screws began to purposelessly thrash the water at her stern into a milky froth.

Christian didn't hesitate. 'Frenssen, take charge!' he yelled above the crazy racket. 'Abandon ship —' He ducked as a shell shrieked above his head and showered down into the sea fifty metres to their front. 'Come on, abandon ship! *Los … los*!'

The men needed no urging. They were over the side in flash, treading water or clambering awkwardly into the dinghies, which were virtually motionless in the shallow water. The noise they made was drowned by the roar of the screws and the clatter of winches over at the stationary troopships unloading the assault force into barges.

Christian waited tensely until Frenssen yelled from the water, 'We're all off, sir.'

'Good, Frenssen,' he cried back, 'I'm coming —' He stopped short, suddenly blinded as the destroyer's searchlight pinned him in the conning tower in its harsh white light. He caught a glimpse of the ghastly headless sailor and Harsch

slumped pathetically in the pool of his own blood. In a moment, he knew, the Amis would flash their light the length of the trapped submarine and see the crew abandoning it. He knew too what would happen then. They would open up with their machine-guns on the fleeing men. Carried away by the crazed, unreasoning bloodlust of battle, they would toss all mercy to the winds. It would be a massacre. He had to put that damned light out.

'Sir,' Frenssen called from the water, 'let's go!… Come on sir!'

Christian didn't answer. Instead he gripped the turret machine-gun in both hands, praying as he had never prayed before that he wouldn't miss, and sighted along the length of that silver beam. He calmed himself, trying to control his breathing. Gently, ever so gently, he pressed the trigger. The gun erupted in his hands. Tracer shot lethally down the beam.

He held on for grim life as the gun chattered and snarled, the gleaming yellow cartridge cases flying to the side, smoking and red hot.

There was the muted tinkling of glass. Someone screamed shrilly. With startled suddenness, the searchlight went out and he was blinded again. Somehow or other he found his way down to the hull; then he was in the water with Frenssen gripping him with a hand like a small steam shovel and they were swimming and paddling their way to the unsuspecting *Amis*...

'George,' Admiral Hewitt declared firmly, 'I outrank you, as you well know. So I am giving you an official order. If you disobey it, I can have you court-martialled. So let's have that quite clear once and for all. You *cannot go* ashore with the first assault wave!'

Sullenly Patton looked at the files of heavily armed men shuffling across the deck of the *Monrovia* in a curious crocodile, each man with his serial number chalked on his helmet and each one holding his hand on the shoulder of the man in front of him. When the embarkation officers with their checkboards yelled an order, each serial went over the side and clambered down the nets into the waiting barges bobbing up and down dangerously below. Every now and again someone screamed out with fear as he lost his grip on the wet rope and fell into the sea. Fortunately, as yet, no one had fallen between the hulls of the barges and the *Monrovia* to be crushed to bloody pulp there. But a stern Admiral Hewitt knew that such tragic accidents happened all the time in operations of this kind, especially during the hours of darkness, and he was not going to let Patton risk his life.

'Well, Harry,' Patton demanded, 'when in Sam Hill's name *are* you going to let me go ashore?'

'As soon as the beach is consolidated and I feel it is safe, George,' Hewitt answered, noting the cherry-red flashes on the horizon which indicated the enemy was now beginning to fire at the invasion fleet. 'Looks like incoming mail.' He crouched a little as the sound of the enemy shells became plain.

'My boys'll go through the Italians like shit through a goose,' Patton boasted confidently. 'A couple of hours and they will have that beach all nice and snug and tied up. Hell, Harry, they'll be holding concert parties there by midnight!'

Hewitt smiled in spite of his worries. 'All right, George. Let's say you land — *with an escort* — at daybreak. How's that suit you, old friend?'

Patton mumbled, but gave in in the end, saying, 'But why the goddam escort, Harry?' He slapped his pistol butt. 'I can look after myself. Did I ever tell you how I shot it out with four Mexicans back in 'sixteen?'

'Yes, George, you did,' Hewitt said firmly. 'Only last time it was *two* Mexicans.' He grinned and Patton did the same. 'Come on, let's see what's going on over there.' He indicated the scarlet stabs of fire to port. 'Last word was that an escort destroyer has forced a German sub to the surface out to port. Now it's probably going in for the kill.'

'Yeah,' Patton agreed, 'let's do that. Let's do *anything* to pass the time. This suspense is sure killing me.'

Together the two senior officers pushed their way through the silent, apprehensive files of assault infantry, their fear of what was to come all too apparent...

Christian stopped swimming and trod water momentarily, as yet another full salvo from the destroyer's guns smashed into the wreck of the U-70, some five hundred metres behind them. It was followed an instant later by great slashes of cherry-red flame, which outlined the dying submarine a stark black, and the tearing, rending, ear-splitting sound of metal being ripped apart. Christian frowned, as the bow of the U-70 reared into the burning sky like the steeple of a steel church. She had been a good boat and it was painful to see her go like this, trapped and shot to pieces without any means of protecting herself. It was like having one's home ruthlessly destroyed before one's eyes.

A hiss. A frantic slithering. The whole length of the hull was wreathed in angry blue sparks. The sea-water rushing into her shattered interior had reached the electric batteries. The water boiled a hysterical wild white and then suddenly, startlingly, she slid back from the shallow water, as if she possessed life of her own and was not going to allow herself to be shot to pieces on the reef. A moment later she had vanished, taking the dead *Kapitänleutnant* Harsch with her.

Frenssen touched his shoulder softly. 'Come on, sir,' he said with unusual gentleness. 'I know how you feel. But we've got to put the lads first. Time's running out.'

Christian pulled himself together rapidly. 'Of course, you're right, you big rogue. The boat's gone, but the *Jungs* aren't. We've got to get home to the Reich. Let's go. You see that barge to the right to the trooper.' He indicated the dark shape of one of the blunt-nosed barges bobbing up and down to the rear of the bigger shape. 'That's the one.'

Frenssen grinned in the darkness. 'The *Amis* won't know what's hit them,' he chortled and momentarily his terrible 'Hamburg Equalizer' gleamed as he raised his fist threateningly;

and then they were off again, swimming or paddling along in their dinghies towards the unsuspecting Americans. Behind them the triumphant destroyer sounded its ship's whistle to celebrate its victory over the U-70.

Gingerly, very gingerly, Christian reached up to grasp one of the wet dripping cargo nets hanging over the side of the barge they had selected. It was obvious that the craft was not fully loaded, for it was bobbing up and down merrily, high in the water. His hand took hold and he glanced to left and right at the pale blobs of faces that surrounded him. He nodded slowly. They nodded back. They were all ready to go. Taking a deep breath, Christian began to climb. The others followed. Like thieves in the night, they commenced this last desperate venture. Behind them the destroyer had ceased its triumphant hooting and was circling the area where the U-70 had gone down, its searchlights flashing off the water. It was obvious the Americans were looking for survivors. In spite of his tension and apprehension, Christian grinned to himself. Little did they know that the survivors of the U-70 were about to commit what used to be called 'an act of piracy on the high seas'.

It was damnably difficult to climb when the barge was bobbing and ducking all the time in the waves. They all paused when they reached the top of the side, waiting for Christian's final orders. Christian cocked his head to one side and listened hard. Above him he could hear voices. He tried to count the individual speakers, to note their position in the craft, to ascertain whether they outnumbered the survivors of the U-70. But it was impossible. The noise of waves slapping against the craft made it too difficult. He nodded to Frenssen. The latter nodded back. Silently Christian began to count off to three. '*THREE!*' he cried and then they were swinging themselves over the top into the confused, surprised throng of heavily armed American soldiers, each one weighed down like a pack animal under his equipment.

A heavy-set American loomed up directly in front of Christian. He lashed out with his fist and yelped with pain as his fist struck a helmet or some other piece of the man's equipment. Frenssen was at his side immediately. The 'Hamburg Equalizer' sent the American reeling back into the barge spitting out teeth, blood spurting from his shattered nose.

That first blow worked as a signal and a wild melée broke out in the bowels of the craft. Christian fought his way through the suddenly cursing, struggling men, trying desperately to reach the tiny bridge of the craft. In a few moments, he knew, they would become aware up above on the troop-ship of what was going on in the barge. He must ensure they were moving by that time. A seaman tried to bar his way. Christian didn't hesitate. He lashed out with his foot. The American shrieked hysterically and went down gasping, hands clasping his injured crotch. Christian sprang over his writhing body and ran on.

He clattered up the iron ladder. A bullet howled off the hull to his right in a spurt of angry red sparks. He looked up. A man was leaning over the bridge, a revolver in his hand. Christian fired, without aiming. The man disappeared from sight, revolver clattering to the deck from suddenly nerveless fingers. Christian gasped and pushed on. From far up above high on the steel wall of the trooper there came shouts of alarm, queries, curses. Christian paid no heed to them. He must get to the tiller — *he must?*

'Hey, you!' Christian spun round. A fat ugly seaman stood there, tommy-gun held menacingly in his big hands.

Christian didn't give him a chance to bring the weapon up to the firing position. He dived forward. The fat American was caught completely off guard. He cursed as Christian's hard shoulder slammed into his fat gut. They went down in a confused heap, the tommy-gun falling to the deck, as the American instinctively wrapped his arms around Christian and squeezed hard.

Stars exploded in front of Christian's eyes. The American's grip was like iron. The man was squeezing the air out of his lungs at a tremendous rate. He'd black out in a minute. He chopped the side of his right hand against the American's exposed Adam's apple. He screamed, mouth suddenly flooded with his own vomit. The grip relaxed at once. Christian didn't give him a chance to recover. He clubbed his fist and smashed it down cruelly on the writhing man's upturned face. Something splintered. Hot blood bathed his hand. The man's head fell limply to one side and then Christian was up, pelting to the little control panel.

With fingers that trembled violently, he felt the various switches and buttons, finding the right ones more by good luck than good judgement. Below his men were still battling it out with the soldiers in a wild confused melée and he could hear Frenssen in the thick of it roaring over and over again, 'Come on, you sons-of-whores, do you frigging well want to live forever?' And once again the 'Hamburg Equalizer' would flash.

Then Christian found it, the starter button for the ungainly craft's engine. Hurriedly he pressed it. Nothing, save a banshee-like low dirge. He cursed furiously. Already he could see high above the dark shapes of other Americans going over the side. A few minutes more and all would be lost. He hit the button again, yelling. 'Frenssen... Frenssen — disengage and drag up the sea anchor!'

'Ay, ay, sir!' Frenssen yelled back cheerfully, 'Just a mo. Bit of unfinished business. *Be with you in second, zero, nothing seconds!*' he gave a mighty grunt and someone in the confused, cursing, swearing, killing throng shrieked with pain.

Desperately he pressed the button again. Someone halfway down the rope netting fired a pistol at him. The scarlet flame stabbed the darkness and a slug howled off the bulkhead just to his right. Christian cursed again as a splinter ripped into his side. Suddenly his shirt was wet with blood.

With all his strength, he jabbed his thumb into the starter button, as the man with the pistol balanced himself precariously on the swaying rope netting and prepared to fire again. Christian broke out in a hot sweat. It was now or never! He gritted his teeth together in his anger and anguish, willing the damned thing to start and bear them away to safety. From below there came the sounds of Frenssen heaving the sea anchor over the side.

Then it came. The whine turned into a high-pitched roar. The roar grew ever louder. The whole of the ugly craft shook and trembled violently. Abruptly the night air was filled with the cloying stink of engine fumes.

'*Come on … come on!*' Christian cried, flashing another look upwards. In the same instant that the man with the pistol fired, the engine burst into full pulsating, joyous life.

Christian let out a whoop of joy. He grabbed the controls. Immediately the craft began to move away. The man with the pistol screamed shrilly as the net was jerked away beneath him. He fell shrieking, arms flailing wildly. He hit the deck like a sack of wet cement bounced and lay still. As the net was ripped away by the departing barge, man after man fell from the height, splashing into the boiling water.

Then they were chugging away merrily at three knots, the men, both German and American, crouched together behind the protection of the steel plating as the slugs howled and whined off the hull. And far above an exasperated, scarlet-faced General Patton was blasting off great angry bursts with his tommy-gun, crying, 'Goddammit to hell... They've stolen my boat — *and the frigging invasion hasn't even frigging well started yet. GODDAMMIT TO HELL!*'

ENVOI

Dawn!

It was 10 July 1943. Already the yellow ball of the sun was peeping up beyond Mount Etna, tinging the sky a soft burnished gold. The night chill was vanishing rapidly. Lying among the rocks of the high ground above the invasion beach at Gela, the damp survivors of the U-70 could feel a new warmth creeping into their bodies. Lazily they puffed at the rich-tasting Lucky Strikes or Camels or crunched on the sickly sweet Hershey bars they had taken from their prisoners before they had kicked the frightened *Amis* out of the stolen barge into the shallows.

Now they waited for *Leutnant* Jungblut's next move. He had saved them from death at sea. Now, they knew, he would take them home safely. Below, the Italian defenders of the coast were moving back in ragged groups, some of them already without weapons, a few minus even their helmets, but all obviously completely demoralized by the American naval bombardment and the beach assault.

Even to the sailors, unversed in land warfare, it was clear that the Italian Army in Sicily was in full retreat. Now it would be up to the handful of German units on the island to attempt to stop the *Amis*. From close by in the interior, a weary but relieved Christian could already hear the rusty squeak and clatter of tanks. The *Wehrmacht* was bringing up the panzers in an attempt to stop the enemy from moving inland.

Another shell shrieked overhead with a roar like an express train racing through some empty station at full speed. Hastily Christian focused his binoculars. The shell smacked down at the water's edge, already littered with beached landing craft and a couple of amphibious vehicles shattered by the mines the Italians had laid. A great black mushroom of smoke shot up into the

perfect dawn sky, together with a jeep, which disintegrated in the process.

'One less,' Frenssen grunted.

Christian nodded and said nothing. He was too busy trying to regain his strength for the next move.

Down below still more landing barges kept chugging in to deposit ever more American soldiers on the shores of Europe. Most of them were tall gangling men in what looked like new uniforms, their helmets and equipment gleaming brightly as if they had just been issued from the quartermaster's stores.

'Cardboard men, Christmas tree soldiers,' Frenssen said scornfully and spat into the dunes contemptuously. He took another swig from the bottle of bourbon he had looted from the landing barge before they had abandoned it. 'Couldn't fight their way out of a paper bag, a frigging *wet* paper bag!'

Christian wasn't so convinced. There were so many of them pouring ashore at Gela. Thousands upon thousands of them, and their invasion fleet moved about its business with disdainful impunity, as if the *Luftwaffe* and the *Kriegsmarine* simply did not exist. So far the Allied invasion of the mainland of Europe had been a complete walk-over.

At the southern end of the invasion beach there was a sudden flurry of movement, as yet another landing barge began to disgorge what looked like cameramen or photographers in uniform (the Americans now wading ashore were all carrying cine-cameras and the like). Hurriedly they were ushered to where a bunch of black soldiers were busy raking the sand clean and straight as if their very lives depended upon it.

Almost immediately another barge followed them in. It ground to a halt in the shallows. As the big ramp came splashing and clattering down, well-fed older soldiers carrying musical instruments began to wade ashore, their highly polished brass instruments gleaming in the rays of the rising sun.

Frenssen's mouth flopped open stupidly, the bottle poised untouched near his lips. 'Holy strawsack,' he gasped, 'what the frig are *they* doing here? Do you think, sir, they're gonna frigging well serenade the troops or something? Shit on the shingle, what kind of an army is that bunch o' pregnant penguins anyhow?' He took a swift, hefty swig of the bourbon, as if he suddenly needed a stiff drink badly. 'What in hell's name is going on, sir?'

The answer to Frenssen's question was supplied almost immediately. For now a third barge, gleaming and freshly painted, unlike the rest, was grinding to a stop in the shallows. Even before it had done so, heavily equipped staff officers, each one carrying a tommy-gun, were dropping into the sea and taking up an aggressive defensive stance.

Hastily Christian focused his glasses upon them. In the same instant that the band struck up smartly and the cameras started to whir, a tall elegantly uniformed officer dropped over the side of the barge. Up to his knees in the surf, carbine hanging loosely from his shoulder, he raised his own camera to his face beneath the gleaming lacquered helmet and began to shoot the memorable scene, *backing* all the way to the shores of Sicily.

'Do you see that, sir?' Frenssen breathed shakily. '*Gross Kacke am Christbaum* ... now I've seen everything!'

But *Obermaat* Frenssen definitely had not seen everything — yet. For now the elegantly clad officer waded back towards the barge. He turned and repeated the landing for the benefit of the cameramen, this time splashing his way aggressively through the surf, *facing* the whirring cameras.

For a few fleeting moments Christian caught a glimpse through his binoculars of the stern wilful face beneath the big helmet with its outsize stars and was impressed by what he saw. For all his posing, this was a man of destiny, he could see that. All that posturing, the camera teams, the brass band, which seemed to be turning the enemy invasion of *Festung Europa* into something akin to a stage farce, could not hide the fact that a great and powerful army had just landed, led by a man who — to judge from the look on his determined, war-like face — would demand and *win* victory.

Suddenly, for no reason that he could fathom then or later, Christian's mind flashed to Harsch the day he had sunk the *Stalin*. In a moment of total recall, he saw the dead skipper's flushed excited face in front of his mind's eye again and heard him exclaim once more in that instant of triumph, '*We've done it. We've done it*, Jungs. *This time I've cured my throatache for good!*'

Now throatache-cured-for-good Harsch lay at the bottom of the Mediterranean, together with the headless rating, in the poor old U-70. To what purpose? What had it all been about? It had not changed the course of the war — not one single iota. All it had meant was the death of more young men.

Somehow Frenssen seemed to sense what was going through Christian's mind, for he took one last slug at the bottle and then tossed it away carelessly into the dunes, saying; 'Cardboard soldiers or not, sir. I think it's about time we was hoofing it. The *Amis'll* be *up* here soon. Somehow I don't think our stubble-hoppers' — he indicated the dark shapes of the German Mark IV tanks rattling down the track towards the beach to challenge the invaders — 'are gonna stop that lot for very long.'

Christian nodded silently and rose to his feet. Frenssen hesitated a moment, watching as Christian began to plod wearily inland, then he said quietly, 'All right, lads, let's follow the, er, skipper.'

A NOTE TO THE READER

Dear Reader,

If you have enjoyed this novel enough to leave a review on **Amazon** and **Goodreads**, then we would be truly grateful.

Sapere Books

Sapere Books is an exciting new publisher of brilliant fiction and popular history.

To find out more about our latest releases and our monthly bargain books visit our website:
saperebooks.com